D1483900

"For now, I will say this one thing, which encapsulates the whole story: I once knew a sailor who was searching for a home. By waving, I hoped to make him and the thousands of others who wandered the world feel as if they had found a place to belong in Savannah, Georgia."

—FLORENCE MARTUS, THE WAVING GIRL

Savannah Secrets

Savannah Secrets

The Waving Girl

GABRIELLE MEYER

Guideposts
Danbury, Connecticut

Savannah Secrets is a trademark of Guideposts.

Published by Guideposts Books & Inspirational Media
100 Reserve Road, Suite E200
Danbury, CT 06810
Guideposts.org

Cover and interior design by Müllerhaus
Cover illustration by Pierre Droal, represented by Deborah Wolfe, LTD.
Typeset by Aptara, Inc.

Printed and bound in the United States of America
10 9 8 7 6 5 4 3 2 1

The Waving Girl

Chapter One

August 1, 1931

My dear cousin Lavinia,

Your heartfelt letter, dated July 25, arrived only a few moments ago. Thank you for your kind words regarding our retirement, and thank you even more for inquiring about my life on Elba Island. I miss it more than I thought I would. The fifty years I lived there seem only a dream now as my brother George and I settle into our new home in the Bona Bella neighborhood, just outside of Savannah. I tend to my flowers, and George putters around the property, mending broken shutters and fixing a leaking roof, but we are both trying to find our new purpose. Our entire lives were spent tending lighthouses, first at our father's knee and then as we took over at Elba Island. It doesn't seem real that our work is done, but, like all things, there is a season.

It will do my heart good to speak of my life on Elba Island with you, but first, I must tell you that contrary to what you have heard in the newspapers (I'm still amazed and humbled you've heard about me all the way in New York City), my life on the island was quiet and simple. Yes, there were moments of excitement, but they were few and far between. I am honored by the attention I have received from the reporters and the city officials, but I do not deserve any of the accolades. They embarrass me more than you will know. I wish to live a quiet, peaceful life, yet people continue to treat me like a celebrity— all but George, of course. (To him, I will always be his little sister, though I'm now sixty-three years old.) I miss the privacy of the island, but more than that, I miss the purpose I found in waving at all the ships that arrived and departed from the Port of Savannah for the past forty-four years.

No matter the hour, nor the weather, I did not miss a single ship. That much of the story you have heard is true. I was never too ill to extend the arm of hospitality. There were nights, if I did not awake on my own, my faithful dogs would wake me to greet the ships. I would light a lantern and wave them in or out. And oh, how they responded. Foghorns, whistles, and the shouts and cheers from the men on deck would make me feel connected to the great big world, if only for a few moments, and help me to forget how very lonely I was.

You ask why I began to wave at the ships and eventually became known as the Waving Girl, but the truth might very well shock you. Only my brother George knows the real reason, though he will take that story to his grave. To this day, George will not discuss a word of it. In my utter grief and devastation, I turned to the one place I could pour out my heart, and that was my diary. When I left the lighthouse, George told me I must burn the diary I kept since I was a girl of nineteen, when the waving began. I wanted to leave the past on the island, so I did as he asked, but now I feel as if I have lost a part of my very own soul. It was the only tangible link I had to those days so long ago, and now it is gone. I have felt myself grieving over them more now than I did when they occurred. This grief has compelled me to share the story with you, knowing I can trust you implicitly. The only thing I ask, dear Lavinia, is that you burn these letters after you read them. I do not wish to bring shame or embarrassment upon my family name—nor do I wish to hurt anyone who is connected to the tragedy. Promise me this, and I shall share the whole tale with you. It is a tale of love, loss, and one girl's undying hope.

For now, I will say this one thing, which encapsulates the whole story: I once knew a sailor who was searching for a home. By waving, I hoped to make him, and the thousands of others who wandered the world, feel as if they had found a place to belong in Savannah, Georgia.

I hope and pray my desire was fulfilled.

Yours affectionately,

Florence

April in Savannah was Julia Foley's favorite time of year. Bright pink azaleas and fragrant blue hyacinths bloomed outside the Downhome Diner as she pushed open the restaurant's heavy door and was greeted by the smell of fresh coffee and warm blueberry pie. The winter chill was long gone, yet the heat and humidity of summer had not yet visited their fair city. Tourists were filling the crowded streets and wandering through the famous squares, but the rush of spring break visitors had subsided and the peak summer travel had not yet begun.

It was as close to perfection as Savannah could offer.

"Julia!" Meredith Bellefontaine, Julia's dearest friend and partner at Magnolia Investigations, waved from a corner booth where she sat with their friend Maggie Lu. "You're just in time. Clarissa was about to leave with the baby."

Clarissa, Maggie Lu's granddaughter, stood near the booth, an infant car seat swinging from the crook of her elbow. She grinned at Julia and turned the car seat so Julia could have a look at little Jacob Philip. He was only four months old, but his bright brown eyes didn't miss a thing as he stared at Julia.

"Isn't he something?" Maggie Lu asked, shaking her head. "I thank the good Lord I have lived to see my great-grandson come into this world. A real blessing," she said as she squeezed Clarissa's hand. "And he couldn't have a better mama."

"Thank you, Gran," Clarissa said, bending down to kiss her grandmother on the cheek. "But I have to run. I promised Jake's daddy we'd be home before he starts his shift at the precinct."

"It was good to see you," Julia said to Clarissa. "And little Jake."

"Bye, Mama!" Clarissa called to her mother, Charlene, the owner of the Downhome Diner, who was standing behind the long counter, pouring a cup of coffee for one of the customers. "I'll see you for supper."

"Oh, let me come and say goodbye to my grandbaby," Charlene said, setting the coffeepot on the warming plate and scurrying around the counter to kiss Jake goodbye. She also gave Clarissa a quick kiss, and they all waved as she left the diner.

"My, my, my," Maggie Lu said as she pulled her cup of coffee into her hands. "That little boy has captured my heart."

Meredith moved aside so Julia could join them in the booth. They were both still smiling after seeing Jake. "He's a doll," Meredith agreed.

Julia settled into the booth and put her purse beside her. "Sorry I'm late. The meeting at church ran longer than I expected. I'm organizing the youth group trip to the convention in Atlanta at the end of the month, and we've had a few issues with finances." A miscalculation in the books revealed they didn't have all the funds necessary to take thirty-three teenagers by bus and put them up in the hotel for a weekend. "We were brainstorming some fundraising ideas."

"No worries," Meredith said as she took a sip of her coffee. Her short blond hair was curled, as usual, and her pretty blue eyes were shining. "Maggie Lu and I were just catching up—and enjoying that great-grandbaby of hers."

Maggie Lu's eyes glowed as she smiled at Julia. "I know you gals are busy. I sure appreciate finding time to just sit and visit with one another."

Julia loved her time with Meredith and Maggie Lu. Since retiring from her position as a judge in the Chatham County Juvenile

Court, she had been running Magnolia Investigations with Meredith and volunteering with the youth group at New Beginnings Church. The work she did for both gave her a sense of purpose, but most importantly, it gave her more time and flexibility to spend with her husband, Beau, than she'd had while serving as a judge. Beau had recently retired as an anesthesiologist, and they were both settling into their new normal. For the most part, Julia and Meredith could set their own hours and enjoy an occasional leisurely meal with their friends at their favorite restaurant in the historic district of Savannah.

The Downhome Diner was a mixture of Southern charm and a fifties retro feel. Warm yellow walls, red vinyl booths and stools, pictures of historic Savannah on the walls, and the best Southern comfort food in town.

"Oh goodness," Meredith said under her breath. "Here comes Beatrice Enterline."

Julia groaned inwardly and had to force herself not to let her feelings show on her face. Despite Beatrice's overzealous behavior, she usually meant well.

"Hello, darlings," Beatrice drawled as she breezed into the diner and lifted a perfectly manicured hand to wave at them. "I thought I'd find y'all here." The outfit Beatrice wore today was as loud as the woman herself. At her age, ruffles and bows should have been left far behind, but for some reason, Beatrice felt the need to affect a Southern belle persona, even though she was a transplant to the South. Her pink sundress had a stiff underskirt, creating a hoop-skirt look. It was a cross between Scarlett O'Hara and a fifties teenybopper.

"Hello, Beatrice," Meredith said, her patience for the director of the Savannah Historical Society far more refined than Julia's. "Won't you join us?"

"Oh, I wouldn't want to impose," Beatrice said. "I just came to tell y'all the most excitin' news."

Julia pressed her lips together, trying to think of a time Beatrice hadn't imposed upon them.

"What do you have to share, Beatrice?" Maggie Lu asked good-naturedly, always eager to hear the latest bit of news about her beloved Savannah. Maggie Lu knew more about Savannah and its history than anyone else in Julia's acquaintance. Her expertise had been used to help solve mysteries several times in the past year since they'd opened their agency.

"Well, since you asked." Beatrice pushed into the booth next to Maggie Lu, her wide skirts sticking out on both sides. She leaned forward, her hazel eyes flashing with excitement. "Regina Terrance just arrived in town! Can you imagine?"

"Regina Terrance?" Julia frowned. The name sounded vaguely familiar, but she couldn't place her. "Why do I know that name?"

"She's just the most amazing author on the planet!" Beatrice rolled her eyes playfully. "She's a *New York Times* bestselling author of half a dozen books, including her breakout narrative nonfiction, *The Bridge to Forgiveness*—it was turned into that movie, do you remember?" She didn't let anyone answer, though Julia did remember the movie. She and Beau had gone to see it. It was the true story of a prisoner of war who was severely tortured during World War II and had returned to forgive his captors years later. "Regina Terrance specializes in bringing lesser-known history to light," Beatrice continued. "She's the author of the latest tell-all about Florence Martus, the Waving Girl of Savannah."

Julia tried not to groan again. "I've heard rumors there was a scandalous book coming out about the Waving Girl, but I didn't believe it."

"Same here," Meredith said, her voice reflecting her own misgivings. "I've heard it's full of never-before-told stories of Florence's life, though I've also heard most of them aren't true."

"When did this book come out?" Maggie Lu asked, a frown on her face. "This is the first I've heard of it."

"Just this week." Beatrice grinned. "And it's already gaining so much attention, Regina Terrance will be in Savannah for a few weeks to film a documentary! Can you imagine? I wonder if she'll want to interview me for the film. I am the director of the Savannah Historical Society, after all." Beatrice ran her hand over her dark, pixie-styled haircut. "I'll have to see my hairdresser."

"What else will she be doing in town?" Julia asked.

"I'm not sure." Beatrice shrugged. "But she's holding a press conference later this afternoon at the Bohemian Hotel, and I plan to be there." She pushed herself out of the booth and rearranged her skirts. "Well, I should be off. There's so much I need to do before I mosey on over to the hotel to introduce myself." She wiggled her long fingers again. "Ta-ta for now."

And just as quickly as she arrived, Beatrice was gone.

"Perhaps we should start meeting at a different restaurant," Julia said, turning her coffee cup up on her saucer and smiling at Charlene as she came over with a coffeepot. "That woman always seems to know when we're here."

Charlene grinned as she set her hand on Julia's shoulder and filled her cup with steaming hot coffee. "Maybe she drives around town looking for your car."

"Maybe I should buy a new car." Julia knew her irritation at Beatrice was a bit petty, but the woman was Julia's complete opposite in every way. It was hard for Julia to take her seriously. "Why doesn't she just call the office and leave a message?"

"It wouldn't be nearly as much fun for her to share the latest gossip with us through a message at the office," Meredith said with a chuckle. "She's harmless, Jules."

"I know." Julia took the first sip of coffee and savored the flavor. "But I could handle a little bit less of her attention."

"Now, what was she talking about?" Maggie Lu asked, her eyebrows still scooped in consternation. "Is someone maligning the name of our sweet Waving Girl?"

"I'm not sure," Meredith said. "I've only heard rumors. I haven't read the book myself, but a few people have said it's full of scandals, all revolving around Florence."

"What kind of scandals?" Julia asked. She was familiar with Florence Martus's life, as much as anyone else in Savannah—but there was so little known about her. She had led a quiet life on Elba Island, waving at ships coming into and leaving the Port of Savannah for over four decades, but had died sometime around World War II. People had speculated about her reason for waving for years, but the stories were all legends. No one knew the real reason. Florence had only said she was a lonely girl, trying to bring joy to others when she started.

"The book tells of a torrid love affair, a family murder, and espionage," Meredith said. "And it has gained a lot of publicity already, especially because it's written by Regina Terrance. Her track record of revealing hidden secrets from important people in history has made her very famous."

"Well, I won't be reading it," Maggie Lu said with a decisive nod. "Any book that suggests Florence Martus was involved in those horrible things isn't worth reading."

Julia glanced at Meredith, wondering if any of the rumors could be true. The partners had been involved in several investigations that had revealed hidden secrets from unlikely suspects. Could Florence be guilty of the things the book suggested?

Unfortunately, there was little that surprised Julia anymore.

"I suppose," she said, "only time will tell." She smiled at Maggie Lu. "Let's hear what's new in your life."

As Julia settled herself in for a nice, long visit, she couldn't shake the unease she felt about Florence Martus and the new book. Something didn't feel right, and she was curious to know why.

Chapter Two

LATE-AFTERNOON SUNSHINE POURED THROUGH THE window in Julia's office at Magnolia Investigations a few hours after she and Meredith had left the Downhome Diner. The room faced the back courtyard, where a small wire table held a potted begonia and a brick patio beckoned Julia to come outside and enjoy the beautiful spring day.

But Julia had a host of emails to return and a few phone calls to make on behalf of her youth group. She was in charge of the bake sale they would host at church on Sunday, between the two services, and she needed to recruit bakers to donate their goodies.

"Julia?" The intercom on Julia's phone made Carmen Lopez's voice echo in Julia's large office. The space used to be the dining room of the antebellum home they occupied. Magnificent wood panels covered the walls from floor to ceiling but did little to absorb the sounds of the intercom. "A potential new client is here to see you and Meredith."

Julia pressed the button on her phone and spoke into the intercom. "I'll be there in a moment."

"*Sí, señora.*" Carmen's Latina heritage was still very much a part of her flavorful personality, though she'd come to the United States with her parents as a child. She had been working for the agency since it opened almost a year ago and had become invaluable to Julia and Meredith.

The fundraiser phone calls would have to wait—as would the inviting patio. Julia finished up one of the emails she was composing and pressed SEND then closed the browser window on her laptop and shut the lid.

With a slight wince at the tightness in her back, she stood and stretched. She also slipped on her shoes, which she often removed when she sat at the desk to work. She didn't wear heels often, and her flats were more comfortable for everyday use. At 5'9", she had a few inches on Meredith and most other women she met. Thankfully, Beau was over six feet, and he liked when she put on a pair of heels to go out for the evening once in a while.

Julia left her office and entered the long, wide hall stretching from the front door to the back door.

A petite woman stood near Carmen's desk in the reception area that used to be the front parlor. The visitor was a diminutive woman, perhaps in her late sixties or early seventies, with deep wrinkles on her thin face. But though she was small, when she caught sight of Julia, her bright blue eyes flashed behind her glasses with a big purpose. "Miss Julia or Miss Meredith?" she asked in an impatient, no-nonsense voice.

"I'm Julia Foley," Julia said as she extended her hand to the other woman. "How may I assist you?"

"I'm Marcella Martus." She gave Julia's hand one hard pump. "And I need you to prove that horrible book about my great-auntie is nothing but a despicable, evil lie."

Meredith left her office at that moment and came into the hall, her eyebrows lifting, no doubt in surprise at the forceful words of the small woman.

"How about we start at the beginning?" Julia asked gently. "First, I'd like to introduce you to my business partner, Meredith Bellefontaine. Meredith," Julia said, "this is Marcella Martus."

"Nice to meet you," Meredith said, shaking Marcella's hand. "Shall we move this conversation to my office?"

Marcella clasped and unclasped her hands, clearly agitated and impatient. "The sooner you can get to work, the better. That book has only been on the shelves for a week, and it's already changing people's good opinions of my auntie. The stories aren't true, I tell you. None of them."

"Please, come into my office," Meredith repeated as she led the way. Julia motioned for Marcella to follow her.

They entered Meredith's office, which faced the front of the house. Her windows looked out on Whitaker Street and the famous Forsyth Park.

"Please have a seat, Ms. Martus." Meredith indicated the comfortable floral sofa in the center of her office and the two olive-colored wingback chairs in front of the fireplace. "Can we get you something to drink? Coffee or tea, perhaps?"

Ms. Martus took a seat on the edge of the sofa and shook her head. "No. And call me Marcella."

Julia sat on one of the olive-colored chairs, and Meredith took the other.

"Now, please," Julia said, "start at the beginning, if you would, Marcella."

With an impatient breath, Marcella pushed her gray hair off her forehead. "My great-aunt was Florence Martus, the Waving Girl. And, until now, I've never had a reason to get involved in what was written about her. Everyone has always treated her memory with utmost respect. From time to time, I've been asked to represent her at different city functions, but I've refrained. Auntie didn't like the attention, and frankly, neither do I." Her mouth tightened, and the fire returned to her eyes. "But I can't sit back and let that author spread false rumors about Auntie Florence. She would be mortified by that book."

"Have you read it?" Meredith asked.

"Yes, and what a waste of my time!" Marcella crossed her arms over her black-and-white striped shirt. A yellowed stain on the fabric caught Julia's eye, and by the look of her faded black pants and scuffed shoes, she wasn't dressed to impress. Yellow dog hair stuck to her pants and black dirt encircled her fingernails, suggesting she worked with soil. Julia took note of all these things, cataloging the information, in case she needed any of it for future reference.

"Neither Julia nor I have read the book," Meredith said. "But we're aware it has been published and that the author just arrived in Savannah to begin recording a documentary."

"What a bunch of hogwash!" Marcella declared, throwing her hands in the air. "That's why I've come to you. I tried calling the author to demand that she retract all her accusations about Auntie Florence, but she refuses to take my calls. The author's note in the back of the book claims she came into possession of some letters, written by Auntie Florence to a cousin in New York City. She said she corroborated the information in the letters with records, newspaper articles, and firsthand accounts, but I want to see the proof." She looked from Meredith to Julia. "That's why I've come here. I want to hire you two to prove the book is a lie and to restore my auntie's good name."

Julia was just as proud of Savannah's history as Meredith, and she knew, without even asking, that Meredith would agree to take this case. The Waving Girl of Savannah was one of the most iconic images of their city. Some even said that Florence Martus was the first hostess of the Hostess City, a name and reputation Savannahians were deeply proud of. The oversized statue of Florence, waving a towel toward the ships in the Savannah River, with one of her dogs by her side, stood on River Street and drew thousands of tourists every year. Little figurines of Florence, Christmas ornaments with her image, books, photographs, and more were sold in shops all across the city. She was at the center of the heart and soul of Savannah. If the stories were false, Julia and Meredith would work tirelessly to clear Florence's name.

"Will you do it?" Marcella asked.

Meredith glanced at Julia, questions in her eyes. "There will be a few things we need to discuss, and we'll both need to read the book, perhaps interview the author, if she'll allow, and then do some fact-checking."

"So, you'll take on the case?" Marcella's eyes glowed with hope.

"Yes," Julia said, with certainty. "We will gladly take the case."

"Oh good." Marcella's shoulders lifted and it seemed a weight had been removed. "But I won't sit back idly, mind you. I'm fixin' to do everything in my power to discredit this author and send her back to New York."

"I would caution you to tread lightly," Julia said to Marcella. "The last thing we want is to anger Ms. Terrance. It might make her difficult to work with."

"Perhaps," Meredith said gently, "you need to refrain from contacting the author while we're doing our investigation. We promise to leave no stone unturned and will exhaust every effort to find the truth."

Marcella squinted, as if weighing the cost of sitting on her hands. "Well," she finally said, "I can't make any promises, but I'll do my best to stay out of your way."

If that was the only reassurance they could get from Marcella, then they'd have to take it.

"I've heard there's a press conference this afternoon," Julia said to Marcella. "Meredith and I will be sure to attend and introduce ourselves to Ms. Terrance. If she's willing to meet with us in private, we'll plan something as soon as her schedule allows."

"Thank you," Marcella said. "My great-auntie Florence would thank you too."

"Do you have any documents that might help us?" Meredith asked. "Diaries, letters, records of any kind from your family?"

Marcella shook her head. "Nothing. I'm not much for history and all that stuff. I know if I ever need anything, it'll be in the museum somewhere, but I've never had the desire to go digging. I generally keep to myself and my home."

"Do you live in Savannah?" Julia asked.

"Yes. I live in the Bona Bella neighborhood, in Auntie Florence's old home."

"Bona Bella?" Julia asked, surprised at the name. "I live in the next neighborhood to the south, very close to Bona Bella."

"How nice." Marcella offered a placating smile.

"Do you have any of your aunt's things?" Meredith asked. "At the house?"

"Some of the old furniture they brought with them from the lighthouse on Elba Island," Marcella said. "My mother wasn't fond of the old stuff and gave most of it away when we took over the house from my grandparents. They inherited it from Auntie Florence and Great-Uncle George."

"That's a shame." Meredith sighed.

Julia knew what Meredith was thinking. She loved old furniture and family heirlooms. Her home was full of them. Even the house Meredith lived in had been inherited from her great-grandfather when she married her husband, Ron. Ron had since passed away, and now Meredith owned several important heirlooms from his family too.

Marcella stood. "If I think of anything or hear anything important, I'll be in touch."

Julia and Meredith also rose, and Julia said, "And if we learn something important, we'll be in touch as well. Did you leave your information with our assistant?"

"Yes. She took it all when I came in."

"Great." Julia smiled, thankful for Carmen's thoroughness.

They walked Marcella out to the front door. She took her leave with little more than a nod of goodbye.

When the door closed behind their newest client, Carmen came out from behind her desk, her brilliant brown eyes large. "Was that Florence Martus's grandniece?"

"Yes," Meredith said. "She's asked us to investigate Regina Terrance's new book about her great-aunt."

Carmen fanned her face with her hand. "I started reading the book last night and it's quite a story. The love scenes between Florence and her Chinese sailor made me blush." She rested her hands on her cheeks. "I had to skip over several paragraphs that were a little more than I was comfortable reading."

Julia's eyes grew wide. "Is the author touting this book as fact, or fiction? I thought it was a biography."

"It reads like a romance novel, with lots of intrigue and suspense mixed in." Carmen waggled her eyebrows. "I can't wait to see what happens next."

"I think the first thing we need to do is get our hands on a couple of copies of that book and see what we're dealing with," Meredith said.

"I think you're right," Julia agreed. "And the sooner the better."

Hopefully, they could find the answers before too much harm was done to the Waving Girl's reputation.

***

The meeting room at the Bohemian Hotel wasn't large, but it was comfortably decorated and boasted a magnificent view of the Savannah riverfront. A narrow table sat positioned at the front of the room, along the windows overlooking the river, while two dozen chairs were lined up in rows for those attending the press conference. When Julia and Meredith entered the room an hour after Marcella Martus had visited them, most of the chairs were full of newspaper and television reporters as well as a couple of city officials and the flamboyant Beatrice Enterline, who had changed and was wearing a bright orange pencil skirt with an equally loud, multi-colored blouse.

A very polished-looking woman with blond hair and a dress suit stood behind the table at the front, talking to Beatrice. She was probably in her midfifties and wore her hair in a twist at the back of her head. She had a bright scarf tied around her neck, and her diamond-studded earrings sparkled in the warm lighting.

Beside her, sitting at the table with a telephone at her ear and a laptop open in front of her was a younger woman, tall and slender, with a pen holding a quick updo at the back of her head. Her hurried movements and irritated attitude as she spoke on the phone were evident, even from where Julia stood.

When the woman hung up the phone, she stood and pulled the pen from her updo and her light brown hair came tumbling over her shoulders. She commanded the room, lifting her chin and looking down her nose at everyone until they quieted. Her gaze lingered on Beatrice until the director of the Savannah Historical Society took a seat. "It's now five o'clock," the woman said, "and I'd like to get this press conference started." She looked over the room, her gaze calculating and sharp. "My name is Allegra Timmons." She spoke in a cultured New England accent, talking much faster than Julia's Southern ears were accustomed to. "I'm a publicist for the Falcon Publishing House, which has had the honor of publishing Regina Terrance's book *The Waving Girl*. I will be coordinating Ms. Terrance's schedule over the next couple of weeks while she's in Savannah consulting on the documentary of Florence Martus's life. She will make several publicity appearances, speak to groups and organizations, and visit bookstores in the area. If you would like to interview

Ms. Terrance, or have any other questions, please contact me. It is my job to make Ms. Terrance's life as easy as possible while she's here." She lifted a stack of business cards and walked around the table. "I'll pass out my card, and you'll find my phone number and email address on it for your convenience."

An eager young woman in the front row jumped up. "Let me," she said, taking the stack of cards from Allegra, "I'll pass them out."

Allegra lifted an eyebrow at the woman. "Thank you."

The woman turned and grinned at the group, pushing her glasses up the bridge of her nose with the back of her hand. With an amazing amount of enthusiasm, she passed out Allegra's cards, smiling at each person and even complimenting Beatrice on her audacious outfit.

"So," Allegra said, her cool, composed voice in control, even with the disruption of the bubbly gal moving through the audience, "I'll take this opportunity to introduce you to Regina Terrance and let her tell you a little more about her reason for coming to Savannah." Allegra smiled at Regina. "Whenever you're ready."

Regina had taken a seat when Allegra began to talk, so she rose now, elegant and smooth, her face a wreath of smiles. "Thank you, Allegra, and thank you, Savannah, for welcoming me to your beautiful city. There's a reason you're called the Hostess City, and I've already felt that warm reception and Southern gentility."

The group clapped, and she dipped her chin.

"Before I open up for questions," Regina said, "I'd like to tell you why I'm here and then introduce you to someone you might see around town over the coming weeks."

She told them about her recently published book and the studio that contacted her to make a documentary film about Florence Martus's life. "The studio has sent a film crew to interview me," she said with a smile, "and perhaps some of you as well."

Beatrice sat up straighter and glanced over her shoulder to grin at the audience. She caught sight of Julia and Meredith and waved, as if they were long-lost friends she hadn't seen in years.

"Before we continue," Regina said, "I'd like to introduce you to the film's producer and director." She motioned to a man sitting in the front row next to Beatrice. "Mr. Frederick Hay-Haynes?" She stumbled over his last name.

"*Hayes*, without the *n*," he said with a smile as he rose. He was a distinguished-looking man with a head of gray hair and a matching gray mustache. He wore a cream-colored button-down shirt, rolled at the sleeves. Over the shirt he wore a khaki-colored vest and matching khaki pants. "It's a privilege to be here," he said, "and to work on this project with Regina Terrance."

The audience clapped again, and Regina smiled. "Thank you for coming, Mr. *Hayes*." She emphasized his last name with a chuckle. "I'll be sure to get that right next time."

"No worries."

"Now," Regina said, "I'd love to answer your questions."

"Oh, me." The eager young woman who'd passed out the business cards raised her hand like a schoolgirl. "Please pick me first."

"Of course," Regina said with a smile.

"I'm Gertie Hanson, from Sheboygan, Wisconsin." She glanced at a newspaper reporter behind her as she pushed her glasses up her nose and said, "Sheboygan is in southeastern Wisconsin, north of Milwaukee, right on the shores of Lake Michigan."

"How nice," the reporter said.

"What is your question, Ms. Hanson?" Regina asked.

"Well"—Gertie clasped her hands together in excitement—"it's not really a question, so much as I wanted you to know I'm your biggest fan, Ms. Terrance. I've read all your books and received an early copy of *The Waving Girl* from your publisher to review it. I used all my savings to come here to meet you and to see Savannah for myself. If I can be of any assistance to you, please let me know. I'll do anything, Ms. Terrance. Absolutely anything."

"Thank you, Ms. Hanson," Regina said with another patient smile. "That's very kind of you. However, Allegra will be here to help, so perhaps you should take the time to enjoy Savannah while you're here. It's a beautiful city."

"Oh, I will," Gertie said with certainty. "Most definitely."

"Any other questions—or comments?" Regina added with a laugh.

"I have a question," someone said at the back of the room.

Julia turned and found Marcella Martus standing near the door.

"Oh no," Julia said under her breath to Meredith. "Why is she here?"

"I'll be happy to answer your question," Regina said.

"My name is Marcella Martus. I'm Florence Martus's grand-niece, and I just have one question for you, Ms. Terrance."

"Oh, how nice." Regina's smile didn't falter. "I was hoping to meet some of Florence's family while I was in Savannah. Are there many of you here?"

"Where are the letters you used to write this book?" Marcella asked, walking up the aisle to slam a copy of the book on the table. "I want to see them with my own eyes."

Allegra rose, her lips pressed in a line.

Regina put her hand out to Marcella. "It's nice to meet you, Miss Martus."

Marcella ignored Regina's hand. "This book is full of lies," she said, jamming her finger against the cover, "and I'm fixin' to prove you made it all up to sell copies."

Regina's mouth fell open.

"Where are the letters?" Marcella asked again. "If they exist, which I highly doubt, I want the handwriting analyzed to prove Florence wrote them."

"They are in my apartment in New York City," Regina said, her smile gone, but her composure still intact. "They're in a very delicate state and cannot be moved."

"You're a liar."

"I beg your pardon?" Regina's eyes grew large.

"Ms. Martus," Allegra said, "I'm going to have to ask you to leave."

"Not until I get the truth out of this woman." Marcella took another step forward. "Where did you get the letters?"

"In a private sale." Regina crossed her arms as she glared at Marcella. "If you know anything about me or my writing, you'll know I'm a collector of rare diaries and letters, which are usually the basis of each book I write. The letters were found hidden in a wall in a house that was being remodeled. A friend of mine heard about them and I made an offer to the owner of the house—someone who has no connection to the Martus family."

"I've seen the letters myself," Allegra said, "though we owe you no explanation. Regina Terrance has a stellar reputation and a proven track record with her other books. Her very first book won the Pulitzer Prize for Biography and was inspired by a true story. Why would she need to make this one up?"

"Reputations can be ruined." Marcella's tone was dry. "Just like you've ruined my auntie's."

"I'm sorry you don't believe me," Regina said, "and I'm sorry the things I shared in the book have hurt you. Sometimes, the truth is hard to accept." She moved away from Marcella. "Now, if you'll please sit down, Ms. Martus, I'll take more questions."

"You're not done with me." Marcella shook her finger at Regina. "I've hired the women of Magnolia Investigations to unearth the truth and expose you to the world." She pointed at Julia and Meredith.

Regina and Allegra, along with the rest of the group, turned to look at Julia and Meredith. Gertie Hanson stood up to get a better look.

Julia's cheeks filled with heat, and she wanted to melt into the floor. Meredith lifted her hands to her forehead, as if she wanted to hide behind her fingers. The only thing Julia could do was offer a cordial smile—the whole while wishing she had one of those vaudeville canes used to pull people off the stage. Marcella Martus should not have come. It would do nothing to help their cause, and she should sit down now before she did more damage.

Regina lifted her chin. "I will gladly answer any and all questions, but I refuse to be bullied by you, Ms. Martus, or by anyone you hire."

Allegra put her hand on Marcella's arm and pointed toward a chair. "If you don't sit down and stop badgering Ms. Terrance, I may have to call security."

"Fine, I'll leave," Marcella said as she turned and walked toward the door. "But I'll get to the bottom of this. My poor dear auntie would be horrified by your book. Simply horrified. I can't sit back and do nothing."

With that, Marcella left the room.

For a moment, no one said anything, but several people eyed the Magnolia ladies with great interest.

Finally, Allegra asked if there were any other questions.

"Should we stay?" Meredith asked under her breath as Regina took another question from one of the reporters.

"Maybe we should leave," Julia said. "We don't want to make her feel ganged up on. We can make an appointment for later, after things have cooled down a bit."

"I think you're right. We're only drawing unwanted attention now."

As quietly as possible, Julia and Meredith left the press conference.

Julia just hoped and prayed Marcella Martus hadn't made their jobs harder than necessary.

Chapter Three

AFTER THE PRESS CONFERENCE, JULIA would have liked nothing more than to go home to Beau and put her feet up, but it was Wednesday and she needed to attend the weekly youth group service. She had to tell the students about the bake sale on Sunday and ask them to bring items to sell.

At half past six, she walked into the youth group room with a smile on her face, eager to check in with the students. She and Beau had not been blessed with a family of their own, but she loved investing in the lives of her church kids. In the early years, when they'd faced infertility issues, she had tried several treatments, but nothing had worked. Through the years, she'd turned her energy instead to her marriage, her professional work, and her volunteer activities with the different churches they had attended. Mentoring and interacting with the teenagers at New Beginnings Church on Wednesday nights was often the highlight of her week.

"Hello, Miss Julia!" Pastor Jay Crispin greeted Julia with a broad, white smile. He wore his thick brown hair shaved close on the sides and longer on the top. It flipped over in a perfect wave that was so immovable with hair product, it never ceased to amaze Julia. He was a young man, just a few years out of seminary, and he had a well of energy that never ran dry. The kids loved him, and he had a way of connecting on their level yet maintaining their respect and admiration. Some of Julia's older friends struggled with the youth pastor's interesting choice of clothes and his jaunty personality but not Julia. Anyone who could engage a roomful of teenagers and teach them about the love and salvation of Jesus while keeping them coming back week after week, bringing friends along with them, was okay in Julia's book. As a juvenile court judge, she knew how important it was for a lot of these kids to have a place to connect and grow in community, and Pastor Jay did a great job.

"Hello, Pastor Jay." Julia smiled as she set her purse under the counter in the snack shop. "I was wondering if I could take a minute sometime tonight and talk to the kids about the youth convention and our fundraising needs."

"Sure thing." He gave a couple of kids high fives as they walked past him, acknowledging their arrival, yet still giving Julia his full attention. "I'll call you up during announcement time."

"Thank you." Tonight, one of the mom volunteers, who hadn't shown up yet, was in charge of the snack shop. Since there was a line of kids waiting, Julia went to work opening the little store. It was a small room, not much bigger than a walk-in closet, in the corner of the youth room. Julia opened the gate over the counter and smiled at the kids.

"Wait a minute while I get the popcorn machine turned on," she said to them as they crowded around the counter, eyeing the candy and soda on display.

Twenty minutes later, the popcorn was made, the rush of kids had been served, and Julia was able to stand by the counter and observe the group as they mingled and waited for the service to begin. It was a nice-sized group of about forty kids, from all walks of life. Like most people, the kids tended to congregate in familiar groups, and it was one of these groups that caught Julia's attention.

Three girls, about sixteen years old, stood off to the side in a close-knit circle, their heads bent together as they spoke. It wasn't the way they were standing or even their judgmental looks that snagged on Julia's awareness. It was the fact that this particular group usually included a fourth member, Olivia Harold, who was sitting all by herself on a couch at the back of the room, phone in hand, obviously pretending not to notice anyone or anything going on around her.

Julia watched Olivia for a few minutes and noticed her glancing up from time to time, watching her group of friends. It was obvious that the three-pack was whispering about Olivia.

But why? What had happened to pull Olivia away from her friends? They'd been an inseparable group since they entered the youth room four years ago as seventh graders. Their families were members of the church, and a couple of them had siblings interspersed throughout the room. For as long as Julia had known them, they'd been by each other's sides.

"Sorry I'm late." The mom volunteer, Nicky, rushed into the snack shop, sans makeup and her hair frazzled, which was unusual for her. "Between tennis, baseball, track and field, and a doctor's appointment, I had four places to be, with four different kids, all at the same time this afternoon."

Julia smiled and gave Nicky a hug, ever amazed at how much a mom did in one day. "Don't worry, I was able to manage on my own."

Pastor Jay called for everyone's attention, and the kids congregated near the front of the room on the couches and chairs set up in a haphazard fashion. The youth pastor wanted the room to be as teen friendly and comfortable as possible, so he had purchased the simple black couches and chairs and moved out the folding chairs that had previously filled the space.

With the scent of freshly popped popcorn still lingering on the air, Julia left the snack shop in Nicky's capable hands and waited near the back of the room until Pastor Jay called her up front.

The three-pack of girls sat on a couch on one side of the room while Olivia remained on the other. But the funny thing was, no one else sat next to Olivia. She had a couch all to herself while the other couches and chairs were overflowing with kids.

Olivia seemed to sink into the corner, folding into herself as she held her mouth in a straight line. She didn't even attempt to laugh or talk with the other kids.

Julia's concern continued to mount. Olivia had always been a popular, well-liked member of the youth group. She was kind to everyone, even the younger kids. As far as Julia knew, she was also active in school, got good grades, and was considered a leader. If everyone was ignoring her, then something serious must have happened.

"And to tell us more about the upcoming youth convention," Pastor Jay said in a loud, excited voice, "please give it up for Miiiiiiiisssssss Julia!" He clapped enthusiastically as he jumped off the small stage in the corner of the room.

The group clapped and shouted for Julia. Several held their hands up, so she gave them high fives on the way to the stage, setting

Olivia and her problems to the side for a moment. She'd talk to her later during small group time.

"Thank you," Julia said, smiling and indicating they should stop their applause. "The youth convention is only three weeks away. We plan to leave the church parking lot at one o'clock Friday afternoon, since you don't have school that day." A couple of kids shouted their approval. "We'll arrive at the convention center in Atlanta by suppertime, grab a quick bite to eat, and then attend the Friday night session."

Several kids began to talk, and she had to wait for them to quiet down before she continued. The next part was extremely important for them to hear. They didn't want to turn away a single student who wanted to attend the convention. And because of that, they needed to make sure their fundraiser was a success. "We're still a little short on funds," she told them, "so I'll need all of you to bring a plate of baked goods to church on Sunday morning. I would like each student who is going on the trip to supply at least two dozen items, whether they're cookies, bars, or cupcakes. We'll also need volunteers to help run the bake sale, so each student will need to sign up for a time slot. The sign-up sheet is over by the snack shop." She looked at their young, eager faces and smiled. "Any questions?"

No one said a word.

"If you think of any, come see me later." She signaled to Pastor Jay, who came back up to the stage.

Julia walked to the sofa where Olivia was sitting by herself. "Mind if I join you?" she asked.

Olivia shrugged but didn't say anything, her gaze still on the stage.

After the youth band led the group in a couple of worship songs, Pastor Jay gave a short sermon on the story of the prodigal son, and then the large group broke up into smaller ones.

Julia was in charge of leading the freshman and sophomore girls' discussion time, so the seven girls of that age gathered on chairs and the floor in front of her sofa. Olivia didn't move, nor did anyone acknowledge her when they came over.

After they discussed the questions Pastor Jay had provided and prayed for one another, the group broke apart.

Olivia pulled out her phone.

Julia turned to her. "You didn't say a word tonight. Is everything okay?"

Olivia shrugged. "I don't have anything to say."

"I'm surprised you aren't hanging out with your friends tonight. Want to talk about it?"

Olivia glanced up at the three other girls standing by a foosball table. They were laughing.

"No," Olivia said. "I don't want to talk about it."

Julia didn't speak for a moment, hoping Olivia would open up with her, but the girl returned her attention to her phone.

"If you change your mind," Julia said, "I'm here to listen."

Olivia nodded. A text popped up on her screen, and she stood and grabbed her backpack, which was near her feet. "My mom's here."

"Goodbye." Julia also rose. "Don't forget my offer."

Olivia nodded again and walked away, barely glancing toward her friends as she left the room.

If Olivia wouldn't tell her what was happening, maybe the others would. Julia walked over to the small group, and when she stopped near them, they smiled at her politely.

"Hi, Miss Julia," Ebony Lester said.

Julia didn't want to appear to be prying, nor did she want to make the girls feel uncomfortable, so she smiled. "Anyone know what's going on with Olivia?"

The girls looked at each other, but their faces were hard to read.

"I can tell something's wrong." Julia looked at each girl carefully. "I was hoping we might be able to help her."

Ebony's big brown eyes looked doubtful.

"Why didn't she hang out with y'all tonight?"

"Olivia's not hanging out with any of her old friends anymore," Heather Cochrane said. "Not here or at school."

"Why not?"

The girls shrugged.

"Did something happen?" Julia was truly perplexed. Last week, the group of four had been laughing and having a great time together. What could have changed so drastically in one week?

Ebony lifted an eyebrow. "Something happened, but I don't want to repeat it to you, Miss Julia."

"We'll just say that Olivia made some poor choices last summer," Elena Sanchez said. "And we all just learned about it."

"Olivia's not who we thought she was," Heather added.

Julia clasped her hands together, a troubled sigh on her lips. Her heart broke for Olivia.

"Let's give her the benefit of the doubt and pray for her, shall we?" Julia suggested. "She probably needs all of us more now than ever before."

The girls looked doubtful again, but Julia was determined to help Olivia, no matter what had happened last summer. She waited until the girls bowed their heads and then said a prayer for Olivia and for reconciliation with her friends.

***

The soft crackle of the fireplace and a warm glow on the walls of the living room drew Julia through the hallway and into the front room of the house, where Beau sat with his feet up on the ottoman, reading a book. He loved big, thick biographies and histories, especially about war or things like the fur trade or the spice trade.

He glanced up now from a thick biography about aviator Charles A. Lindbergh and smiled at Julia. "Hi."

"Hi." She loved seeing his smile at the end of a long day. No matter where they lived, his smile always felt like home.

She slipped off her flats and went to the couch where he sat. She curled up next to him and he put his arm around her, kissing the top of her head.

"How was your day?" He slipped a bookmark into his book and put it aside.

"Long and very eventful. What about you?"

"I mowed the lawn and went to the golf course." He chuckled. "So not quite as eventful as your day. When I got home I repaired the railing on the back deck and grilled some veggie burgers. There's a plate in the refrigerator for you."

"Thanks." She'd had no time to eat supper between the press conference and youth group. They usually planned on being apart for supper on Wednesday evenings, but Beau always saved something for her to warm up when she returned home.

Julia watched the fire jump and waver in the fireplace. It was an unusually cool evening for the beginning of April, and the heat felt nice. A log fell and embers flew up the chimney. She and Beau loved real wood fireplaces. It had been one of the features they had requested when searching for houses sixteen years ago when they came back to Savannah.

"Want to talk about your eventful day?" Beau asked.

Julia let out a sigh as she told him about Regina Terrance and her new book about the life of Florence Martus. She told him all about Marcella Martus and her appearance at the press conference and how Julia was afraid they had alienated Regina even before talking to her. "You should have seen the way she looked at Meredith and me," Julia said. "Like we were just as confrontational as Marcella Martus. We're labeled even before she's met us."

When she was finished telling him about *The Waving Girl*, she told him about the shortage of funds for the upcoming youth trip and then the situation revolving around Olivia Harold and what her friends had said about her at youth group.

"Wow," Beau said after a couple of seconds. "It *was* an eventful day. Sounds like both Florence and Olivia are dealing with the same problem."

Julia sat up and looked at her husband. "How so?"

"Both of them are suffering from a tarnished reputation."

"The only difference is, Olivia made some kind of choice that hurt her reputation, while Florence didn't."

"Maybe," Beau said. "Maybe not. You don't know yet if Florence is guilty of the things in the book—but you also don't know if what those girls at youth group told you is true, either. Until you talk to Olivia, you won't know for sure. And even then, you might have to use your best judgment to discern if she's telling the truth."

Julia agreed. She was a bit ashamed at how quickly she had assumed Olivia was guilty, just because her friends said she had done something wrong. Julia didn't know how the girls heard about Olivia's transgressions, nor whether or not Olivia had actually committed whatever she was accused of. Besides, it wasn't up to the girls, or Julia, to pass judgment. As followers of Christ, they shouldn't be so harsh with their reactions or self-righteous indignation.

"It's kind of sad that I've already made assumptions, based on what little I know about each situation." Julia put her arm up on the back of the sofa and rested her head in her palm. "I assume Florence is innocent because everyone has always looked upon her as a shy, simple woman who lived a quiet, peaceful life on an island. But I've been involved in enough legal cases and enough investigations to know that looks can be deceiving." She shook her head. "And I didn't even question Olivia's friends before I assumed the worst about her."

"I don't think you assumed the worst," Beau said, putting his hand on Julia's knee. "You've always given people the benefit of the doubt. That's why you were such a great judge. You waited to pass judgment until you had all the available evidence before you. I've always admired that about you."

"I haven't always made the right judgment calls."

"No. But you try hard." His gaze softened. "Even if your first response was to believe Olivia was guilty, you would have no trouble changing that opinion, if given the right information. And, if she was guilty, you have an unwavering belief in redemption. You would believe in her to do better next time. You see the hearts of people, and you cheer them on. That's something I know you'll share with the girls in youth group."

She leaned forward and gave him a kiss and a smile. "Now I know why I love coming home so much."

He winked at her.

"But you're right," she said, taking his hand in hers. "Our first instinct as humans is to judge. It takes intentionality and patience to change that instinct, and I've done that with your help. Now I need to teach the kids in youth group do the same." Beau always helped her see the other side of a situation. "I appreciate how you often examine something from as many different perspectives as possible."

He smiled. "We're a good pair, aren't we?"

"The best." She snuggled into his side again, loving the feel of his solid muscles and the smell of the cologne he wore. "You're the best part of my day."

He opened his book again and kissed the top of her head one more time before he started to read.

Julia's mind returned to both Florence and Olivia. She wanted to believe the best about both of them, so she'd wait until she had all the facts and evidence before she would accept that either one was guilty of whatever they were accused of.

Before then, she'd hope and pray that they were both innocent.

Chapter Four

August 9, 1931

Dear Cousin Lavinia,

I received your last letter, and thank you again for your kind words. Knowing I will have a safe place to tell my story has given me so much joy this past week. I have not spoken of these events to anyone for over forty-four years. Some days, I wonder if it was all a dream. But then I look at the scar on my forearm and remember it was very real. The events that led to my waving left indelible scars in my life—but not all of them are physical. The ones on my heart and soul are deeper and more profound. Thankfully, no one ever saw those.

Because you have promised to destroy these letters once you receive them, I will endeavor to tell you the whole story, with as many necessary details as possible, so you will understand the decisions I made. It is my prayer that you will not judge me harshly. My brother never understood, and neither did my mother or father. As an older woman looking back, I can now see why they struggled with my choices. At the time, I thought I knew everything. Now, I realize I was simply a naive nineteen-year-old girl who had far too much faith in humanity and love.

To give you a better idea of the events leading up to my waving, I'll start at the very beginning. My father was a sergeant in the United States Army, and at the close of the Civil War, he was stationed at Fort Pulaski in Savannah, Georgia, as an ordnance sergeant. I was born at Fort Pulaski in 1868. I was the youngest of his six children. Soon, my father was put in charge of the lighthouses at Cockspur and Elba Islands. We lived on Cockspur Island, near Fort Pulaski, until a hurricane destroyed our cottage in 1881. By then, all of my siblings but my brother George and me had left the lighthouse to seek their own lives. So, in 1881, my father moved my mother, brother, and me to Elba Island. It was a lonely childhood, but unique. I knew nothing else, though I read many books and often longed for an adventure to take me away.

My waving story began at the blush of dawn in June of 1887, just a couple of months shy of my nineteenth birthday. George was manning the lighthouse, since my parents were away on a very rare vacation. I heard his voice yelling for me in my sleep, and when I opened my eyes, I immediately saw the trouble. Out on the river, within sight of my bedroom window, a dredge was on fire. Already, flames had engulfed the boat. I threw on my clothes and rushed out to join George, who was rushing toward the burning dredge.

It was a race to save lives. George and I did not even stop to communicate what we would do. We jumped into the water and swam to the dredge. Having been raised near the water, we were both strong swimmers. Men were trapped in the inferno, screaming and calling out for help. Instinct took over, and I never once considered my own life. All I could think was to save those men. It was the hardest thing I've ever done, and the scar on my arm is from that day. I do remember thinking how thankful I was that my parents were away. My father's heart had been weak for several years, and if he had been there, he would have worked alongside. I shudder to think of what might have happened if he had.

We worked for several hours rescuing over thirty men on that dredge, swimming them to safety. One man succumbed to his injuries and died, but the others were soon transferred to the hospital in Savannah.

All but one.

His name was Hai Ching. He was a Chinese sailor who had started to work on the dredge earlier that summer. The Chinese Exclusion Act of 1882 prevented all Chinese citizens from immigrating to the United States, but many still worked and lived in America. There was a strong prejudice against the Chinese, and there had been for as long as I could remember. My father told me it started in the 1840s in California during the gold rush when so many were seeking better lives, and by 1868, they were barred from immigrating to America altogether. The hospital in Savannah refused to accept Hai Ching as a patient, but I could not bear to see him suffer. He was only twenty-two years old and had lived as an orphan on ships almost all his life. He spoke flawless English, with a strange mixture of accents. He was a man without a home or a nation.

George did not approve of bringing Hai Ching into our home, but my parents were away and we didn't know what else to do, so there was little other choice. Burns covered Hai Ching's hands, chest, and neck. He was delirious with pain that first week. When Mother and Father returned home, they agreed we had done the right thing, though they were leery of having Hai Ching on the island. What would people think? What might they do? Would Father be in trouble? Would people start to talk? We were not allowed to tell anyone Hai Ching was in our home, but who would I tell? I only left the island on occasion to go into Savannah to shop, and very few people came to visit us.

Father and Mother agreed I was doing a fine job caring for Hai Ching's wounds and that it was the right thing to do, so they allowed me to continue, but, sadly, they were constantly on guard.

It took weeks for Hai Ching to recover. I read to him often, and he told me tales of his life at sea. I had never met anyone like him. He opened my eyes and filled my heart and mind with wonder. I laughed, I cried, and I sat amazed as he talked. He could go on for hours and hours, and I could have listened to him all day.

And in return, he listened to me tell him stories of my childhood and my limited experiences. He never made me feel as if my small world was any less important than his big one. I didn't have much experience outside the island, but I could share my hopes and dreams—things I'd never told anyone before. He seemed to love my innocence, my simple way of seeing the world. My perspective was unsullied and so full of hope in the common man. He often told me he had never met anyone like me either.

Sometimes, when I think back to those days, I think of how naive I must have sounded to him. I think of how brave and bold I was to sit for hours with a stranger and pour out my heart—but, at the time, it did not seem strange or unusual. It felt right. Being with Hai Ching was as easy to me as breathing, and we soon became very good friends. I wondered how I had ever lived on the island without his company. He filled my days with excitement and purpose and gave me hope, for the very first time, that my life might be more than an island.

But it is getting late, and I cannot tell you my whole tale in one letter. I wonder if I could do it justice in a thousand letters.

Perhaps now, knowing a little more of my story, you are having second thoughts about learning the rest. I will stop for now and wait until I hear from you again. If you'd like me to continue, I will do so. If not, I will simply let the rest live on in my heart and mind and take it to my grave with me, where it will be safe forever.

Remember, dear Lavinia, to destroy this letter the moment after you've read it.

Yours truly,
Florence

A slow, steady rain dripped outside the windows of the Mansion on Forsyth Park, a gorgeous hotel housed in a sprawling Victorian Romanesque mansion in historic Savannah. It sat opposite Magnolia Investigations, on the other side of the park, and was often the site of the monthly luncheon hosted by the Savannah Historical Society. The mansion was made of beautiful red brick and terra-cotta and boasted a hundred and twenty-five guest suites. It was a must-see building on many Savannah tours.

On Thursday, Julia and Meredith sat at a round table with eight other women, enjoying the hotel's Savannah Honey Glazed Chicken. It was a specialty of the hotel and one of Julia's particular favorites. It was served with dirty rice, roasted heirloom carrots, and bacon and red pepper relish. A glass of sweet tea sat near the top of her plate and was refilled by one of the servers.

Beatrice presided over the luncheon with her usual flair. She sat at the head table with Regina Terrance, Allegra Timmons, and Frederick Hayes. Though Regina was the guest of honor, from where Julia sat, she noticed Beatrice did most of the talking.

"I'm eager to hear Regina Terrance's presentation," one of her tablemates said to Julia. "I haven't read the book, have you?"

Julia had started to read the book that very morning. The story opened on a cool, summer morning when Florence awakened to the smell of smoke and men's voices crying for help. In a daring scene, Florence and her brother saved thirty men from a burning dredge in the Savannah River. "I just started it," Julia told her.

"What do you think?" The woman's eyes were wide with curiosity. "Do you think it's all true?"

Julia shrugged. "I'm not going to make any judgments yet. I'm eager to hear Ms. Terrance tell us more."

"The same here, dear," the woman agreed. "I'm not even going to read it until I hear a little more about it."

The dishes were taken away, and dessert was served. It was a decadent chocolate cake, too rich for Julia to finish. After the cake, coffee was poured and Beatrice finally rose to introduce their speaker.

"I'm thrilled, simply thrilled," she gushed, "to welcome today's guest speaker to the podium. Regina Terrance is the author of six bestselling books and dozens of award-winning articles. She's here to talk to us about her newest nonfiction narrative, *The Waving Girl*, an in-depth look at the life of our very own Florence Martus." Beatrice wore a purple fascinator on her head made out of feathers and various other decorations. It waved and bobbed as she spoke. "Please join me in welcoming Regina Terrance."

The room, full of about a hundred members of the society, clapped politely for Regina. There was a reserved air about the audience. Florence was a dear Savannah icon. If the stories were true, her fans would have to deal with the disappointment.

"Thank you," Regina said as she came to stand behind the podium. She was dressed in an aquamarine skirt and suitcoat, with a navy blue shirt underneath, and several layers of gold necklaces. Her blond hair was down today and perfectly styled. Everything about her spoke of professionalism and glamour. Julia couldn't help but wonder if she dressed like that every day, even when she sat at her computer to write. It was hard to picture Regina Terrance in yoga pants and an oversized T-shirt, her hair quickly thrown up in a ponytail, as she typed away.

"It's an honor to speak to the Savannah Historical Society," Regina said. "Your respect of and reputation for historical accuracy and preservation is world class. I know I will learn invaluable lessons from all of you while I'm here. My life and writing will be better because of it."

Beatrice beamed from her spot at the head table, but Meredith and Julia shared a look. Was Regina being sincere or simply flattering everyone so they would fall for her charm?

"I'm here today to talk about my recent book, *The Waving Girl*."

A movement near the side of the room caught Julia's attention, and she tapped Meredith's arm. "Look," she whispered.

The young woman, Gertie Hanson, was sitting at a table with a group of older, sophisticated women. She stuck out in her jean jacket and ponytail, a large digital camera slung around her neck, while all the other women were wearing suit coats and jewels, their hair professionally sculpted and styled.

"I wonder who invited her," Meredith whispered back.

The luncheons were for society members only, though each was allowed to bring one guest a year. Julia had assumed Gertie didn't know anyone in Savannah.

Regina told the audience how she had acquired the letters and how she had used them, along with other historical records, to recreate the life of Florence Martus. "I don't want to give away all the details," she said with a cultured laugh, "or you wouldn't need to go out and purchase your own copy."

The audience laughed, and Julia was amazed at how captivated everyone seemed to be by Regina.

"I know the book comes as a complete surprise to all of you." Regina's face softened, and her voice took on an empathetic tone. "It's hard to see our heroes and heroines fall from grace. There are ever so many of them who have disappointed us lately, aren't there? It seems the very people we want to hold up as role models and pillars of moral strength and integrity are the ones who crumble under our expectations—even dozens or hundreds of years later."

Regina went on to tell them about the documentary crew. She didn't give away any details about the book itself or the historical resources she used to corroborate the content. She hinted at several scandals but left many things unsaid, Julia imagined that every person in the room couldn't wait to get their hands on a copy and see for themselves.

When she came to the end of her speech, she asked if anyone had any questions.

Julia raised her hand.

Recognition twitched in Regina's face as she looked at Julia, but she continued to smile. "Yes?"

Julia stood and smiled at Regina. "My name is Julia Foley."

"I'm so glad you could come today, Julia," Regina said with little emotion.

"Thank you for speaking to our group. It's been fascinating."

"Thank you for having me."

"You've said your story is based on letters written by Florence Martus to her cousin, correct?"

"Yes." Regina watched her closely, as did Allegra Timmons, whose back went rigid when Julia began to speak.

"I'm wondering if the entire story is true or if you used some literary license to make it more interesting. I imagine a lot of writers are forced to add a few fictitious details to keep the reader turning the page."

Regina cocked her head to the side, her smile turning a little more pointed. "Are you suggesting I made up parts of the story?"

"I'm not suggesting you did," Julia said, not wanting Regina to go on the defense. "I'm just wondering if everything is factual, or if some of it was elaborated to make for a more compelling book."

"The story is true, to the best of my knowledge." Regina put her hands on the sides of the podium, as if bracing herself. "I had to round out the edges, so to speak, to make everything fit together nicely. It is, after all, a nonfiction narrative. Florence didn't give all the details of her love affair with Mr. Hai Ching, but one can easily read between the lines and fill in the blanks. That's all I've done."

"So the love scenes, for instance," Julia said with a little more confidence, "are purely imagined on your part. Florence didn't say in her letters that she and Hai Ching were intimate."

"Of course she didn't," Regina said, as if Julia was a simpleton. "A lady didn't talk about such things in her generation."

Some of the women giggled at Regina's remark, but Julia disregarded their response.

"So then," she went on, "it might also be safe to assume that Florence didn't talk about being a spy, either, and that you had to 'round out the edges' in that part of the tale as well."

Allegra started to rise from her spot, and Regina shook her head. Allegra sat once again, and Regina looked down at the podium for a moment, as if composing her thoughts. "One would need to read the letters to understand the depth of Florence and Hai Ching's love affair as well as her carefully coded words that confess her involvement in espionage. She didn't need to be explicit for me to understand what she meant. And with a little bit of research to confirm my suspicions, I feel very confident that everything I've written is as accurate as humanly possible, without Florence writing the account for herself."

"But the letters aren't on public display, are they?" Julia asked. "We'll have to take your word for it."

Regina shook her head. "No, they're not." Then she nodded. "And yes, you will."

Allegra gained Regina's attention and pointed at her watch.

"I'm afraid I've run out of time," Regina said to the group. "It's been a pleasure to be here today. I will be holding a book signing event at Bookin' It Bookstore later this week. I hope all of you will join me there."

Beatrice stood and clapped her hands with gusto. The audience was a little slower to applaud their speaker.

Regina waved goodbye as she, Allegra, and Frederick rose and walked toward the door.

Julia took her seat again. In a court of law, even a shadow of a doubt by a jury could allow a defendant to go free. And Julia had more than a shadow of a doubt that Regina's story was completely true. In a nonfiction book, it was a big risk to "read between the lines" as Regina had just admitted to doing. She had just confessed that Florence had not been explicit about the love affair or the espionage—and if she hadn't, then perhaps there were other parts of the story Regina had fabricated or interpreted for her own purposes.

"I wonder why she won't admit the book is a work of fiction," Julia said to Meredith. "Then she could get away with interpreting the letters. Why does she insist it's all fact?"

"Because she's known for her factual stories." Meredith watched the small group leave the room. "If someone can prove that this story is based on lies or half truths, then her other stories might be scrutinized closer."

"But didn't she just admit it's based on half truths?"

Meredith shook her head. "She said she confirmed her suspicions with research."

"But what research did she do? What sources did she use?"

As Beatrice started the monthly business meeting, Julia excused herself from the table to go to the ladies' room.

Under all her refined behavior and polished manners, Regina Terrance was hiding something. Julia was determined to discover what that was.

Chapter Five

THE DECOR IN THE MANSION on Forsyth Park was elegant and beautiful but a little too dark for Julia's taste. Hidden alcoves, long, heavily wallpapered halls, and mood lighting were some of the features the decorator had used to give the space a mysterious ambiance.

Julia left the well-lit ballroom where they held their luncheon and was immediately cast into the shadows of the interior of the hotel, made even darker by the gloomy weather outside. The ladies' room was down a narrow corridor and around the corner, so she headed in that direction. Light from the front lobby drew her attention. Allegra stood near the front door, her arms laden with a stack of folders, a messenger bag slung over her shoulder and a cell phone in hand. Her attention was on Gertie Hanson, who stood in front of Allegra, speaking with animated hands and face. Julia was too far away to hear the words, but Allegra was shaking her head no. Was Gertie offering her assistance once again?

Julia couldn't imagine being such an avid fan of anyone that she would use her time and money to travel and meet the celebrity. But, then again, hadn't she gone to see the homes of famous people? Abraham Lincoln's home in Springfield, Illinois, George Washington's in Mount Vernon, Paul Revere's in Boston, and Louisa May Alcott's in Concord? Just last night, Beau had mentioned his desire to go to

Little Falls, Minnesota, one day to see the boyhood home of aviator Charles A. Lindbergh. Was that much different than Gertie coming to Savannah to meet her favorite author? How much more enjoyable to actually meet the person, instead of just see the house where they once lived?

Julia smiled to herself at the thought and proceeded down the hall.

But another movement and conversation caught her attention and made her pause.

In one of the shadowed alcoves off the hall, a man and a woman stood close together in a heated argument. Julia didn't want to eavesdrop, so she walked faster and pretended she didn't notice—but the man's voice was raised, and it was hard not to hear.

"What about me?" he asked. "What do I get out of this?"

"Quiet," the woman said, speaking in a strained voice. "Do you want someone to hear you?"

"I don't care who hears me." His voice became louder. "I didn't sign up for this cat-and-mouse chase."

"Shh." The woman started to move out of the alcove, and Julia's eyes grew wide. It was Regina Terrance. "I don't want to talk about this again," she said to the man. "You have a job to do, so do it and stop complaining."

Frederick Hayes followed her, his jaw so tight a muscle jumped in his cheek. "Stop playing games with me, Regina, you know what I wa—"

Regina saw Julia, and she put her hand up to Frederick's chest to silence him.

Frederick stopped talking midsentence and turned to look in the direction Regina was staring.

Julia paused, embarrassment rushing up her neck and warming her cheeks. She hadn't meant to eavesdrop, but it looked as if she had come to do that very thing.

No one said a word, but then Regina lifted her chin and straightened the lapels of her jacket. Gone was her cool, sophisticated charm. A scowl tilted her brow as she pushed past Julia and walked toward the front lobby.

"Pardon me," Frederick said to Julia as he brushed past her and followed Regina.

Silence filled the corridor as Julia's mouth slipped open, and she stared after the pair.

Her embarrassment soon melted away, and in its place curiosity rose up.

What had they been fighting about? Their mannerisms and body language had indicated the fight was more than professional—but how much more? They'd been standing awfully close in the alcove. What had Frederick meant when he said he hadn't signed up for this cat-and-mouse chase? What cat-and-mouse chase? Hadn't he come to town to film a documentary about Florence Martus? What else could he be doing here? And what had he meant when he asked Regina what would he get out of this? Wasn't he being paid? Or was there something else he wanted? Something more personal?

Questions were still stirring in Julia's mind when she returned to the ballroom a few minutes later.

The business meeting was well underway as she slipped into her seat next to Meredith.

"What happened to you?" Meredith asked quietly as the treasurer of the society read off the expense report for last month. "You have that look on your face."

"What look?" Julia whispered back.

"You've been intrigued by something."

"I have a look for that?"

Meredith grinned. "You have a look for everything."

Julia tried to hide a chuckle. A few of the women at their table gave Julia and Meredith pointed glances.

"I *am* intrigued," Julia said close to Meredith's ear, "but I'll tell you about it later. Let's stop by the library before we go back to the office. I'd like to see what Rebecca knows about our Waving Girl."

Meredith nodded. They had come to rely on their friend Rebecca Thompson, a librarian at the Live Oak Library, as one of their greatest resources. Rebecca and her husband were experts at Savannah's history and loved to help Julia and Meredith solve all sorts of mysteries.

It was past time they asked Rebecca about Florence Martus. If anyone knew the truth about Savannah's first hostess, it would be Rebecca.

The meeting droned on and on. Beatrice loved being the center of attention and often brought up inconsequential matters that didn't need to be discussed at the luncheons.

When they were finally able to escape, Julia and Meredith walked out into the drizzling rain under their umbrellas. Usually, they walked to the Mansion from the agency, but it had been raining when they came today, so they had taken Julia's car. They got into it and shook out their umbrellas before pulling them into the vehicle.

"Someone needs to tell Beatrice we don't come to these luncheons to discuss the toilet paper brand used in the welcome center downtown," Julia said with a sigh. "I don't care if it's one ply or two or how much more each roll costs if we go with standard or luxury grade."

Meredith laughed. "I find her entertaining."

Julia looked at her friend out of the corner of her eye. "I wish I felt the same."

"Just try it sometime," Meredith encouraged Julia. "Stop watching the clock and just view the whole thing as a performance. Beatrice is actually a really amusing entertainer. Because at the end of the day, that's all she's doing. Putting on a show."

Julia rolled her eyes.

"Now, tell me," Meredith said, changing the subject. "What happened when you left the ballroom?"

"Oh!" How could she have forgotten? "I heard Regina Terrance and Frederick Hayes in an awkward conversation in one of the alcoves."

"Awkward? How?" Meredith's voice rose an octave. "As in a romantic rendezvous?"

"I don't know." Julia shrugged. "They were having a heated argument." She told Meredith everything she had heard and then the way Regina had brushed past her, as if Julia wasn't worthy of her attention.

"Interesting," Meredith said. "I'm sure she was caught off guard when she saw you and didn't know how else to deal with the situation."

"I agree." Julia took a right and then a block later took a left onto Bull Street.

"Did you start reading *The Waving Girl*?" Meredith asked.

"This morning, but I didn't get far. What about you?"

"Last night." Meredith gave Julia a sheepish look. "I admit, I was so engrossed in the story, I stayed up way past my bedtime to keep reading."

"Really?" Julia was surprised, since Meredith was usually such an early-to-bed person.

"Whether the story is factual or not," Meredith said, "Regina is a good writer. I kept telling myself I needed to put the book down and go to sleep, but I couldn't stop reading. The love affair between Florence and Hai Ching starts very soon after the story begins, and it's both sweet and heartbreaking."

"I know." Julia couldn't deny Regina was a good writer, or that the story was intriguing and well told. "I'm just getting to the part where their friendship changes into romance, and they're trying desperately to hide it from her parents and brother."

"Wait until you see what happens next," Meredith said. "It's so sad."

"Don't ruin it for me." Julia parked across the street from the Live Oak Library. The library had been organized by the Colored Library Association of Savannah, which was founded in 1906 by a group of conscientious African-American men, leaders in their communities. The beautiful brick building was built and dedicated in 1914. Large pillars flanked the steps, and as the partners passed through the front doors, they were greeted by a wide-open room smelling of old books and buried secrets.

"Well, if it isn't my favorite female detectives," Rebecca said with a smile as she set down a piece of paper she'd been holding and stood to greet Julia and Meredith. She was working behind the circulation desk, which was a long wooden counter with a computer and barcode scanner.

"Hello, Rebecca," Julia said. "How are you?"

"I'm good. What brings you two into the library on this gloomy day?"

"We're here to learn everything we can about Florence Martus," Meredith said. "Have you heard about the new book?"

"Who hasn't?" Rebecca shook her head. "Kelvin has gotten a lot more questions about the Waving Girl on his Savannah River history cruises because of it."

Kelvin, Rebecca's husband, offered river cruises for a big excursion company and was known as "the Voice of the Savannah." He was considered to be an expert on the Savannah River, both its history and its geological formations.

"He's been fielding questions about Florence Martus from several newspapers," Rebecca continued, "and he was even approached by the documentary film crew who took his tour and asked if they could interview him on film."

"Did Kelvin mention what questions the film crew asked?" Julia wondered.

"Just basic information," Rebecca said. "Nothing unusual, at least, not that I recall."

"What do you know about Florence Martus?" Meredith asked Rebecca.

The library was quiet that day, with the rain probably keeping people at home. There was an older woman looking through a stack of magazines on a nearby table, and a younger woman browsing the shelves near the back, but that was all Julia noticed.

"Why don't we take a seat?" Rebecca suggested.

She led them to a grouping of comfortable chairs on the side of the building, within sight of the circulation desk. Green lamps were turned on and offered a pleasant glow while the rain continued to fall outside the large, leaded windows.

"We've been hired by Florence Martus's grandniece to try to prove the book is fictitious," Julia explained to Rebecca. "So any information you might have to help us, or any resources you might know of to point us in the right direction, would be wonderful."

"I'm happy to share everything I know." Rebecca clasped her hands in her lap. "After Kelvin came home and told me about the film crew and the book, we were both curious. I did a little research on my own, just to refresh my memory. I can't find anything that would justify that author accusing Florence of murder, espionage, or a forbidden love affair."

"That's what our client says," Meredith said. "We need to be able to verify the truth."

"What I do know is that Florence waved at over fifty thousand ships during her forty-four years on Elba Island, from 1887 to 1931," Rebecca said with admiration in her voice. "By day, she waved a white towel or other linen, and by night, a lantern. She loved dogs and would often have one at her side. She said they would wake her at night when they heard the ships coming. She didn't miss a single one, not even when she was ill. Seamen from all over the world knew who Florence was, even if they didn't know her by name. She was the Waving Girl of Savannah, and her likeness could be found in taverns, warehouses, and ports of call all over the world." Rebecca smiled. "Some people say she's better known on the seven seas than she is right here in Savannah. There are several accounts of sailors and seamen who couldn't wait to see her at the lighthouse, whether coming or going. They would start on one end of the ship's deck and walk along to the other, waving to her until she was out of sight. They blew whistles and foghorns and always greeted her as fondly as she greeted them."

"Every day for forty-four years," Meredith said.

"Every single day." Rebecca nodded. "People thought that perhaps she was a simpleton, but when newspaper reporters interviewed her later on in life, they found her to be a very sweet, gentle, and intelligent woman."

"What happened when she left the island?" Julia asked. "How long did she live in retirement?"

"Twelve years. She and her brother moved to the Bona Bella neighborhood."

"I just learned that from Florence's grandniece," Julia said, leaning forward in her chair. "That's close to where I live."

"When they arrived," Rebecca continued, "they were greeted by a 'welcome to Savannah' committee, comprised of several leading businessmen, as well as the mayor of Savannah at that time. She was quite the celebrity, and she was dearly missed on the river."

"Is it true she burned her diary when she left the lighthouse?" Meredith asked.

"Yes, unfortunately," Rebecca said. "No one knows why. About five years after she left the island, a reporter spoke to her and learned that she had kept a diary and a log of all the ships she'd waved at. She recorded the ships' names, where they were from, and what kinds they were. He asked her why she burned it, but she said she didn't think it would have anything of value for anyone else."

"Still," Meredith mused, "that's an odd thing to do."

"I agree." Rebecca tapped her fingers on the table. "And when people asked her why she waved, she never gave a real answer. Over the years, people have come up with some wild reasons but none as explicit as Regina Terrance—and none that actually claim to be the real story."

"Do you think any of Regina's claims are true?" Julia asked Rebecca.

Rebecca let out a long sigh. "My gut tells me they're not, but I can't say for sure."

"Do you think the letters Regina said she used actually exist?"

"I suppose anything is possible."

"Do you know anything else that might help us?" Meredith asked. "Any family records?"

"I have been searching through all my files," Rebecca began, "but I haven't found anything. For as special and important as Florence is to Savannah, there's really very little information about her life. You could look online. There are a few things about her family there, but again, a lot of it is hearsay. I think the Savannah Historical Society might have a few records. You could ask Beatrice for access to those things."

It was the last thing Julia wanted to do, but if it helped their case, she would.

A library patron stepped up to the circulation desk, and Rebecca had to excuse herself to check the young woman out.

"Well?" Meredith asked Julia. "Would you like to contact Beatrice, or should I?"

Julia lifted her eyebrows and tilted her head. "Must you even ask?"

Meredith smiled. "Consider it done."

"While you do that," Julia said, "I'll contact Allegra Simmons and see if we can schedule a meeting with Regina. Maybe if it's just us she'll be less evasive, since she won't be trying to sell us her book."

"I have a feeling that woman is always trying to sell something." Meredith stood and Julia followed.

As important as this case was, they had other business matters and other clients to deal with back at the office. When Julia had a spare minute, she'd continue to read Regina's book. Though she tried to convince herself the only reason she wanted to read it was to help their client, she couldn't deny that Regina wrote a very intriguing story.

Chapter Six

SUNDAY MORNING, JULIA STOOD BEHIND a line of banquet tables the youth group had set up in the fellowship hall of New Beginnings Church. The tables were laden with all sorts of delicious baked goods provided by the teenagers and their families. Julia had even solicited Carmen's help. Carmen loved to cook and took advantage of any opportunity she could find to try out a new recipe or two. When Julia had told her she needed baked goods, Carmen had brought over dozens of caramel rolls, cinnamon rolls, and cookies.

"Thank you for supporting the youth group," Julia said to Naomi Markham, the senior pastor's wife and one of Julia's friends. She had purchased four dozen cookies and a pan of Carmen's caramel rolls.

"Thank you for all of your hard work, Julia," Naomi responded. "You've done so much to help the youth group. Ed really appreciates all your help."

"It's my pleasure." Julia smiled as she put the money into the cash box. "The kids bless me more than I bless them, I'm sure."

Naomi took her treats off to the church kitchen, no doubt planning to store them there until she and Pastor Ed went home after the second service.

A dozen youth group members spread out around the tables, visiting with the congregants as they looked over the offerings and asked the students about their youth convention. Julia loved organizing fundraisers like this one, in which multiple generations came together to get to know one another better.

Olivia Harold stood near a white-haired woman, a smile on her face as she nodded at whatever the woman was saying.

Julia had been watching Olivia and Ebony Lester. The girls had been inseparable two weeks ago, but today, they didn't even acknowledge each other. Julia had hoped that whatever had come between them would have blown over by now, but it was clear it had not. If anything, they were more distant today than at Wednesday night youth group.

As the first service people started to trickle out, the second service people began to arrive. A steady stream of shoppers circled the bake sale items, and within the hour, almost everything had been purchased and the cash box was full.

Julia walked around the tables, moving the remaining items to a more central location, and caught Olivia's eye. She smiled at her, and Olivia smiled back, but it didn't reach her eyes.

"How are you?" Julia asked her, quiet enough that the others might not hear them. The students had congregated at the opposite end of the tables.

"Fine," Olivia said, though she didn't sound or look fine.

"I noticed you and Ebony are still fighting."

Olivia glanced toward Ebony and shrugged one shoulder.

"I want to help." Julia had known Olivia since she was a toddler running around the church nursery. Over the years, they'd gotten to know one another well, both in and out of church, since Julia and Beau were friends with Olivia's parents. It hurt Julia to see Olivia's friendships suffering. "You can trust me."

"I thought I could trust Ebony too, but it turns out I was wrong."

"What happened?" Julia had spent most of her legal career working with kids. She had seen almost everything. "There's nothing you can tell me that will shock me or make me think less of you or Ebony."

Olivia looked up at Julia, pain in her eyes. "I guess you'll hear about it. I might as well tell you the truth so you don't believe their lies."

"Do you want to talk about it here, or should we go somewhere more private?"

"What does it matter? They've all heard about it."

The fellowship hall had quieted down quite a bit, and most of the congregants had left. Two of the parent volunteers were helping the remaining shoppers, and the students were busy visiting. None of them seemed to be paying attention to Julia or Olivia.

"Last summer," Olivia began, "I started to date a boy a couple of years older than me. My parents didn't know." She stopped and swallowed but didn't meet Julia's gaze. "I wasn't supposed to start dating until I turned sixteen, but Tyler Toby was the most popular kid in school and I didn't want to tell him I had to wait. So, I went out with him."

Julia kept her expression neutral, and Olivia continued.

"When my parents found out, they told me I had to break up with him. By that time, I was ready to be done with him anyway. He dated a lot of girls before me and had a lot more *experience*." She emphasized the last word, and Julia nodded in understanding.

"He was upset," Olivia said, "but he knew I couldn't keep disobeying my parents. We still talked at school and texted all the time. But when I turned sixteen a couple of weeks ago, he asked me out again." She ran her finger along the edge of the table closest to her. "I didn't want to go out with him again. I knew that this time I wouldn't have an excuse to break up with him. And I also knew that if we started to date again, he'd want me to do things I don't want to do. So I told him no."

"You made the right choice, Olivia."

Olivia looked up at Julia for the first time since she started to tell her the story. "I know what Tyler wants, and I don't want to date someone who'll pressure me like that."

Julia smiled. "I'm proud of you for taking a stand. You're making the right choice."

"But none of it matters." Tears filled Olivia's eyes, and she looked down again. "When I told Tyler I didn't want to date him again, he started to spread nasty rumors about me. He said I did things—" She choked on her tears and impatiently wiped her cheek. "Everyone believes him." She jerked her head toward Ebony. "Even my best friends believe him. I think Ebony always liked Tyler, so she'll do anything to make him notice her—even spread his lies to all my church friends." She bit her bottom lip as she composed herself. "She won't even let me tell her the truth. Every time I try to talk to her, she ignores me. She's turned everyone against me—and she's supposed to be my friend."

Julia's heart broke for Olivia. She had seen enough in her courtroom to know the telltale signs of an honest confession and one that was full of lies and half truths. Olivia was telling her the truth. "I'm sorry."

Olivia shrugged again. "My parents are mad at me because I dropped out of softball. Ebony's on the team, and she's been horrible. I wanted to drop out of youth group and not go to the convention, but they're making me stick to my church activities."

"Have you told them what's happening?"

"I disobeyed them last year when I dated Tyler and lied to them about it. I need to earn back their trust." She wiped another tear. "I should've never dated Tyler to begin with. He's nothing like everyone thinks."

"You need to at least try to talk to your parents." Julia had watched enough families over the years to know that parents valued a child's honesty, even if it was hard to hear. "Tell them the truth before they hear the lies. Trust them to discern your heart. I know your parents. They'll listen to you."

The youth group students broke out in laughter at something someone said, and Olivia glanced in their direction. Her eyebrows were heavy with pain and disappointment.

"What about my friends?" she asked. "How will I get them to believe me?"

Julia wished she knew. "It'll take time." She put her hand on Olivia's arm. "And you might have to make new friends."

Olivia's mom stepped out of the sanctuary and caught Olivia's eye. She motioned for her to come to the sanctuary for the second service.

"Is it okay if I leave?" Olivia asked Julia. "Do you need any more help with the bake sale?"

Julia shook her head. "I don't think so. You can join your mom."

"Okay." She started to walk away but then turned and looked back at Julia. "Thanks for listening—and believing me."

"Anytime, Olivia. I hope things go well with your parents."

Julia let out a long breath. She would remember to keep Olivia in her prayers. The girl had some damage to repair because of her strained relationship with her parents, but harder still would be the act of forgiving those who were spreading rumors about her. Forgiving someone who hadn't asked for forgiveness might just be the hardest thing to do.

***

Another storm passed through Savannah that night as Julia sat in bed, her pillows propping her up while her reading lamp shone over her shoulder, illuminating the book in her hands. Her warm comforter was tucked up around her waist, and her readers were perched on her nose.

The storm blew outside, and rain beat against the window. Beau puttered around in the bathroom, and Bunny, the rescue cat they had brought home last fall, was curled up next to Julia on the bed.

But it was the book in Julia's hands that had her complete attention. Her eyes were wide as she read one page and then the next. Whether or not the story was true, it was a compelling and intriguing read. Regina Terrance painted Florence as a restless, young, adventure seeker who was tired of her life on the island. The book portrayed her father as a cruel and authoritative figure in her life, in complete control of Florence, her mother, and her brother, George. Not only did John Martus dictate the actions, words, and behaviors of his family, but he also dictated what Florence and her mother wore, what they cooked, and even how they spent their time. He detested idleness and forbade Florence from reading books, telling her they were frivolous and a waste of time. They never had visitors, and when supplies were needed, he was the one to leave the island to get them. By Florence's nineteenth birthday, the book claimed she had not left the island since they'd arrived there six years before. Even when her older sister was married, they didn't attend the wedding. Florence's father had tried to stop his daughter from marrying and leaving them, but she had disobeyed his orders and was then shunned.

"And Regina got all this information from the letters?" Julia asked herself. She was skeptical, to say the least. The book also claimed Florence and her brother were severely abused, both physically and mentally, made to fear the outside world so they would never want to leave the island.

Beau flipped off the bathroom light and walked around to his side of the bed. He took off his bathrobe and lifted the comforter to get into bed.

Julia glanced up at him as he got settled under the covers, his back propped up against a bank of pillows. He turned on his reading lamp and pulled out his biography of Charles Lindbergh, by A. Scott Berg. It was a thick, hardbound book with a black-and-white picture of a young Lindbergh on the cover. Beau was about halfway through the book and had told Julia several things she hadn't known about the world-famous aviator who had taken his small monoplane, the *Spirit of St. Louis*, and flown solo, nonstop from New York to Paris in 1927.

Beau glanced at her and then pointed at *The Waving Girl* in her hands. "Is it any good?"

"As a novel, it would be fascinating, but as a nonfiction book about a dearly beloved Savannah heroine, it leaves a lot to be desired."

He smiled. "I believe you."

"It's just hard to reshape my opinion about someone as innocent and genuine as the Florence Martus I've always heard about."

"When I was in the clubhouse today I overheard some guys talking about her."

"Really?" Julia put her finger in her book and turned to look at Beau a little closer. "What did they say? Were they talking about the book?"

"One man said his wife had told him about Florence—at least the Florence the book portrays." He shook his head. "The guys weren't even questioning whether it was true or not. They were discussing how Florence's work as a spy for the Chinese government had assisted China in their trade relations with the United States. They said she kept a journal of all the ships coming and going from the Port of Savannah because she was a member of a network of spies along the US coastline. Her waving was actually a series of signals she gave to the Chinese ships coming into port."

"Then why did she wave at all the ships?"

"They said she waved at all the ships so the government wouldn't catch on to her. But when she waved at the Chinese ships, it was different. They were watching her for messages."

Julia frowned. "That sounds nothing like the Florence Martus everyone in Savannah loves." She pointed at her book. "And all that came from this book?"

"I don't know." Beau shrugged. "That's what I overheard at the clubhouse today."

"I'm familiar with the Chinese Exclusion Act of 1882," Julia said, "but I don't know a lot about Chinese and US relations beyond that."

"It's rarely been good. In the 1880s it was so violent there was an attack on Chinese miners in Wyoming and twenty-eight men were killed. That sparked a wave of similar assaults across the American west. In the 1890s, Chinese people had to carry a residence permit if they lived in the US, or face deportment. They were prevented from immigrating to America well into the 1940s and, even after that, it was limited. There were all sorts of issues with exporting and importing, US missionary involvement in China, and more."

"Do you think China had spies in America?"

"I wouldn't be surprised. I'm sure America had spies in China too."

"Do you think Florence could have been a spy?" Julia still couldn't wrap her mind around such a thing. From all accounts, Florence was shy, gentle, and soft spoken. If she was a spy, she had been a really good one. No one would have suspected her.

"I don't know. I suppose anything is possible."

"I need to finish this book and then keep digging for the sources Regina claims to have used. If I can see them with my own eyes, I'll believe it. But until then, I won't be convinced."

"Have you spoken to the author?"

Julia shook her head. "Not since the society meeting. I called her publicist and left two messages. I also emailed her, but she hasn't responded. There's a book signing this week, and I plan to go and see if I can arrange a meeting with her while I'm there."

"It sounds like book sales are going well for her."

"Yes." Julia sighed. "The title is listed in the top fifty books on Amazon right now."

"Wow. That's pretty impressive."

"Very impressive—and also sad. How many people reading the book will search for the truth?"

"Unfortunately, not many." Beau held up Lindbergh's biography. "This is another man who had a lot of speculation about his life, especially about his involvement with Germany during World War II. People remember that he tried keeping America out of the war because he believed Germany was unbeatable, but do they know that after Pearl Harbor Lindbergh worked as a civilian airman in the Pacific and shot down at least one enemy plane? He taught the American pilots how to ration their gas and engaged in several combat missions. Sometimes, it's nice to just read the facts and not have some talking head interpreting them for you."

"Is Lindbergh's biography well written?"

"It's exceptional. It won A. Scott Berg the Pulitzer Prize for Biography in 1999, and it was a *New York Times* Best Seller. He does a magnificent job in telling the story without slanting the reader's opinion one way or the other. He neither paints Lindbergh in a good light nor a bad light but simply tells the history of his life." Beau chuckled. "Talk about a man who had misinformation spread about him from day one."

"How'd he deal with it?"

"Ignored it. And when he was on his deathbed, he told his wife not to spend the rest of her life defending him."

"Sometimes it takes just as much courage not to defend yourself as it does to stand up and fight." Julia's mind went to Olivia, and she wondered if it would be better for her to ignore Ebony or to stand up and fight for herself.

"Speaking of defending oneself, I saw you talking to Olivia today." Beau was so good at keeping track of Julia's cases and the things that concerned her. And sometimes, like now, it was as if he knew her thoughts. "Did you get her to open up?"

Julia told Beau what Olivia had shared with her, knowing he was a safe place to confide. "I encouraged her to talk to her parents."

He nodded. "That's a good place to start. Hopefully, this will all blow over in time."

"I hope so too."

"In the meantime," Beau said as he slipped his book open, "we both have some reading to do."

Julia smiled, remembering how she used to think a quiet night at home with a book in hand would be boring. Now, she liked nothing better.

Chapter Seven

Oh, Lavinia,

You've made this old woman smile. Your letter dated August 15th was a balm for my melancholy soul. The rain and humidity have been incessant here in Savannah, and they have done nothing for my mood or my rheumatism. But when I read your letter, it was like a ray of sunshine burst forth into my dreary little world, and now, I will take a break from darning stockings and return to a different time and place, one laced with the scent of hyacinth and gardenias, of river water and foghorns, of hopes and dreams. Of a time when everything seemed possible and nothing was yet out of my reach.

I'm so happy you're curious about Hai Ching and, as you put it, our "book-worthy love story." But that is what has put a smile in my heart. It wasn't book-worthy, nor was it so out of the ordinary. Our bond grew as all such bonds do, through mutual respect and admiration, through shared values and beliefs, and through common goals and dreams. It was as simple as breathing in and out. Instinctual. Something you

71

don't need to be taught or reminded to do. That was how our love felt. There were no fireworks, no bells ringing, no signs spelled out in big letters in the sky. Over a very short amount of time, my soul recognized something familiar within him and our hearts were knit together. It was love, pure and simple, and once I found it, I never wanted to let it go.

My father and mother were not blind, though I thought I was hiding my feelings well. Three weeks after Hai Ching's arrival, he was well enough to join us at our kitchen table to eat meals with the family. It was the first time my parents saw our interaction, and looking back, I'm certain our affection for one another was evident. How could it not be? How could I hide the smiles or ignore the way my heart fluttered whenever I looked into his eyes? How could I stop from hanging on his every word or repeating exciting things he had told me to my parents?

After that first meal, I saw the way my parents looked at one another with concern, and then my father called me into his office to talk.

I wish you could have known my father. He was a strong, authoritative figure, with certain expectations regarding our behavior, but he was also good and kind and loving. He ruled with a firm hand, though his grace and mercy were limitless. He was a man of deep and abiding faith, and understood the dire consequences of sin. He taught freely from the Word of God, but his message was not all about condemnation. He also taught me about the love and steadfast faithfulness of God.

My respect and admiration for Father knew no bounds. The way he put my mother and his children first was always something I could count on, even when that meant making decisions for us that I didn't agree with. He had tried to stop my sister from marrying a man he did not trust or like, but she eloped with him and suffered the consequences. It grieved my father, but he told us we must turn our backs on her and the life she chose to live with her husband. But when she returned to us, ten years later, knowing she had made a mistake, my father freely forgave her and helped her create a new life for herself and her children.

So, when my father told me he was turning all of Hai Ching's care over to my mother, I knew he was trying to protect me. Maybe not from Hai Ching, because he seemed to truly respect and admire the man I fell in love with, but from myself. From my own innocence and naivete. He knew a life with Hai Ching would be out of the question, and I was too young to understand the consequences. He wasn't stupid. He was trying to keep me from a life of hardship, but at the time, I saw him as only overbearing and unjust.

From that point on, I was not allowed to be alone with Hai Ching. I was not allowed to enter his room, take care of his needs, or seek out his company. If I wanted to visit with him, it had to be in the open, with my brother or parents present. As you can imagine, I was angry and disappointed, but I respected my father too much to disobey him.

There were still times when Hai Ching and I found ourselves alone, when my brother was called away or we happened to be walking around the island at the same time. We never did anything I am ashamed of, but he did kiss me, and it was the most wonderful experience of my life. I'm not ashamed to say that he is the only man who has ever kissed me. Does that shock you? Once Hai Ching came into my life, I never once wished to be kissed by anyone else again.

Two more weeks passed and Hai Ching's wounds had healed enough that there was no longer any threat of infection, and his pain had decreased to manageable levels. He was working just as hard as my father and brother on the island, trying to repay his debt for our care, and my father decided it was time for him to leave us.

On a dark, sultry night, with no moon and only the stars as light, I sat on the porch after supper to catch my breath and try to accept the fact that Hai Ching would soon be gone. I had known the day would come, but those five weeks with him had somehow felt like a lifetime, and I had started to believe they would continue on for an eternity.

Hai Ching found me there, alone, on the porch, and he was just as sad as I was. He whispered that he loved me and he couldn't imagine his life without me. We clung to one another, heedless of my parents and brother just inside the house. That's when Hai Ching asked me to be his wife. He did not want to leave me any more than I wanted him gone. I knew it would not be an easy life, but I believed, with all my heart, that we could make it work. Love has a way of doing that. It gives you hope that together, you can overcome any obstacles.

I quickly learned I was wrong.

But that part of the story will have to wait until my next letter. George will be coming home soon, and I must get his supper prepared. Besides, if he knew I was telling you this story, I'm afraid he'd advise me to quit now, before I divulge the worst of it.

Just as you have done with mine, I have also destroyed your letters. I cannot take the chance that George will find them, though he rarely reads my correspondence. It would disappoint him if he knew I still held these memories so close to my heart.

Until next time, sweet Lavinia, I remain,

Yours truly,

Florence

Sunshine warmed Julia's neck as she sat in a booth at the Downhome Diner, waiting for Meredith to arrive. She held *The Waving Girl* in her hands, unable to put it down. She'd bypassed the intimate trysts between Florence and Hai Ching as they hid from her father and was now reading about the night her father forced Hai Ching to leave the island. A more wretched and heartbreaking scene Julia had never read before. John Martus's cruelty and disdain for Hai Ching seemed relentless, and it was this abuse that Hai Ching desperately wanted to save Florence from. They were both scared of her father, and, according to the book, rightfully so.

"Julia." Meredith was sitting on the bench directly across from Julia, but Julia hadn't noticed her come into the restaurant, nor take a seat. "Care if I interrupt?"

Julia slipped a bookmark into place and set the book on the table, a little embarrassed to be found so engrossed in it. "I can't put it down."

"I've had the same trouble." Meredith reached inside her purse and pulled the book out. "I take it out whenever I get a chance. In the waiting room at my dentist appointment, while I was standing in line at the store, and even when I was in the car wash."

"What do you make of it?"

Meredith put her book back in her purse and shrugged. "It's well written, that's for sure, and leaves me wondering what will happen next."

"Good morning, ladies." Charlene smiled and held up the coffeepot. "Care for a cup?"

Both Julia and Meredith turned their cups right side up and thanked Charlene for the coffee.

"What will you have this morning?" Charlene asked.

"I'll have biscuits and gravy," Julia said, not needing to look at a menu. She'd been craving them for days.

Meredith smiled at Charlene. "And I'll have your breakfast scramble."

"Coming right up." Charlene turned to walk away but paused and smiled when her mother entered the diner. "Morning, Mama."

"Morning, baby." Maggie Lu gave Charlene a quick hug and then she noticed Julia and Meredith sitting in the booth. "Morning, you two."

"Good morning, Maggie Lu." Julia moved over on the bench seat. "Would you like to join us? We were going to call you today and see if we could meet with you."

Maggie Lu was tall and carried herself with an elegant, regal air. She wore a pair of slacks and a pretty blue blouse today. She looked like she was on her way somewhere important, but she nodded. "Sure I will. I don't need to be at the ladies' aid meeting for another hour. I was just stopping by for a quick cup of coffee."

"Perfect." Julia patted the seat next to her.

They chatted for a few minutes. Meredith told them that her son Chase had recently come to visit and that Carmen had also come over. They sometimes met at Meredith's house when he was in town and cooked meals with each other. Meredith was in favor of that, since she loved spending time with both of them and enjoyed being on the receiving end of their delicious food. Julia had thought that the two of them would be a little more serious by now, but they were taking their time, and neither one seemed to be in any hurry.

Maggie Lu told them she'd babysat little Jake so Clarissa could have an afternoon off. She glowed when she spoke about her great-grandson, and it made Julia's heart warm to see her friend so happy.

"What about you?" Maggie Lu asked Julia. "What's been happening in your corner of the world?"

Julia took a sip of her coffee. "Meredith and I have been working on several cases, including the Waving Girl one, but it's been hard finding information about Florence Martus. She seemed to be a very private woman."

"Oh, she was indeed." Maggie Lu nodded. "I remember my Granny Luv telling me a story about Miss Florence's seventieth birthday. What a day it was."

"What happened?" Meredith asked.

"To celebrate her seventieth birthday, in August of 1938, the Propeller Club of the Port of Savannah arranged to have a party at Fort Pulaski, where she was born." Maggie Lu accepted a cup of coffee from Charlene and squeezed her hand in thanks. Then she continued. "Granny Luv said there were over three thousand people there that day. Among those who attended were the mayor of Savannah, as well as a congressman who said Miss Florence was 'the sweetheart of mankind.'" She paused, her eyes bright with wonder. "Can you imagine? There were lots of bands there that day. Granny Luv said the police band, the US Navy band, and the Marine band all paraded through the fort. A Coast Guard cutter, the *Tallapoosa*, even saluted her from the Savannah River."

"That's amazing," Julia said in awe.

"Telegrams were sent to her from sea captains all over the world, and many politicians made speeches. One of them called her a 'symbol of the world.'" Maggie Lu shook her head. "She was quite a woman. Granny Luv said that when she was called upon to give a speech, Florence was just a little bit of a thing, all shy and reserved. She was so overcome with emotion, she scribbled on a piece of paper and one of the politicians read her note. It said, 'This is the grandest day of my life.'"

"What a wonderful way to celebrate her birthday," Meredith said. "What must it have been like to come from a lonely life on an island and then to be pursued by reporters, honored with a celebration of that magnitude, and have people recognize you wherever you went?"

"It goes to show that you can make a difference in this world through a simple act of kindness." Julia wrapped her hands around her warm coffee cup. "I think that's the most important lesson Florence taught everyone."

"Did you know a ship was named for her during World War II?" Maggie Lu asked.

Julia shook her head. "I know one of the Savannah Belles Ferry boats is named after her." There were four ferries that operated on the Savannah River, and each was named after an important woman in Savannah history. The *Florence Martus* floated alongside the *Juliette Gordon Low*, named for the founder of the Girl Scouts, the *Susie King Taylor*, named for the first Black army nurse, and the *Mary Musgrove*, named for the early Savannah native who served as an intermediary between the Muscogee Creek Indians and the European colonists.

"And let's not forget the statue at the end of River Street," Meredith added.

"I remember when they put up that statue," Maggie Lu said. "It was commissioned in the early 1960s and was created by the same man who made the famous statue in Washington, DC, of the marines raising the flag on Iwo Jima. Everyone agreed that the statue should be on the river, still welcoming ships into Savannah."

"And so it is." Julia took another sip of her coffee. "Florence is a symbol of hospitality and kindness for everyone in Savannah—and around the world."

Charlene came to the table with Julia's and Meredith's breakfast.

Steam rose from Julia's plate of biscuits and gravy.

"Do you want something to eat, Mama?" Charlene asked.

"No, thanks, honey. I already had my breakfast." She pointed at the coffee. "This will do for now. I can't stay much longer."

Charlene patted her mother's shoulder and left the table again.

After waiting for Julia and Meredith to bless their food, Maggie Lu asked, "Are you having any luck finding answers about the book?"

Julia shook her head. "Not much. Rebecca is looking for records, and Meredith called Beatrice to see if she could find something in the historical society archives."

"I'm starting to think that the only way we can know for sure," Meredith said, "is if we see the letters Regina Terrance has in her possession."

"*If* she has any letters," Maggie Lu said with a raised eyebrow. "She could easily be making it all up."

"But why?" Julia asked. "Why would she do that?"

"To sell books?" Maggie Lu offered.

"But she could have written about anything." Julia sliced her fork through the fluffy biscuits. "Why Florence? Why now?"

"Maybe because there's a rising interest in lesser-known historical figures," Meredith suggested. "Just think about it. *Hamilton* has taken Broadway by storm; *The Other Alcott* is about Louisa May Alcott's older sister; *Before We Were Yours* is about the real-life scandal of Georgia Tann, who kidnapped and sold poor children to wealthy families; and *The Aviator's Wife* is about Anne Morrow Lindbergh. There are dozens and dozens of books like those, telling the story of the people who were overlooked in history."

Anne Morrow Lindbergh's name piqued Julia's interest, especially because Beau was reading a biography about her husband.

"Maybe Regina wanted to cash in on the current trend," Meredith offered. "Find a lesser-known historical figure and give her a bigger-than-life story."

"I think you might be onto something," Maggie Lu agreed.

Julia took a bite of her biscuits and gravy, savoring the rich, creamy flavors. "We're planning to attend the book signing tomorrow," she said to Maggie Lu after she swallowed the first bite. "And we won't leave until we've had a chance to speak to her."

"I hope she agrees to meet with us." Meredith put a little salt on her breakfast scramble. "I think she'll be more agreeable in private."

"I hope you're right." Because Julia was running out of ideas.

Chapter Eight

BOOKIN' IT BOOKSTORE WAS A quaint shop tucked into the historic district in downtown Savannah. The building was made of brick and had a large plateglass window in front filled with a huge display of *The Waving Girl*. Already, several people were walking into the store when Julia and Meredith arrived.

"Looks like we found the right place," Julia commented as they walked down the sidewalk toward the building.

"And it looks like Regina has a lot of fans in Savannah." Meredith repositioned her purse under her arm. "I wonder what people are thinking about the book."

"We'll probably find out in a minute."

They waited for a couple of women to enter the store and then followed them inside.

The place was filled with people browsing the shelves or standing in small groups visiting. Toward the back of the long, narrow building, a group had gathered, and Julia caught a glimpse of Regina in the midst of them, sitting at a table with several stacks of her books on it.

A sign near the door had a schedule of events.

"It looks like she'll be signing books for the first half hour," Julia said to Meredith, "and then she'll be speaking to the group before signing books again."

"Should we get in line to speak to her now, or later?" Meredith asked.

"Might as well get in line now. It might be harder afterward."

They walked around several tables and shelves and joined the group waiting to speak to Regina. Allegra was standing close to Regina, alternately speaking on her phone and keeping an eye on her author.

"There's Gertie," Meredith whispered to Julia. "Regina's superfan."

Julia nodded. Gertie was a few spots ahead of them in line, clutching her book to her chest as she eagerly watched Regina visit with other readers. Her dark hair was in the ever-present ponytail, but today she was wearing a cute sundress and light cardigan sweater.

"And look who else is here," Meredith said on a sigh, nodding to the person just behind Gertie. "Marcella Martus."

"That's not good." Julia had hoped they could speak to Regina without Marcella's interference.

Marcella turned and caught sight of Julia and Meredith. She stepped out of line and joined them.

"I'm happy to see you've come," she said. "I was afraid you wouldn't show."

"Of course we're here." Meredith offered a reassuring smile.

"I haven't heard anything from either of you," Marcella said, looking from Meredith to Julia, frustration in her gaze. "What have you learned?"

"We've been reading the book," Julia said, "to see what the claims are."

"You're reading that garbage?" Marcella's voice was louder than necessary, and a few of the people standing closest to them turned in her direction.

Julia found it a bit hypocritical that Marcella would judge them for reading something she herself had read.

"We thought it best," Meredith said in a quiet voice, probably hoping to bring Marcella's volume down. "We needed to see what the story is about so we can hold it up to the facts we gather."

Julia quickly filled Marcella in on the information they had gleaned from Rebecca and Maggie Lu. "Our assistant is doing an online search as well," Julia offered, "to see if she can find more about Florence that way, but it takes some time because she has to find original sources. Otherwise we don't take it into consideration. The internet isn't the best place to look, though, since anyone can write anything and post it like they know what they're talking about."

"Have you spoken to Regina?" Marcella asked. "And demanded she show you the letters?"

"Not yet." Julia glanced toward the table to see if Regina was listening to their interaction. Thankfully, she and Allegra seemed distracted by Gertie. "I've tried contacting her and Allegra several times, but they haven't returned my inquiries. I'm hoping to speak to them here and schedule a meeting soon." Julia glanced at Meredith and could see her friend was also uncomfortable with Marcella's presence. She looked back at Marcella. "We feel this is a very delicate situation, and we don't want to insult the author. If she respects us, then perhaps she'll trust us with the truth."

Marcella snorted. "I don't think she knows the definition of the word."

"We think it would be best if you don't have any more interactions with Regina," Meredith said to Marcella, as gently as possible. "We know how upset all of this makes you—"

"Upset is too kind a word for how I feel." Marcella crossed her arms. "And if you're trying to tell me to stay away from her, you'll be sorely disappointed. Remember, I hired you—not the other way around."

Meredith closed her mouth.

It took everything within Julia not to tell Marcella that they could drop the case if they wanted to. "We're not trying to control your actions," she said instead. "We just want to do our job well, and we're concerned that if we upset Regina, she'll be even more difficult to work with."

"Be that as it may," Marcella said, turning back to face Regina's table, "I'm not leaving here until I speak to her again."

Allegra came around the table to stand by Gertie's side. "Perhaps, if you'll allow me," she said, "I can show you to a seat in the front row so you'll have the best view of Regina during her talk, and you can give someone else a turn in line."

Gertie pursed her lips together as if she was thinking over the offer and then nodded. She stepped away with Allegra at her side, and they went to the chairs.

The person in front of Marcella greeted Regina and gushed about the book, calling it a gem and a masterpiece.

Marcella stood with her back to Julia and Meredith, tapping her toe.

Julia sighed as she shared a look with Meredith. Marcella was proving to be one of their most difficult clients, and there was nothing they could do to stop her from confronting Regina. Perhaps the partners should discuss whether or not they should drop this case. If Marcella was going to remain belligerent and not let them do their job, there was no point in continuing.

"Thank you so much," the woman ahead of Marcella said to Regina. "This is the best book I've read this year. I'd love to see it turned into a movie."

"Thank you," Regina said. "That's quite a compliment."

The woman moved away, her signed book in hand, and Regina glanced up to see Marcella. The look on her face instantly changed, and the smile she had been wearing slipped out of place. "Hello, Ms. Martus," she said. "What can I do for you?"

"You can show me those letters."

Regina crossed her arms, and Julia could see she was trying hard to hold her composure. "I'm sorry to disappoint you—again—but I will not be making them public."

"Then why not just tell the world the book is fiction?" Marcella placed both hands on the table.

"I will not be addressing this with you again," Regina said. "If you would like me to sign a book, I'd be happy to do that for you. If not, please step aside so the next person—" She paused when she noticed Julia and Meredith standing behind Marcella. "Oh, I see."

Julia smiled, hoping to convey that her intentions were good.

Allegra came to the table and glared at Marcella, her displeasure much more evident than Regina's. "Ms. Martus, I will have no trouble asking you to leave if you make a scene."

"I have no intention of making a scene." Marcella didn't move from where she leaned on the table. Julia couldn't see her face, but she was certain Marcella wasn't smiling. "I want answers."

"And I want you to leave, Ms. Martus." Regina stood. "You've come with an agenda, and I see you will not take no for an answer."

"I want you to show me those letters, or—or—" Marcella stammered.

"Or what?" Regina asked, leaning toward her. "Or what, Ms. Martus?"

"Or"—Marcella breathed heavily—"you'll regret you ever wrote that book!"

Regina's eyes opened wide. "Are you threatening me, Ms. Martus?"

Others in the store had stopped what they were doing to watch the scene unfold. No one said a word.

Marcella was visibly shaking as she removed her hands from the table. "Yes, I am. I'll do whatever is necessary to see those letters."

Julia closed her eyes briefly. The last thing they needed was for their client to be threatening the very person they were investigating.

"Marcella," Meredith said gently, putting her hand on Marcella's shoulder. "Perhaps you should go home and cool off."

Marcella yanked her shoulder away from Meredith's hold and pointed at Regina. "I want to see those papers within the week or you'll be sorry."

Regina lifted her chin and looked down her nose at Marcella. "I refuse to be threatened. Allegra is calling the police, Ms. Martus. I'd advise you to leave before they get here."

Without another word, Marcella turned and stormed out of the bookstore, knocking over a pile of books on the table in her anger.

Julia and Meredith stood motionless as they faced Regina. Julia's pulse was beating hard, and she had to remind herself to close her mouth.

Regina leveled her glare on them. "I know she hired the two of you to do her dirty work. Should I be worried that you'll threaten me too?"

"We have no intention of harming you, or anyone else," Julia said, knowing they still had an audience and not wanting their reputations as detectives to be tarnished. "We're simply curious about the book, Ms. Terrance. That's all. We're just looking for the truth, and we know you're the best person to ask."

Regina's chest rose and fell a couple of times before she uncrossed her arms and seemed to be calming down.

"We were hoping for a private meeting with you," Meredith said. "A time to get together to just talk."

Regina smoothed back her hair and glanced at Allegra. "I don't believe my schedule will allow for a meeting with you. Now, if you'll excuse me, I'd like to freshen up before I give my talk."

Allegra showed Regina to the ladies' room at the very back of the building and the store soon filled with chatter once again, though several of the people kept their curious—and somewhat hostile—gazes on Julia and Meredith.

"I have a feeling most of the people in this store think we're the bad guys," Meredith said to Julia.

"I have a feeling you're right." Julia tried to put a smile on her face as she glanced around at Regina's fans. "And I think your question has been answered. It appears that the book has gone over very well with most people."

"Maybe it's time to discuss whether or not we should continue with this case. When we can no longer represent our client without hurting our business, then we have a problem." Meredith sighed.

"I agree. But whether or not we do this for Marcella, I'm far too invested in this case to back down now. I can call her and express our concerns. Perhaps I can get her to calm down."

Meredith pointed to the chairs. "Do you want to stay, or should we go?"

"Maybe we should stay. I think the damage has been done. Might as well see if Regina has anything more to share that we haven't already heard."

They walked to the chairs and sat down.

People continued to talk all around them, clearly troubled by the scene with Regina and Marcella.

Gertie glared at them.

Julia was a bit troubled herself. She hated working for someone who was a wild card. What did Marcella intend to do if Regina didn't share the letters?

She wasn't sure she wanted to find out.

***

The next morning, Julia pulled into a parking space behind Magnolia Investigations just as Meredith was arriving. Julia smiled and waved at her friend and business partner and then grabbed her purse and briefcase as she got out of her car.

"Good morning," Meredith called out to Julia. "I see Carmen beat us to work again today."

"She usually does." Julia loved that Carmen was always on time and diligent about her work but also a joy to work with. The younger woman added a little spice to the office and was almost always a burst of sunshine to her day.

The scent of freshly brewed coffee met Julia as she entered the back door.

"*Hola, amigas,*" Carmen said as she walked through the front door with a watering can in hand and met them in the long, central hall. "I have some juicy gossip for you this morning."

Julia didn't like to encourage Carmen's gossiping, but it usually had something to do with their work, so she indulged her this time. "What have you heard?"

Carmen clutched the watering can, her brown eyes shining with her news. "Do you remember my friend, Manuela, who works at the front desk at the Bohemian Hotel?"

Julia searched her memory but couldn't recall someone named Manuela, so she shook her head.

Meredith took a mug from the cart in the hall and poured herself a cup of coffee. "I think I remember you talking about her before."

"Well"—Carmen leaned forward in a conspiratorial posture—"I was talking with her on the phone early this morning, and she told me the most interesting thing I've heard in weeks. Apparently, the cops were called to the hotel late last night by Regina Terrance."

"*What?*" Julia was now completely engaged in Carmen's gossip.

"What happened?" Meredith asked.

"Manuela told me there's a guest at the hotel who requested to change rooms and specifically wanted a room on the fifth floor, facing the riverfront. The front desk met her request, but then the next day, which would have been yesterday, Regina Terrance complained to the front desk that the woman they moved had been stalking her and was now in the very next room!"

Julia anticipated the answer before she asked, "Did she mention the guest's name?"

Carmen frowned and scrunched up her face in thought. "It was a Scandinavian name—Gertie Anderson or Johnson—"

"Hanson?" Meredith asked.

Carmen snapped her fingers. "That was it. Anyway, after Regina complained to the front desk and they said they couldn't force Gertie to move out of her room, because she hadn't technically done anything wrong, Regina insisted on calling the police to file a complaint. She also asked that they keep an eye on Gertie. She said Gertie's been stalking her since she arrived in Savannah. Manuela said that Gertie follows Regina's every step. Regina asked to be moved to another floor."

"Wow," Julia said. "I hadn't realized Gertie had become such a problem."

"She seems pretty harmless to me," Meredith said. "Why would Regina need to call the police?"

"Manuela overheard the conversation when the police came, and she said that Regina wanted the police to go see Gertie and give her a 'talking-to,' as she put it. Let her know Regina was serious and wanted Gertie to stop following her."

"Did they talk to Gertie?" Julia asked.

Carmen nodded. "That's what Manuela said—and Gertie was quite upset, as you can imagine."

"Well, that's unfortunate," Meredith said. "Gertie doesn't seem like a threat. She just seems like an enthusiastic fan."

"Maybe Regina knows more about her than you do," Carmen suggested. "It seems strange to me that she'd call the police unless she thought Gertie was a real problem."

"Maybe." Julia lifted her eyebrows. "Maybe not. Perhaps Regina is more of a diva than we thought."

Meredith smiled at Julia and shook her head. "Or maybe she's just nervous about an overly energetic fan following her every move. I know it would make me uncomfortable."

Julia shrugged.

"What if it was Beatrice following your every move?" Meredith asked with a sly smile.

Julia rolled her eyes. "She already does!"

The three of them laughed as the front door opened and Allegra Timmons entered.

Julia and Meredith immediately sobered, and Carmen turned to see what they were looking at.

"Hello, Ms. Timmons," Julia said, unable to hide her surprise at seeing Regina's publicist. "Welcome to Magnolia Investigations." Maybe Allegra was there to finally set up an appointment to meet with Regina—but wouldn't it have been easier to call or email?

"What can we do for you?" Meredith asked.

Carmen took the watering can and quietly slipped out the back door, no doubt to water the wax begonia on the courtyard table.

Allegra glanced around the hall with no smile on her face. "Is there someplace private we can speak?"

"Of course," Julia said. "There's a conference room through this door."

Julia led Meredith and Allegra into the room across from her office. After Meredith closed the door, Julia asked, "What can we do for you?"

Allegra held her cell phone in hand and lifted her chin, looking down her nose at Julia and Meredith. "I've come here to ask you to cease and desist your investigation into *The Waving Girl*. It's clear your work is only making Marcella Martus more upset and confrontational. We can't afford for her to lose her head over this situation."

Julia and Meredith just stared at Allegra. Julia didn't know what to say.

"I don't know what you're telling her," Allegra said, "but she's becoming a problem, and I don't need any more problems right now. The Savannah police are already dealing with a different situation concerning Regina. I'd hate to have to call them again about Ms. Martus."

"We have advised Marcella, on two separate occasions, to keep her distance from Miss Terrance," Julia said to Allegra. "We have not told her anything she doesn't already know."

"If anything," Meredith added, "Marcella is upset because we haven't discovered more."

"There's nothing to discover." Allegra glanced at her phone impatiently. "I don't have time for this."

Meredith looked at Julia.

Allegra sighed. "I want you to stop this nonsense now, before something horrible happens. Regina has no intention of making the letters public, and everything she wrote in her book is true. That's all you need to know."

"Are there really letters?" Julia asked. "Truly?"

"Yes." Allegra puckered her lips. "I've seen them with my own eyes—and I'm not in the habit of lying."

"We tried contacting you to meet with Regina," Julia continued. "Could we set up an appointment with you now?"

"Regina Terrance doesn't owe you, or anyone else, any explanations. Read the book. You'll learn everything you need to know."

Julia clenched her teeth. What was the harm in a conversation?

"I need to leave." Allegra glanced at her phone again, clearly distracted. "Regina doesn't even know I came here. But it's my job as her publicist to put out fires, and Marcella Martus is threatening to turn into a forest fire. I'd hate to see her do something stupid. My advice to you is to stop this foolishness and let this go."

"I wish we could," Julia said. "Unfortunately, Miss Terrance has maligned the name and reputation of one of Savannah's most beloved citizens, and unless we have proof that her book is based on facts, we won't stop searching for the truth—even if we stop working for Marcella. Nothing we have found corroborates Regina's story."

Allegra straightened her back and tossed her head. She didn't even bother to say goodbye as she took her leave.

"Can you imagine the gall she had to come here and ask us to cease and desist?" Julia had to force herself to calm down. "She acts like we're the ones causing trouble. I wouldn't stop working on this case now for anything."

"I'm sure she's worried," Meredith suggested. "Especially after what happened with Gertie. No doubt she's stressed out and trying to keep her author safe. Marcella *did* threaten Regina."

"Marcella seems as harmless as Gertie." Julia couldn't imagine either woman causing any real trouble. "I just think Regina's worried Marcella will hurt her book sales."

"Either way, we should try to talk to Marcella again and convince her to leave Regina alone," Meredith said as she walked toward the door. "It will be better in the long run."

Julia nodded her agreement but already knew it would be almost impossible to convince Marcella Martus to sit back and do nothing while her great-aunt's name was being dragged through the mud.

Chapter Nine

THE YOUTH ROOM WAS HOT as Julia stood on the stage that Wednesday night, facing the students with a big smile. "I'm happy to report that from the bake sale on Sunday, we have raised half of our youth convention goal!"

Everyone cheered and some of the kids clapped. Only Olivia appeared to be uninterested as she sat alone on one of the back couches.

"I have a plan to raise the second half," Julia continued. "This next Saturday, the owner of the Downhome Diner, Miss Charlene, has agreed to let us use part of her parking lot to hold a car wash fundraiser. We'll meet at ten in the morning and work until four. Miss Charlene has offered to donate lunch to anyone who comes to help."

There were more cheers and clapping. "We'll work in two-hour shifts, and I hope that everyone who plans to attend the convention will sign up for one of the time slots." Julia motioned toward a clipboard Pastor Jay held up for the kids to see. "Please sign up tonight. A reminder text will go out on Friday evening so you won't forget." She smiled. "Thank you."

"Thank you, Miss Julia." Pastor Jay handed the clipboard off to a student, and then he took the stage once again.

Julia moved to the back to sit next to Olivia. Olivia gave Julia a tentative smile. Julia returned the smile and took a seat.

After Pastor Jay preached about the call to unconditional love, Julia's small group gathered around her for discussion time.

"What did you think of Pastor Jay's message?" Julia asked, watching Ebony, Sally, and Elena for their response to the message, as well as Olivia.

The girls didn't even look in Olivia's direction, but neither did any of them meet Julia's gaze. As a courtroom judge, Julia had learned the hard way that it could be difficult to get teenagers to open up, especially to such general questions. Pastor Jay usually had a handout with prepared questions ready for discussion, but Julia tried to personalize it and let the girls lead the discussion as much as possible.

"Is it always easy to love unconditionally?" Julia asked them. "What about when someone is being hard to love? What if they have a bad attitude or they're treating you unkindly?"

"Why do we have to love someone who's being unkind to us?" Ebony asked. "Why can't we just ignore them?"

Julia smiled at her. "That's a great question. Wouldn't it be easier just to push someone aside instead of deal with them?"

Most of the girls nodded.

"What if Jesus had done that?" Julia asked them. "What if He came to earth and said all of us sinners were too complicated and difficult to deal with—and then left? Where would we be?"

The girls didn't respond.

"The Bible tells us to love one another, as Christ has loved us. We're supposed to be like Christ. It also says that God is love and that His love never fails. The love of God is sacrificial, not selfish. We don't have to earn it, and since it's a gift, it should be freely given to others." Julia looked from one girl to the other. "It isn't always easy, but we must love at all times and be as Christlike as possible."

"Even when someone isn't being a good Christian?" Ebony asked, her gaze slipping to Olivia.

"What is a 'good Christian'?" Julia asked. "Aren't we all sinners, saved by God's grace? If our friends and family ask for forgiveness, it's our responsibility to forgive them. That, more than most things, demonstrates unconditional love."

"What if they don't ask for forgiveness?" Ebony challenged. "What if they're not sorry for what they did? What if they lie to you?"

Olivia stood and glared at Ebony, anger and pain radiating from her face. "I've never lied about what happened with Tyler! He's the liar, but you believe him over me."

Ebony glared back, and Julia held her breath. At least they were talking to each other.

"I can't sit here with a hypocrite," Olivia said. "Ebony, all you've done is spread lies about me. If anyone should ask for forgiveness, it's you—not me." She rushed out of the circle and went toward the door leading to the hall.

Ebony rolled her eyes and shook her head at her friends, who were clearly on Ebony's side.

"So," Julia said, feeling torn between running after Olivia and talking to her friends. "How long have you all known Olivia?"

Sally shrugged. "Since we were little girls."

"And how many times has she lied—especially about something so important?"

The girls looked between each other, but no one answered.

"Maybe you should rely on your friendship and give Olivia the benefit of the doubt." Julia's voice was grave as she spoke to them. "Not only because we're called to love unconditionally but because friendship is priceless. Olivia doesn't need your harsh judgment or shame. She needs you all to behave like the young women Christ has called you to be."

"But what about what she did last summer?" Ebony asked. "I don't want to hang around with a girl like that."

Julia's mouth slipped open in surprise. "Ebony, Olivia is the same girl she's always been. All of us are sinners, saved by God's grace—you included. Besides, she told you nothing happened. Why won't you believe her?"

"Why would Tyler lie?" Ebony frowned. "He's the most popular boy in school. Everyone likes him."

"Just because someone's popular doesn't always mean they're trustworthy." Julia couldn't help but think of Regina Terrance. Just because she was a popular author, people took her word as truth. "You know Olivia far better than you know Tyler—and besides, if Olivia committed this sin you've accused her of, hasn't Tyler also done the same? Both of them need your love and forgiveness, not just the boy you've put on a pedestal. Give Olivia the benefit of the doubt and try to help her—not hurt her more."

Julia rose from the couch, frustrated and sad that these girls had somehow missed the very essence of their Christian faith: redemption, grace, and mercy. "I'm going to go check on Olivia. I'd love it if y'all would examine your hearts and see if you have some unconditional love in there for your friend."

The girls didn't say anything as Julia walked across the youth group room and entered the hallway. Olivia was sitting in the corner, her knees tucked up to her chest, her forehead resting on her knees.

"Hey, Olivia," Julia said.

The girl lifted her face, and tears were streaming down her cheeks. "I don't want to be here."

"I'm sorry for what happened in there." Julia would have gotten on the floor next to her but wasn't sure she could get up very gracefully if she did. Instead, she leaned against the wall and gave Olivia some space. "Want to talk about it?"

"No." Olivia wiped her cheeks. "What does it matter?"

Julia was silent for a second and then said, "Did you talk to your parents?"

She nodded. "I talked to them on Sunday night, after I talked to you at church."

"And what did they say?" Julia had been praying for her since she'd learned about Olivia's problems.

A gentle smile warmed Olivia's face. "We had a good talk. They had already forgiven me for dating Tyler last summer, and they were glad I told them what's happening now."

"See?" Julia smiled. "I knew they'd believe the best about you."

"It felt good to talk to them."

"Did they have any advice?"

She took a deep breath but shook her head. "They think I should just try to ignore everyone. But how can I when I go to school with them and then see them on Wednesdays and Sundays here at church? What you just saw in there?" She gestured toward the youth room. "That was Ebony being nice to me. At school, she's a lot meaner."

Julia thought about all her experience on the bench and as an investigator. She thought specifically about Florence Martus and how things could be proved one way or the other if they could go right to the source. Since Florence was dead, the only thing they had was the letters. If they could just see the letters, then they'd know if Regina was lying or not. Maybe Olivia needed to go to the source of her problems. "Have you tried talking to Tyler? Explain to him how you're being treated and ask him if he'll clear your name?"

"I'd rather die than talk to Tyler about this."

"It doesn't have to be a big deal. Next time you have a quick minute with him, tell him you don't appreciate the rumors being spread about you. Ask him to set the record straight. What's the worst thing that could happen?"

"He'd tell more lies about me."

Julia shrugged. "Maybe, or maybe he might realize you're a real person, with real feelings, and think twice about what he's saying."

Olivia looked doubtful.

"Either way," Julia continued, "keep your chin up. There are so many other people in this world who could use your friendship." She smiled at Olivia. "I know it might be hard, but try to love Ebony and the others unconditionally, and forgive them even if they don't ask for forgiveness."

Olivia sighed and wiped her cheeks again. "I'll try."

"What do you say? Should we go back in and join the others?"

Again, Olivia looked doubtful, but she stood and followed Julia back to the youth room.

Julia would need to talk to Pastor Jay about this problem within the youth group. Maybe it was time to talk about the danger of passing judgment on God's people. A story or two about how Jesus welcomed sinners and outcasts into His inner circle might be a timely lesson. The youth pastor wouldn't be remiss to talk about removing the planks from their own eyes, either.

***

The next day, Julia found herself staring out the window of her office at Magnolia Investigations, thinking about Olivia and her friends. It felt like an injustice that a person's reputation could be tarnished by a bunch of lies. How was Olivia supposed to convince everyone she was innocent unless Tyler told them the truth?

But more than that, why did the girls in the youth group feel so self-righteous?

"Julia?" Carmen stuck her head around the office door, breaking into Julia's troubled thoughts. "Beatrice is here to see you and Meredith. I sent her into Meredith's office."

Beatrice.

Julia sighed. She didn't feel like facing Beatrice today. It usually sapped Julia's energy to be in her presence, and today, she was on short supply. She'd been awake far too long the night before reading *The Waving Girl* and had been up early this morning to get her car into the shop to get an oil change. She'd spent most of the morning catching up on business emails and returning phone calls to clients.

She waved at Carmen. "Thanks. I'll be right there."

She left her office and grabbed a fresh cup of coffee on the way to Meredith's office. Beatrice's voice was loud as it seeped into the hallway. Something had her excited and all atwitter, but then again, when wasn't Beatrice that way?

"Oh, Julia," Beatrice said when Julia entered Meredith's office. "I'm so glad you're here. I'm just fixin' to burst with the information I found for y'all."

Julia forced herself to smile as she took a seat on the sofa in Meredith's office, making sure not to spill her coffee. "What brings you in today?"

"Well"—Beatrice sat on the edge of her chair, her lime-green jumper surprisingly complimenting the olive-green chair she sat on—"first, I had the honor to be interviewed by the film crew in town. They asked me all I knew about Florence Martus, but the truth is, I didn't know much more than I learned in the book."

"You shared the information in the book?" Julia asked, her eyes wide in horror.

"It's all part of the same story, isn't it?" Beatrice asked. "Besides, the director, Frederick Hayes, told me what he wanted me to say."

"He gave you a script?" Meredith asked.

"More or less." Beatrice fluttered her hand, as if waving away the topic. "But that's not why I came. I found something in the historical society archives and thought you'd like a copy."

"What did you find?" Julia leaned forward and took the flash drive Beatrice handed to her.

"It's an oral history Florence gave in the late 1930s. I made a copy for you, since Meredith asked me to look for information about

Florence, and I made one for Regina, since she asked me to give her anything I happened to find for you." Beatrice laughed, as if it was all fun and games. "She's quite worried about you two." She shook her finger at Julia and Meredith, like she would at disobedient children. "You're not making her time in the Hostess City very welcoming."

"We've hardly had a chance to even talk to her," Julia said. "We haven't done anything to make her visit here uncomfortable."

"Marcella Martus has." Beatrice raised her eyebrows. "And since you're the ones feeding Marcella all the information, I blame you."

"We haven't fed anything to Marcella," Meredith protested.

"Clearly, Regina has been talking to you about us." Julia tried not to let her frustration with Beatrice show.

"We've had several very lovely conversations." Beatrice's smile was a bit smug. "I even hosted her, Allegra, and Frederick at my house for supper."

"That's strange," Meredith mused. "We've tried to schedule a meeting with Regina several times now, and we've been told she doesn't have the time."

Beatrice lifted a hand and shrugged but didn't give a response.

"Let's take a listen to the oral history." Meredith stood and took the flash drive from Julia. She pulled her laptop off her desk and plugged the flash drive into a USB port.

As Meredith worked at getting the oral history ready, Julia took another sip of her coffee, trying not to show her irritation.

"Here we go." Meredith set the laptop on the coffee table near the sofa and pressed PLAY on her media player.

"Hello," said the female interviewer on the crackling recording. "Today is Wednesday, June 17th, 1936. I'm here as part of the Federal

Writers' Project, under the Works Progress Administration, a New Deal program of the United States government. We are taking oral histories of thousands of Americans in an attempt to capture the history of our great nation. I'm in the living room of Miss Florence Martus, also known as the Waving Girl of Savannah. Hello, Miss Martus."

"Hello," said a quiet voice.

Julia glanced up at Meredith, a smile on her face. Florence's voice was so gentle and sweet. It matched the image Maggie Lu had painted of her at her birthday celebration at Fort Pulaski.

"Miss Martus," the interviewer continued, "those in Savannah, and most of the seaports around the world, know you simply as the Waving Girl. But for those who do not know who you are, can you please tell me why you are known as the Waving Girl?"

There was a slight pause and then Florence said, "Do I speak into this?" The interviewer must have nodded, because there was no audible response, and then Florence spoke again. "For forty-four years, from 1887 until 1931, I waved at over fifty thousand ships entering or exiting the Port of Savannah from my front porch on Elba Island. My brother George was the lighthouse keeper there after our father passed away."

"You waved at every single ship?"

"Yes," Florence said in her unhurried Southern accent. "To my knowledge, I did not miss a single ship."

"That's remarkable."

Florence didn't respond to the interviewer's remark.

"Before I ask you about your life growing up as a lighthouse keeper's daughter, I have another question. There are many legends about why you started to wave, and many people have asked you this question over the years, but I'll ask it again. Why did you wave at those ships for forty-four years, Miss Martus?"

There was another pause and Julia could almost imagine the small, unassuming Florence carefully gathering her thoughts before she spoke. "I once knew a sailor who was without a home. Through him, I realized there were hundreds of other men sailing the world's oceans without kith or kin. I hoped that by waving at them, they felt like they had someone, somewhere, who cared."

There was another pause and then the interviewer spoke, clearly moved by Florence's sincerity. "You're a remarkable woman, Miss Martus."

Florence giggled.

"Did it bother you that you were called the Waving *Girl*, even when you became a mature woman?"

"Oh goodness, no. I was not much more than a girl when I began to wave—though, at the time I felt much older than my nineteen years. The name stayed with me, and, if truth be told, it made me feel young. It still does. Youth brings with it a sense of possibility and limitless faith. If being call the Waving Girl can restore some of that youth to me, I will gladly wear the name for the rest of my life."

Julia, Meredith, and Beatrice listened as the interviewer continued by asking Florence to tell her a little about her early life, her years on the island, and her experiences with the ships. She shared all the things Julia had already learned about her, or had previously known. Not once did she hint at any of the scandalous things Regina wrote in her book, nor did she seem to be the type of woman who could easily hide those things. Her voice was so soft and gentle, it was difficult to make out a few of her words. She came across as being very shy and private, though a bit of passion filled her voice when she spoke about the waving.

When the recording came to an end, Julia sat, very quiet, as Meredith closed her laptop.

"Bless her heart," Beatrice said. "What a sweet soul."

"She seems nothing like the woman portrayed in Regina's book," Meredith said.

Beatrice nodded slowly. "I'd have to agree with you."

"What did Regina think of the recording?" Julia asked Beatrice.

"She didn't show much interest in having it," Beatrice confided. "I wonder if she even listened to it."

Julia and Meredith shared a look but didn't comment.

"How could she write about Florence the way she did," Beatrice asked, "if she did all the research she claimed? It wouldn't take much research to realize this sweet woman could not be a spy!"

"Now you can see why we've been on this case," Julia said. "And why Marcella Martus is so upset."

Beatrice leaned forward, her eyebrows scrunched together. "I'm upset now too. And to think, I fed the film director with the information he wanted to hear!"

"You can always help us," Meredith offered. "Continue to look for more information to help our case."

"And stop helping Regina and Allegra promote the book," Julia said. "The more people who read it, the more the lies are perpetuated."

Beatrice stood, a fierce determination in her gaze. "You're right. As the director of the Savannah Historical Society, it's my duty to uphold the *real* history of Savannah." She wilted back into her chair, her face white. "But I asked her to be the keynote speaker at the historical society's fundraising dinner this Friday night."

"Is there any way you can rescind the invitation?" Julia asked.

For the first time Julia saw Beatrice truly troubled and uncertain. Her hand hovered near her throat as she shook her head. "I don't know—but I'll have to find a way. After listening to this recording, I can no longer support Regina's book in good conscience." She swallowed hard and then rose to her feet again. "I need to leave. I'm sorry, y'all."

Julia and Meredith stood to see her out. "Goodbye," they called in unison.

When the door was closed behind Beatrice, Julia smiled at Meredith. "At least we have Beatrice on our side now."

Meredith shook her head. "See, she can be an ally—sometimes."

"I just hope she doesn't make Regina as angry as Marcella has."

Only time would tell.

Chapter Ten

September 1, 1931

Dear Lavinia,

I'm sorry I left my waving story hanging in such a precarious place. George came home soon after I set down my pen, and I was glad I had paused. I know he would ask me to stop telling my story, but now that I've begun, I cannot quit until it is all on paper.

I've thought a lot about how I would share this next part of the story. I want, so desperately, to make you understand. I also want to justify my choices, but the truth is, I would probably make the same decisions all over again if I thought they would lead to my happiness. Unfortunately, they did the opposite—but I am getting ahead of myself.

When Hai Ching asked me to be his wife, I was overjoyed. I foresaw a future together exploring the world and then settling down to create a home and start a family. Hai Ching was going to leave the next morning, so we decided to tell my father that night.

I remember how hot it was, how loud the katydids were singing, and how the air was so thick and still. Funny how certain details stick with you, long after the event has passed. I hardly remember what we said to my father, but I remember the weather.

My father was very disappointed in us. He told Hai Ching that he, out of everyone, should know better than to fill my head with unrealistic hopes and dreams. Hai Ching tried to defend himself by telling Father that he loved me, but Father would not listen. He told Hai Ching he was being selfish and idealistic. He asked Hai Ching where we would live, how he would support me, and how we would overcome racial barriers. Hai Ching didn't have the answers, but he said we could overcome any obstacle we faced.

I believed him, with all my heart. Isn't that the power of love? It's full of hope, belief, and an unparalleled amount of optimism.

Father told Hai Ching he must leave and never return. I cried, begging my father to let us try—but Father was adamant.

Hai Ching just stood there, clasping his hat in his hands. He looked helpless and hopeless. And I saw him, as if for the first time. I had a glimpse into his heartache and pain. I had believed my father trusted and respected Hai Ching, but I saw that his belief in Hai Ching only went so far. He would never entrust me to Hai Ching's care.

Father forced Hai Ching to leave—he didn't even give us time to say goodbye. My mother was also crying, and George had made himself scarce. I pulled on my father's arm, begging him not to send Hai Ching away. But Father's face was red with anger, and he would not be swayed. He was embarrassed by my hysterics and kept telling me he had raised me better than that.

Hai Ching stood in the yard and looked at me as Father hauled me back into the house. Looking back, I wish I would have taken that time to say goodbye instead of carry on as I did. But I was so upset I couldn't think straight.

Father railed at me while Mother sat in the corner, weeping. I didn't listen to Father, and when he was spent, I raced to my bedroom to be alone with my tears and grief.

Hours passed, but I could not sleep.

The house eventually settled and I sat near my window, looking out on the dark, loveless world around me. It was then that a pebble hit my window, and I saw Hai Ching standing in the yard.

My heart leaped in my chest, and I had to force myself not to tear through the house to get to his side. Instead, I tiptoed out and rushed into his arms. He begged me to run away with him, but it was already so close to morning, I knew we'd never get far enough away before my parents discovered we were gone. Instead, I promised I would send Hai Ching a signal when I felt it was safe for me to leave. I would wave a towel by day or a lantern by night. Hai Ching hoped to return to the dredges on the river, and they came by at all hours. When Hai Ching asked me what my parents would think seeing me do such a thing, I told him I would tell them I was waving at the ships to welcome the sailors to Savannah. I would do it for as long as it would take for Hai Ching to see me.

We embraced, and he left. I went back to my room and began to plan my escape.

A week passed before I saw my opportunity. My father's health had deteriorated that week, since our fight and Hai Ching's departure. One morning, he could not get out of bed and I knew it would be my chance to flee. I began to wave at the ships that day, and that night, I waved a lantern.

Hai Ching must have been watching from wherever he'd been staying, because that night, moments after I extinguished the lantern, he appeared in the yard again. I was prepared this time. I had packed a suitcase and tucked it under my bed. When I saw Hai Ching, I tiptoed out of the house again. My heart was breaking, knowing I was leaving my parents and my home, and based on my sister's treatment, I knew I was turning my back on my family for good.

The moment I joined Hai Ching in the yard and our hands clasped, my father appeared at the back door, breathing hard, his face white. He demanded to know what was happening, so I told him. I was leaving with Hai Ching, and no matter how much he protested, I would not be swayed. My heart was pounding so hard, I thought it would burst out of my chest.

Father commanded me to return inside, but I refused. He came into the yard to grab my arm—but at that moment, Hai Ching stepped forward to stop him. Father lost his footing and fell, clutching his chest. He hit his head on a rock and I could see, by the light of the moon, that he was no longer conscious. I called out his name and fell on the ground beside him—but there was nothing I could do.

He died in my arms.

I will never be able to communicate the utter devastation I felt at his death. I knew it was my fault—all my fault. I knew he was not well, yet I had pushed him to his limit. When I looked up at Hai Ching, I could see he felt just as guilty—but when I tried to speak to him, he shook his head and backed away from me.

"They'll blame me," he said. "No one will listen to me."

Terror filled his face, and I knew that he was right. If he stayed, and people knew what had happened, they would blame Hai Ching. The horrible things that were happening to other Chinese men and women across the country would happen to him too.

I called for him, but he disappeared into the darkness.

My mother and brother heard me sobbing, and they came outside to find my father in my arms. As you can imagine, we were all horrified to lose him. I explained what had happened, that I was trying to run away, though I did not tell them Hai Ching had come for me. For all they knew, I was running away on my own. I couldn't risk them blaming Hai Ching. I took all the blame, though my mother tried to convince me that it wasn't my fault, that Father's heart was weak and he was already failing. I learned later that his heart had given out.

I wanted so desperately for Hai Ching to know he wasn't at fault—that the guilt was all mine. It was because of my *disobedience that Father died. I couldn't bear to break my mother's heart again by marrying Hai Ching, but I didn't want him to live with the belief that he had killed my father hanging over his head. So I did the only thing I knew. I waved by day and by night to get his attention—for forty-four years, I waved. I hoped and prayed he was still working on the dredge, and he would see me and come to me—even if it was for but a moment, and I could tell him it wasn't his fault.*

But he never returned and I never heard from him again, from that day until this one.

Perhaps you wonder how long I held out hope. The answer is, I never gave up hope. Even now, there is a place in my heart that hopes that Hai Ching will find me again and that we will be able to finally put the past behind us. I hold on to hope, because I realized a long time ago that hope is the thing we live for. It gets us out of bed, energizes us to do our work through the day, and gives us the faith we need to close our eyes at night.

I will never give up hope. It's all I have left of the love I shared with Hai Ching.

So now you know my waving story, dear Lavinia. I hope I have conveyed it in a way that paints Hai Ching in a good light, because he is not to blame. Perhaps, like my mother said all those years ago, I'm not to blame either. But I'll never know for certain. Would my father have died from his heart ailment if I had not broken it first? I wish I could have one more moment with him to tell him I love him and to ask for forgiveness. But I cannot, and I must console myself with the knowledge that he knew I loved him.

Thank you for allowing me to share this story with you. Please, when you think of Hai Ching, do it with a smile, because that's how I think of him. And, I cannot stress this enough: please destroy this letter after reading it. I cannot risk George ever knowing I shared the story with you. I could not live with the disappointment I know he would feel. Though he does not blame me for what happened that night, we still do not speak of it.

I'm sure you have other questions, and I will answer them if you do, but I have told you the whole story, leaving nothing out.

Now you know that I once loved a man without a home, and by waving, I hoped to make him, and everyone else, know that someone cared.

Your faithful cousin,

Florence

Julia sat in the wingback chair in front of the empty fireplace in her office at Magnolia Investigations, *The Waving Girl* in her hands. She had come to the ill-fated night when Hai Ching and Florence had tried to run away together, but her father had intervened and Hai Ching had hit John Martus over the head with a rock, killing him instantly. The attack was so brutal, Florence had become scared of Hai Ching, and when he tried to pull her away from her father, she had screamed for help. Hai Ching had run away, disappearing into the dark as Florence's mother and brother arrived on the scene. In the days that followed, the family told the coroner that John had fallen and hit his head on a rock. No one had questioned them.

The clock in Julia's office ticked softly as the minutes flew by and she continued to turn the pages. She had other work to accomplish but could not pull herself away.

The book claimed that, after the funeral, Florence began to long for Hai Ching once again, hardening her heart toward her father's death, blaming her father for trying to interfere. When Hai Ching got word to her several months later, he had returned to China. It was at that time he confessed to her that he was a spy for the Chinese government and that the best way she could honor their love was to work with him. He promised to return to her, when it was safe, but until then, he gave her a series of signals to use to pass along information to certain vessels that came into the Port of Savannah. It would require her to wave at all the incoming and outgoing ships, so no one would grow suspicious.

Julia closed the book, unable to continue reading. It was one thing to accuse Florence of a love affair, another entirely to accuse her of covering up her father's murder and becoming a spy for a foreign country.

"Knock, knock," Meredith said as she opened Julia's office door. "Mind if I come in? Rebecca's here to see us."

"Come in." Julia rose and set *The Waving Girl* on her desk, uncertain if she'd ever pick it up to read again. She'd had enough.

Meredith entered Julia's office with Rebecca close behind her. Julia smiled at their friend. It wasn't often that Rebecca left the library to stop by and see them. If she found information, she usually emailed it to them or called to let them know. "What brings you to Magnolia Investigations today?"

"I found something and wanted to deliver it to you in person." Rebecca pulled a folder out of her large tote bag. "And I'm on my way to meet Kelvin for lunch, so I thought it would be easier just to stop in."

Julia moved her laptop to the side of her desk, and the women joined her to stand around it to look at the piece of paper Rebecca pulled out of her folder.

"I was looking through the microfilm recently," Rebecca said, "and came across this obituary from August 1887, so I made a copy for you."

"Obituary?" Julia asked, scanning the document. It was clearly a copy of a newspaper article from the *Savannah Morning News*, the old typeset words a bit smeared with time.

Meredith began to read it out loud.

"'It is with deep regret and mourning that we report the death of Sergeant John Martus, keeper of the lights at Elba and Cockspur Islands, who passed away at his family's home at Elba Island last

Friday night. It was reported that Mr. Martus suffered from a heart ailment after contracting scarlet fever just after the war. The coroner confirmed his death was due to heart failure.

"'Mr. Martus was well known to all who plied the Savannah River and will be dearly missed. He was born in 1828 in Kirrlach, Baden, Germany, and arrived in New York City in 1842. Sgt. Martus enlisted in the US Army when he was only 14. He met and married Rosanna Cecelia Decker of Philadelphia around 1848. At the close of the War Between the States, he was a disabled decorated war veteran who was appointed Ordnance Sergeant at Fort Pulaski. After the repairs were completed at Fort Pulaski, Sgt. Martus was assigned keeper of the lights at Elba and Cockspur Islands.

"'Left to survive his death and keep the lights are his wife, Rosanna, his son, George, and his daughter, Florence, among other children and grandchildren.'"

"The coroner confirmed heart failure as the cause of his death," Julia said, almost to herself.

"And not by Hai Ching hitting his head with a rock," Meredith added, "as Regina's book suggests."

"I haven't read the book," Rebecca said, "but I heard that Regina claimed John Martus was murdered. That's why I brought this to you personally. It's proof that at least that part of Regina's book is falsified."

"We should probably call Marcella with this information," Meredith said.

Julia groaned. "I'd rather not add more fuel to her fire. The last time I spoke to her, to ask her to refrain from contacting Regina or we'd have to stop working for her, she struggled to agree."

"I doubt she can do more damage at this point," Meredith said.

"I wouldn't be so sure." Julia crossed her arms as she reread parts of the obituary. "I suppose we should call her though. She deserves to know the truth."

"Would you like me to do it?" Meredith asked.

"I'll do it." Julia sighed.

"I've got to run," Rebecca said. "I hope this helps."

"Thank you, Rebecca," Julia said. "I'm sure it will."

"You're welcome. I'll let you know if I find something else."

"Let me walk you out," Meredith offered.

They left Julia in her office, and a couple of seconds later she had Marcella on the phone.

"Hello, Marcella," Julia said as she took a seat behind her desk. The copy of *The Waving Girl* still sat on the corner of her desk.

"Do you have some information for me?" Marcella asked.

"Rebecca Thompson from the Live Oak Library just brought us an obituary for John Martus, dated August 13, 1887. Contrary to what Regina's book claims, John died from a heart ailment—and not by trauma to the head. The coroner even confirmed the report."

"I knew it!" Marcella's tone was full of glee. "Just one of many lies we'll uncover."

"I wish we had more for you right now. This has been a tough case to crack."

"You don't have to worry about that," Marcella said. "I just alerted the media that I'll be holding a press conference tomorrow at three. I have a few tricks up my sleeve for Regina Terrance."

Julia sat up straighter, her senses on full alert. "You're holding a press conference?"

"Yes, tomorrow in Ellis Square."

"What do you have to share?"

"I've uncovered something everyone will be interested in hearing about." Marcella's laugh was full of glee again, almost like a child who had a secret she wanted to spill.

"What have you uncovered?"

"Nope," Marcella said. "I won't be telling you—at least not now. You'll have to come to my press conference like everyone else."

"Marcella, I think it's in your best interest to tell us what you've found, since you hired us to help you with this investigation."

"Consider yourself unhired. I've got it from here."

Julia couldn't believe her ears. "You're discontinuing our services?"

"You heard me right. I'm taking matters into my own hands. You and Meredith can get on with your other business—unless you want to come to the press conference tomorrow."

They were too deep into the investigation to stop now. "Of course we'll be there."

"Good. I'll see you then." Marcella hung up the phone right as Meredith reentered Julia's office.

"Did you talk to Marcella?" Meredith asked, taking a seat across from Julia's desk.

Julia stared at Meredith for a few seconds, allowing the information Marcella had given her to soak in. "She just fired us."

"What?" Meredith frowned. "Why?"

"She said she's taking matters into her own hands. She's holding a press conference tomorrow to reveal something she discovered."

"Oh dear." Meredith put her hand up to her forehead. "I don't like the sound of this."

"Neither do I. That's why I told her we'd be at the press conference tomorrow."

Meredith sighed. "I almost feel like I'm watching a train wreck in motion. I want to stop it, but it's beyond my power."

"Yet you can't look away."

"Exactly."

Julia both dreaded and anticipated Marcella's press conference. What had she discovered that Julia and Meredith hadn't?

Chapter Eleven

A LIGHT BREEZE RUFFLED JULIA's hair as she and Meredith stood in the crowd in Ellis Square, one of the larger and least parklike of all the squares in Savannah. It was located close to historic downtown at the entrance to City Market, near River Street. The square was a popular place for community parades, concerts, and other gatherings. A large water fountain sprayed up from the concrete in one corner where children were running and playing, and a glass building in the other corner housed a popular visitor center. Originally built in 1733, the square was first called Market Square and was home to several markets, as well as the slave auctions before General Sherman's march into Savannah. In the 1950s, the city had built a large parking garage on the square, but it had recently been demolished and the square reestablished.

Tourists filled the square, since several popular restaurants and the American Prohibition Museum were nearby. A single microphone and amplifier were set up on the concrete, and Marcella Martus stood nearby speaking to a reporter from the *Savannah Tribune*.

"I wonder if Regina will show," Julia mused as Meredith stood next to her, shading her eyes as she watched the growing crowd.

There had to be at least fifty people standing around the microphone, waiting for Marcella's press conference to start.

"I doubt it, but I've been surprised before."

"Look who just showed up." Julia nodded toward one of the streets, where Gertie Hanson materialized. She wore another sundress, without a cardigan this time. Her high ponytail bounced when she walked, and she wore her digital camera around her neck. She pushed her glasses up the bridge of her nose as she glanced around the square.

Meredith looked in the direction Julia indicated. "That girl doesn't look like she could hurt a fly. I wonder if the police took Regina's request seriously."

"Who knows? Some people never cease to amaze or surprise me."

Gertie noticed Julia and Meredith and moved toward them.

"Looks like she'll be joining us." Julia put a welcoming smile on her face.

"Hello!" Gertie said to them, her eyes bright and animated. "I was hoping I'd see you two here. Isn't this terribly exciting? What could Ms. Martus have to say? I know she doesn't like Regina Terrance, but maybe she's called this press conference to finally show her support for Ms. Terrance's book."

Julia hated to be the one to ruin Gertie's optimism. "I guess we'll have to wait to see."

"Is it true you two are private detectives?" Gertie asked. "That must be awfully fascinating work."

"I'm Julia Foley," Julia said, extending her hand. "And this is Meredith Bellefontaine."

"Hello," Meredith said, shaking Gertie's hand.

"I'm Gertie Hanson—and I already know who you two are," Gertie said with a grin. "I'd like to be a private detective someday. Like the ones I read about in books."

"It isn't always quite as exciting as the books and movies make it out to be," Julia said. "But it's rewarding and fun to investigate—"

Just then, Marcella tapped on the microphone and the crowd grew quiet. She wore an outdated dress suit that must have been new in the 1980s, but she didn't seem to care. She stood at the microphone with dogged confidence and determination in her face.

Julia held her breath, almost afraid of what Marcella might say.

"Thank you all for coming." Marcella looked at the crowd, scanning the faces and squinting hard. "It looks like our intrepid author decided not to show. She's probably afraid of what I have to say."

"Not Regina Terrance," Gertie said as an aside to Julia and Meredith. "She's not afraid of anything." The respect and awe in Gertie's voice were hard to ignore.

"I have called this press conference today," Marcella continued, "because I am disappointed at the positive reception Regina Terrance's book has received, especially by this city. Everyone should be ashamed of themselves. After three weeks, the book is on the best-seller lists and gaining more and more attention. Florence Martus was a symbol of hospitality, innocence, and simplicity. The book Regina Terrance published paints Florence in a far different light and is full of misinformation and lies. It's a travesty to our city and to Florence's memory."

Gertie's back went rigid, but she kept her eyes narrowed on Marcella.

"I have asked Ms. Terrance to show me the letters that she claims are written by Florence and filled with all the nonsense she put in her book. But she refuses to show them to me, thereby proving she is a liar."

"Regina Terrance isn't a liar!" Gertie blurted out and then threw her hand over her mouth as if the words came out of their own accord.

Marcella's gaze landed on Gertie, and she scowled. "I can see Regina's number-one fan is here to heckle me."

Gertie's face turned crimson and she lowered her chin, glancing around.

"For those who don't know," Marcella continued addressing the crowd, "I live in the home that Florence and her brother, George, occupied between 1931 and 1943. In my quest to prove that Regina's book is full of lies, I began searching through my great-aunt's possessions to see if I could find any proof that the book is fiction." She lifted her chin and straightened her shoulders. "And I found something everyone thought was long gone! In the attic of my home, in the hidden compartment of a steamer trunk's lid, I found the diary Florence kept while living on Elba Island! The diary she claimed to have destroyed when she left the island in 1931."

A rush of conversation rose up around Julia and Meredith.

Marcella waited a couple of seconds for the initial information to sink in to her audience. "The diary holds the true story, and it's proof that Regina's book is fake."

Gertie's mouth fell open. "It can't be!"

"I have personally read the entire diary," Marcella said into the microphone, "and I can confidently stand before you and say that

Florence is exactly the woman we've always known and loved. She was sweet, gentle, and kind. She wasn't a murderer, a spy, or even a rebellious teen wanting to be free from her loving family." Marcella paused to look around at the crowd again. "I am asking Regina Terrance to immediately rescind her claim that her book is fact and categorize it as fiction, which it clearly is." She clasped her hands together. "Now I will take a few questions."

A dozen hands shot into the air, including Gertie Hanson's.

"Yes, Ms. Hanson?" Marcella asked smugly, with hardly a glance in Gertie's direction.

"Where is this so-called diary?" Gertie asked. "I want to see it."

"Oh, really?" Marcella's eyebrows rose high on her forehead. "Don't you believe I have it in my possession?"

"No, I don't."

"You would believe an author over the grandniece of Florence Martus? You would believe that Regina possesses some obscure letters, found in a wall in New York City, over the claim that I found Florence's personal diary in her very own home?"

Gertie opened her mouth to respond but quickly clamped it shut again, breathing hard.

"Where is the diary?" someone called out from the crowd.

Marcella's self-satisfied grin almost looked malicious. "I'll show everyone the diary as soon as Regina Terrance shows us the letters."

Julia glanced at Meredith, and they shared a bewildered look.

"That is all for today," Marcella said to the crowd. "I will be happy to produce the diary as soon as Ms. Terrance produces the letters." And, with that, Marcella stepped away from the microphone. She was soon bombarded with several people who went up to speak to her, but Julia and Meredith stayed where they were.

Gertie's lips pressed hard together, and her nostrils flared. She pushed her way through the crowd and walked toward River Street.

"Well," Julia said, letting out a breath, "I didn't see any of that coming."

Meredith shook her head. "Do you think a diary actually exists, or do you think Marcella is bluffing?"

"I guess we won't know, unless Regina reveals the letters."

"Maybe Marcella will show us the diary," Meredith suggested. "We can ask."

"We can," Julia agreed, "but I doubt she'll show it to anyone."

"I wish I could be there when Regina hears about this." Meredith hiked her bag farther up her shoulder. "At least we have the Savannah Historical Society fundraiser to look forward to tonight. Maybe we can get Regina to finally talk to us there."

"Remember," Julia warned, "we're not working this case anymore. We have other clients to assist."

Meredith grinned. "That doesn't mean we're going to stop trying to solve the mystery."

Julia grinned back at her. She wasn't so sure Regina would want to talk, but that had never stopped her and Meredith before.

***

Savannah's Ships of the Sea Maritime Museum was housed in the old Scarbrough Mansion in the downtown historic district and was the location of the black-tie fundraiser Beatrice had organized for the historical society. Julia walked up the front steps and into the large Greek Revival house on Beau's arm. He wore a black tie and tuxedo, while Julia wore a silver gown and a pair of black heels.

"There's Meredith and Quin," Julia said to Beau after they checked in at the reservation table and received their dinner tickets. The meal would be served later in the North Garden Assembly room, which was an open-air space in the two acres of beautiful gardens behind the house.

Meredith and her friend, Quin Crowley, were standing just off the main hall in one of the galleries housed in what would have been a formal parlor. The house boasted nine such galleries and was full of Savannah's rich maritime history. The house had originally been built in 1819 for one of the principal owners of the *SS Savannah*, which was the first steamer to cross the Atlantic that same year.

"Hello," Meredith said to Julia and Beau as they approached.

Quin and Beau shook hands, and Julia smiled at him. Quin was a corporate attorney who had moved to Savannah from Columbus, Georgia, a few years back, after the death of his wife. Though he had shown interest in Meredith from the start, she appeared to be taking the relationship slowly. Julia didn't ask Meredith too many questions about it, but she was thankful Meredith had his friendship.

"Hello, Julia," Quin said to her. "You look lovely tonight."

"Thank you." Julia smiled. "It's always nice to have a reason to dress up."

"I've tried to convince her to dress like this every day," Beau said with a wink at Julia, "but she claims it wouldn't be conducive to her work."

"Especially tomorrow." Julia laughed. "I'll be helping the youth group with a car wash fundraiser at the Downhome Diner."

"What are you raising funds for?" Quin asked.

"We're taking the youth group to a convention in Atlanta, and we're a little short on funds." Julia appreciated that Quin was taking an interest. It showed that he cared about Meredith's friends—she just hoped Meredith saw it too.

"Thank you for reminding me." Meredith laid her hand on Julia's arm. "I'll be sure to come by and get my car washed."

"Let me know when you're heading there," Quin said. "I'd like to support the youth group too."

Meredith smiled at him. "I will."

"We appreciate the support," Julia said. "The kids are really looking forward to the convention." At least, most of them were. She couldn't help but remember how much Olivia didn't want to go.

Dozens of people mingled throughout the galleries, admiring some of the paintings and models of ships important to Savannah's history. Julia, Beau, Meredith, and Quin moved from one piece to the next, admiring and commenting on the artifacts. It had been many years since Julia had been to the museum.

Quin showed Meredith special attention, asking her opinions, seeking her knowledge, and generally enjoying her company. Julia couldn't help but notice, and she even nudged Beau a couple of times when Quin and Meredith shared a tender smile with one another. Quin couldn't keep his eyes off Meredith—yet Meredith seemed to be oblivious. Or, if she noticed, she didn't let on.

"Seems like a happy coincidence that Beatrice planned this event for the Maritime Museum," Meredith said at one point, "given the recent development with Florence Martus. It's a nice touch." Meredith had been the president of the Savannah Historical Society before Beatrice, and Julia had always admired how Meredith had gracefully handed over the reins.

"And there she is now." Julia's back straightened as Beatrice glided toward them wearing an evening gown reminiscent of a sailor's uniform with large, white lapels and navy blue stripes. On her head, she wore a jaunty sailor's hat.

"Thank you all for attending," Beatrice cooed as she stopped near the foursome, glancing over her shoulder before leaning in to speak to Julia and Meredith. "Have either of you seen Regina?"

Julia shook her head, but Meredith nodded. "I saw her near the model of the SS Savannah."

"I tried to be tactful and told her I had changed the program and we would no longer need her to speak tonight." Beatrice sighed. "But she insisted."

Julia couldn't help but wonder how "tactful" Beatrice had actually been.

"I'm sure it will be fine." Meredith tried to comfort Beatrice. "I doubt she could do more damage."

"I hope you're right." Beatrice's eyes opened wide. "Did you hear about Marcella Martus? She found Florence's diary!"

"We were at the press conference when she shared the news," Julia told her.

"How marvelous." Beatrice grinned. "Hopefully all this Regina Terrance business will go away."

"One can hope." Julia caught a glimpse of Regina, Frederick, and Allegra. The three walked close to one another, talking as they meandered through the gallery across the front hall. "There she is."

Beatrice and Meredith turned to look, and at that moment, Regina and Allegra glanced up. Regina wore a beautiful evening gown in a dark purple shade, while Allegra wore something a little less formal but just as sleek. Frederick was in a tuxedo, like most of the other men. They drew close to one another to whisper, and then Frederick disappeared while Regina and Allegra walked toward Julia, Meredith, and Beatrice.

Beau and Quin had found something of interest in the opposite corner of the room and had made themselves scarce.

Julia didn't blame them.

People mingled and visited all around, but Julia, Meredith, and Beatrice didn't say a word as Regina and Allegra approached. Neither woman looked excited or pleased to see the Magnolia detectives.

"A little birdie told me the news," Regina said to Julia and Meredith, a hint of disgust in her voice. "Marcella Martus claims she found Florence's diary."

"That's what we heard," Julia said.

"I suppose you found the diary for her." Regina looked as polished and composed as ever, though she lifted her chin a little more.

Meredith shook her head. "Marcella said she found it in her house."

"Have you seen it?" Allegra asked.

Julia shifted on her feet, remembering why she liked flats better than heels. "No, we have not."

"I don't think it exists." Regina smoothed the front of her gown. "I think she's lying."

No one said a word. Beatrice fidgeted and actually kept her mouth closed.

"The press is starting to hound me," Allegra said. "Not only the press from Savannah, but from several other prominent cities around the country. If we don't put a stop to Marcella soon, she'll hurt the sales of the book, and that's the last thing we need."

"Her claims will soon die down," Regina offered. "If she doesn't produce the diary, people will stop caring. My book will stand on its own two feet—just like the others. My reputation as a historian is flawless. I have a Pulitzer Prize to prove it."

For the first time, Julia could see beyond Regina's facade—and she didn't like what she saw. The woman was proud and conceited.

A man caught Regina's eye, and she waved at him. Julia recognized him from the historical society board of directors, though she hadn't met him before.

"If you'll excuse me," Regina said. "My public is calling." She left the group and joined the man across the room.

Allegra took a step closer to Julia and Meredith. "I can see you haven't done as I've suggested."

"And what is that?" Julia asked, feigning ignorance.

"Cease this infernal investigation on Marcella's behalf. This is really getting out of hand."

"Unfortunately," Meredith said, "Marcella is no longer using our investigative services."

"She's doing all the work on her own," Julia added. "And I have a feeling you haven't heard the last from her."

"This is ridiculous." Allegra pursed her lips. "I have better things to do with my time than worry about Marcella Martus, of all people."

"I'm sorry you feel that way." Meredith's voice was filled with empathy. "But try to see things from Marcella's point of view. Regina Terrance's book has hurt her deeply."

Allegra rolled her eyes. "Then Marcella needs to get over it. This is the twenty-first century. People can only pretend to be good for so long." She let out a disgruntled sigh.

As she walked away, Julia looked from Meredith to Beatrice, who looked a little stunned.

"She's not very nice, is she?" Beatrice asked. Then she sighed. "I need to run, y'all. I have to check on the caterers. They were planning to serve vanilla mousse, instead of chocolate. Can you believe that?"

Beatrice set off to find the poor caterers as Meredith moved closer to Julia.

"What do you make of Regina's response to Marcella's news?" Meredith asked.

"I think she's worried, though she hides it well."

"I think you're right. And if she's worried, then that means she's lying about the letters."

The author was still talking to the board member, laughing and laying her hand on his arm in a very familiar way. It was clear the two were flirting, even from where Julia was watching.

Frederick Hayes came around the corner, with two glasses in hand, and stopped short at the sight of Regina and the board member. Anger simmered in his gaze as he watched Regina continue to flirt.

"Uh-oh," Julia said under her breath to Meredith. "Look over there."

Meredith glanced in the direction Julia indicated.

"Remember the conversation I overheard between those two at the Mansion?" Julia spoke quietly.

"Something about a cat-and-mouse chase and him not getting what he came here for?"

"Yes, and her telling him to just do his job and stop complaining."

"I wonder what kind of relationship they have," Meredith mused.

"By the jealous look on his face, I'm thinking it's romantic."

"That was fast."

Julia shrugged. "There's no time limit to falling in love."

"I wonder if it's love. Maybe he's just infatuated."

"It looks like it might be one-sided, if her behavior is any indication."

Regina continued to flirt with the board member, despite the fact that Frederick was watching them.

Instead of walking away, Frederick approached Regina and shoved the glass in her face. She stopped laughing and, instead of a smile, she sent daggers toward him with her eyes.

Frederick downed his drink in one gulp and then turned and walked out the front door.

Regina watched him leave—her gaze falling on Julia and Meredith after Frederick disappeared. She simply lifted her chin at them and went back to flirting.

Chapter Twelve

CLOUDS COVERED THE SKY ON Saturday morning as Julia stood in the parking lot of the Downhome Diner with about a dozen of her youth group students. A few parents had also volunteered, allowing for four stations to be set up, so they could wash multiple vehicles at the same time. Earlier, when the car wash had first opened, Meredith and Quin had come to get their vehicles cleaned. After that, they'd gone into the diner for a late breakfast and Julia hadn't seen them exit yet.

Beau had come to help as well, and Julia enjoyed having him there. He joked with the teens and greeted several members from their church as they pulled into the parking lot to support the youth group. He also handled all the cash, which Julia appreciated the most. It gave her the opportunity to connect with the students as they worked, something she enjoyed about helping with the youth group.

The first shift was almost finished, and the second shift would be starting soon. Julia had greeted Olivia earlier that morning, but she hadn't had time to talk to her about her troubles with her ex-boyfriend. Ebony and the other girls had taken the second shift, probably to avoid spending time with Olivia, but it helped to ease the tension that was usually hovering around them on Wednesday nights.

"Come and get some refreshments," Charlene called out to the kids as she and two of her waitresses came out of the diner, with large trays of glasses of lemonade and cookies. Several tables had been set up under the shade of an ancient oak tree, and that's where Charlene and the others set the treats.

"We'll need to take our break in sections," Julia told the students. "Group one can go first."

Olivia was in group one, so when she and the others finished the SUV they were washing, they went over to the table. Julia met them there, a smile on her face for Charlene.

"Thank you for all your support," Julia said to her friend. "I appreciate it more than you know."

"No problem." Charlene's rich, melodic laugh carried on the gentle breeze. "You and Meredith have been such a blessing to my mama, I wanted to be a blessing to you."

"We're the ones blessed by Maggie Lu," Julia said. "She's been a great help to us since we met her."

"You've given her so much hope. If it hadn't been for you and Meredith, Mama and I might not be reunited, and she wouldn't know Jakey." Charlene shook her head. "And what a travesty that would be."

Charlene was referring to one of the first cases Meredith and Julia had undertaken after starting their agency. Charlene had come to them, looking for help in locating her mother, who had been in hiding for several years. Not only had they found her, but they'd also unlocked a decades-old mystery.

"Anytime you and Meredith need something," Charlene continued, "you know who to call."

"Thank you, again."

Charlene went back into the diner with her waitresses, leaving Julia to chat with the kids. She worked her way around the table, not wanting to draw too much attention to Olivia.

"Thank you for all your hard work," she said to her. "You look like you know what you're doing out there."

Olivia smiled. "I like to help my dad wash our cars on Saturdays. It's always been 'our' time."

"That's a nice tradition." Julia loved to hear stories about parents bonding with their children over daily chores. There was something sweet and simple about the act of serving together.

Another breeze blew across the parking lot, shifting the Spanish moss in the tree branches above their heads. Some of the students finished their treats and went back to washing cars, allowing others to come over to the table. While there was a little lull, and no one was close enough to hear, Julia asked Olivia, "Have you had a chance to talk to Tyler?"

Olivia took a sip of her lemonade and didn't meet Julia's questioning gaze. "I talked to him yesterday after school, in the parking lot."

"Was he receptive to you?"

Olivia's laugh was cynical. "He thought it was a big joke. He laughed at me."

"I'm sorry, Olivia."

She shrugged. "I didn't really expect him to listen. But at least I said what I wanted to say. A few kids were standing close enough to hear us, so I'm kind of hoping they heard." She shrugged again. "But I don't think they'll tell anyone the truth. Not many people are interested in the truth when a lie is more exciting."

Julia was finding that to be true with *The Waving Girl* book too. "I'm proud of you for doing the hard thing. That takes a lot of courage."

Olivia finally looked at Julia. "It kind of makes me feel stronger, you know? Like I stood up for myself. Even if Tyler won't tell the truth, and even if Ebony won't believe me, at least I'm not letting them walk all over me."

Julia's heart warmed at Olivia's revelation. "I think the best thing you can do is to try to move on. Make your life what you want it to be—not what other people say it should be."

"Like this youth conference in Atlanta," Olivia said. "I was really looking forward to it, until everything happened with Ebony. After that, I didn't want to go, because I had to spend the weekend with her. But I realized that there will be hundreds of other kids there from all over Georgia. Maybe I can make some new friends."

"That's the spirit." Julia grinned. "And maybe it'll give you a chance to get to know some of the other youth group kids better. Not all of them attend your school."

Olivia nodded. "I'm actually looking forward to it now."

"Good." Julia gave Olivia a side hug. "I'm so happy to hear it."

"Thanks for talking to me, Miss Julia." Olivia's eyes shone with new hope. "I don't know if I could have done it if you didn't talk to me."

Tears sprang to Julia's eyes, even though she wasn't much of a crier. She loved watching God work through people, and it was especially wonderful to allow God to work through her. "I'm here for you, anytime you want to talk."

"I know." Olivia finished her lemonade and stacked the cup with the other dirty ones in the bin Charlene had provided. "I better get back to work."

Olivia bounded off toward the parking lot again, a new spring in her step. A couple of the kids in her group smiled at her when she approached.

Beau was standing near the entrance to the parking lot, and he caught Julia's eye. He winked at her and gave her an encouraging smile. She knew, without even talking to him, that he would say he was proud of her.

It was wonderful, the way God had orchestrated His creation. An act of giving could benefit not only the receiver but also the giver.

Julia was just happy she had been available to be part of Olivia Harold's story, and she would keep praying that Olivia would have the courage to do what was best, even if it was hard.

***

The weekend had been refreshing and productive. Exactly what Julia had needed. On Monday morning, she walked into Magnolia Investigations with renewed vigor and a revived sense of purpose. The aroma of freshly brewed coffee gave her an extra boost of energy.

Carmen met her coming into the back of the office, the ever-present watering can in hand as she completed her morning chores. She grinned. "Hola, amiga. You're looking happy today."

"I am happy, Carmen."

"That's why I love coming to work here," Carmen said. "You and Meredith are two of the happiest people I know. I've worked in some pretty crummy places and haven't always liked who I worked with."

Julia wrinkled her nose, thinking about some of the people she'd had to work with in her years as a juvenile court judge. "Same here. It's nice to have a workplace you look forward to going to every day."

"Amen!" Carmen laughed and pushed the back door open, just as Meredith was pulling it open from the outside. The two of them laughed, and Carmen held the door to let Meredith enter.

"Good morning," Meredith said, a smile on her sunny face.

"You look happy too," Carmen said. "How was your weekend?"

"Excellent. Carter and Sherri Lynn brought Kaden and Kinsley to visit yesterday. I hadn't seen them in a couple of weeks, so we had lots of catching up to do. The kids are growing so quickly, it's almost hard to believe. And smart! They're so smart. They constantly amaze me."

Julia loved hearing Meredith talk about her grandchildren. They brought her so much joy. She was always happier after one of their visits.

"Saturday seemed kind of special too," Julia teased Meredith. "At least from where I was standing in the parking lot. It took you and Quin over two hours to finish your meal."

Meredith's cheeks turned a becoming shade of pink, but she ignored Julia and said to Carmen, "What about you? How was your weekend?"

Carmen's eyebrows were raised high. "Two hours?"

Rolling her eyes, Meredith shook her head. "I'm talking about you now."

Carmen and Julia laughed, and then Carmen said, "My life is the same old, same old." She grinned. "I did spend some time with

Harmony on Saturday. We went to the park and then baked a birth-day cake for her foster mom. It was the highlight of my week." Carmen had been mentoring Harmony for quite some time through the Boys & Girls Club. The seven-year-old's mother was in prison, and her father had disappeared. Since Carmen's own story was similar, going from one foster home to the next after her parents died in a car accident when she was ten, she'd taken a special inter-est in Harmony's life and been a wonderful friend to the little girl.

Julia put her hand on Carmen's arm. "Harmony is blessed to have you."

"She's such a sweet girl. I feel lucky to have found her. She's good for me. Helps me remember to count my blessings." Carmen didn't usually get too sentimental, hiding behind her frank and honest comments. She seemed to grow uncomfortable now, because she made a face and said, "Those begonias won't water themselves."

She bustled out the door, and Julia smiled at Meredith. "That girl has a heart of gold."

"And you're the one who discovered it," Meredith reminded her, "when she came into your courtroom. Not everyone would have given her the benefit of the doubt—and a job."

"A lot of people look on the outside and see the crime or poor behavior. The truth is, most of the time, the child or teenager is just crying out for love and attention, and doing it any way they can. Carmen just needed someone to believe in her." Just like Olivia had.

"It's a gift, Jules. Not everyone has the ability."

Julia wasn't overly thrilled to get sentimental either, so she went to the coffee cart and poured a cup for Meredith, and then one for herself.

The front door banged open and Julia jumped, almost spilling her coffee. Marcella Martus stood on the threshold, panic in her eyes.

"Marcella." Julia set her cup down and went to the woman, who was clearly distraught. "What's wrong?"

"I-it's Regina." Marcella was breathing heavily, and she put her hand to her chest. "She's gone missing."

"What?" Julia and Meredith asked at the same moment.

"Last night," Marcella explained, swallowing hard. "There are cops everywhere. They've already been at my house questioning me."

"Why would they question you?" Julia asked.

"Because Allegra said I threatened Regina, and now that she's missing, I'm the number-one suspect."

"That's ridiculous," Meredith said, placing a calming hand on Marcella's arm. "Take a deep breath and start at the beginning."

Marcella did as Meredith directed and took several deep breaths. "Apparently, Regina was last seen sometime last evening. She went to supper with Allegra and then back to her hotel room. This morning, when Regina didn't meet Allegra in the lobby, Allegra went looking for her. All her personal items were in her hotel room, including her cell phone and purse, but she was gone."

"And they have no other clues or suspects?" Julia asked.

"I don't know. I don't know," Marcella said, her eyes not focusing on Julia but on some distant spot. "Allegra said I'll go to prison."

Meredith rubbed Marcella's arm. "Don't worry."

"How can I not worry?" Marcella swallowed again. "I was home all alone last night with my dog. I live alone. I don't have anyone to give me an alibi."

"When was the last time you saw Regina?" Julia asked.

"At the book signing. I haven't seen her since then." Marcella put her face in her hands. "And I threatened her! I threatened her!"

Julia glanced at Meredith and saw concern in her eyes.

"I need your help again," Marcella said, finally looking up to focus on them. "I need you to help prove I'm innocent. I didn't wish Regina Terrance ill. I was just bluffing. I don't even have Florence's diary. It was a lie to get Regina to show me her letters."

"Of course we'll help you," Meredith said. "We'll go to the hotel immediately and begin our investigation."

"The police questioned me for over an hour. Allegra was adamant that I had something to do with Regina's disappearance." She shook her head. "I wouldn't hurt a fly."

"I believe you," Meredith said. "And we'll do everything in our power to prove you're innocent."

"Oh, thank you." Marcella's relief was visible. She wiped her face, and Julia noticed her hands were shaking.

"Just go on home," Julia said. "We'll call you if we need you."

"Try to get some rest," Meredith suggested. "And don't talk to anyone, other than your lawyer."

"My lawyer?" Marcella's eyes opened wide. "I don't have a lawyer."

"You might want to get one." Julia sighed. "Just as a precaution."

"I'll need a lawyer?" Marcella's hands shook even harder.

"You might not," Meredith said. "But it's never a bad idea to talk to one."

Tears filled Marcella's eyes, and Julia had a strong suspicion that the woman didn't cry easily.

"Try not to worry," Meredith said. "We'll go immediately to see what's happening."

"Thank you." Marcella wiped her eyes and nodded. "I'll just go on home to Jemma."

"Good." Julia and Meredith walked to the front door with Marcella and said their goodbyes.

When Meredith closed the door, Julia let out a long breath. "It looks like our case suddenly took a surprise twist."

"Who would want to abduct Regina Terrance?"

"I don't know—but we'll need to find out if we're going to prove Marcella is innocent." Julia poured her coffee into a to-go mug and grabbed her purse. They had a long day ahead of them, and she'd need all the caffeine she could get.

Chapter Thirteen

THE PARKING LOT OF THE Bohemian Hotel was swarming with police officers, newspaper reporters, and curious onlookers when Julia and Meredith stepped out of Julia's car. Heat radiated up from the asphalt as the two of them walked toward the front door.

A section near one of the main-floor guest room windows was cordoned off with police tape, and a few officers were guarding it.

"I wonder what that's about," Julia mused as they entered the hotel lobby.

More police officers were there speaking to hotel staff, including Barry Pratt, one of the officers they'd worked with on previous cases. He was chatting with a coworker when he saw Julia and Meredith enter.

"Hello, ladies," he said as he left his coworker and approached them. "Are you working the case?"

"We were hired by Marcella Martus," Meredith explained.

"Ah," Barry said. "We questioned her earlier."

"She told us." Julia glanced around the lobby. "We thought we'd come and talk to a few people."

Gertie Hanson sat on a chair, her hair in a high ponytail, holding her thick, black-rimmed glasses. Her face was red and puffy, and she was sobbing uncontrollably. One of the hotel staff members sat next to her, running her hand over Gertie's back.

"Can you tell us why the police have sectioned off an area outside?" Meredith asked Barry.

"That was the room Ms. Terrance was staying in. Her window was open, and there are a few broken branches on the bush outside. It looks like Ms. Terrance left her hotel room that way, whether on her own or with an abductor."

"Is there video surveillance?" Julia asked.

"None on that side of the building." Barry rested his thumbs in his belt. "She was last seen around ten thirty last night. She was supposed to meet her publicist at nine this morning here in the lobby. Around quarter after nine, Ms. Timmons went to Ms. Terrance's room, and when Ms. Terrance didn't respond to her knocks or phone calls, Ms. Timmons asked the front desk to help her get into the room. That's when they found the open window and Ms. Terrance missing."

"And nothing was stolen?" Meredith asked.

"Not that we can tell." Barry shrugged. "And no ransom note or any other correspondence from an abductor."

Julia frowned, remembering something Carmen had told them the previous week. "I thought Ms. Terrance was staying on the top floor."

"She was," Barry said, "but she moved down here after there was some trouble with another guest."

"Oh, that's right." Julia remembered Carmen mentioning that Regina had requested a room change.

"Was she having a problem with Ms. Hanson?" Meredith nodded toward Gertie, who was making quite a scene.

"So, you've heard about the incident?"

"We have."

Gertie must have seen Julia and Meredith, because she cried out and jumped off the chair. She raced across the lobby and grabbed Julia's hand. "You've come. Oh, I'm so happy to see you."

"Me?" Julia asked, frowning.

"Both of you." Gertie took Meredith's hand as well, turning her back to Barry. "If anyone can find Regina, it's you."

Almost everyone in the lobby stopped what they were doing to stare at Gertie. Julia glanced at Meredith. Why would Gertie think they were the best people for this job?

"I'll tell you all I know, and I know a lot." Gertie let go of their hands and wiped her tears away. She put her glasses back on. "I've already spoken to the police, but they don't think Regina has been abducted."

"We didn't say that, Ms. Hanson." Barry looked like he was about to lose his patience. "We said we haven't ruled this an abduction *yet*. It might be that she left of her own accord, which isn't a crime."

"Out the window? Without her purse, cell phone, or personal belongings?" Gertie pursed her lips as she gave Barry a look.

"If she didn't want anyone to try and stop her—or see her leave—she could have gone out the window." Barry spoke slowly, as if to a child who couldn't understand. "And a person isn't obligated to take her things with her."

"Meanwhile," Gertie said, ignoring Barry, "Ms. Terrance has gone missing and who knows what's happened to her?" Tears gathered in her eyes again. "I can't sit back and let her be harmed, if I can do anything about it." She straightened her spine. "I will help you. I'll do whatever you need me to do. But we must find Ms. Terrance."

"Thank you for your offer," Julia said, "but beyond asking you some questions, I don't think there's anything you can do to help us."

"Please," Gertie begged. "Let me help. This might be my only shot at being a detective, like in the books and movies."

"We'd love to talk to you," Meredith said gently. "And then we'll let you know if there's anything else we need."

Meredith's promise seemed to pacify Gertie. She nodded. "I'll tell you anything."

"Can we go sit down?" Julia asked.

"Yes, yes," Gertie said. "We can go to my room. It's on this floor."

Julia frowned again. Hadn't Gertie been moved up to the top floor?

They followed Gertie down a hallway. Two police officers were standing outside a doorway leading into a guest suite.

"That's Ms. Terrance's room," Gertie said. She stopped at the door right next to Regina's room. "Here's mine."

"I thought you were on the top floor." Meredith pointed up.

"I was," Gertie said. "But I asked to be moved down here when I heard Ms. Terrance had moved."

"I'm sorry to be blunt," Meredith said, "but isn't that why Regina asked to be moved—so she could get away from you?"

Gertie laughed, as if it was inconsequential. "I paid the night auditor to move me to the first floor."

Julia studied her. "Why?"

"For this very reason. I was keeping an eye on her."

"For what purpose?" Julia was having a hard time understanding Gertie's motives.

"She's a famous author," Gertie said. "People say the meanest things about her in their reviews. I knew she'd need my protection, in case someone like Marcella Martus wanted to hurt her."

Julia and Meredith didn't respond. It was a huge jump to go from bad reviews to needing protection. Ironically, Regina had asked the police to keep her safe from Gertie.

Gertie's room was simple and tidy. The bed was made, there were only a few personal items on the nightstand, and everything was in order. Gertie motioned for Julia and Meredith to take the seats at the small table near the window, and she sat on the edge of the bed.

"What can you tell us about last night?" Julia asked, taking out a pad of paper and a pen.

"I'll tell you exactly what I told the police. After supper, Ms. Terrance came back to the hotel around nine o'clock."

Meredith raised her hand. "You saw her?"

"Of course I did. I ate at the same restaurant, and I followed them back to the hotel. We all walked."

"We?"

"Ms. Terrance, Ms. Timmons, and me." Gertie crossed her legs and leaned forward. "Of course, I didn't walk *with* them—but well behind them, so they didn't know I was there. Ms. Terrance doesn't like to know when I'm following her." She looked around, as if afraid of being overheard. "About an hour after we got back to the hotel, I heard a man's voice in her room."

"Do you know who it was?" Meredith also leaned forward.

"I think it was Frederick Hayes. He comes to her room all the time. He's also staying here in the hotel somewhere, but I don't know where." She waved her hand like it didn't matter to her. "Last night they were fighting. I couldn't hear everything they said, but Mr. Hayes accused her of cheating on him." Gertie's cheeks grew pink, and she dropped her gaze. "It wasn't hard to figure out they were mad at each other."

"How long did he stay?" Meredith asked. "Could he have taken her?"

"He didn't stay long. Maybe twenty or thirty minutes."

"What happened then?" Julia was watching Gertie carefully, studying her for any signs of guilt.

"I heard the shower run, and then the television turned on. About midnight, the television went off, and I went to sleep." Gertie frowned. "But I woke up about three fifteen when I heard something funny. At first, I didn't know what it was, but then I heard it again. It sounded like metal on metal, and then a little while later, a thump. I went to the window because it sounded like it was coming from the parking lot. I saw something, but it was so dark, I didn't know if it was a bush or a person. I made sure my window was locked and went back to bed." She folded her hands together and looked at Julia. "But I wish I would have called the front desk or the police or someone, because this morning, Ms. Terrance was gone. And"—she stood up, went to the window, and looked outside—"by the light of day, I can see there is no bush or anything where I saw the dark figure last night. It had to have been a person."

"What does Ms. Timmons or Mr. Hayes have to say?" Julia asked Gertie. "Have you spoken to them?"

"No, but I've heard other people talking about them today. Both deny any wrongdoing, and Ms. Timmons is adamant that Marcella Martus kidnapped Regina."

"Yes, we know." Julia stood and went to the window. The police were still guarding the scene, but there was really nothing that Julia could see that was out of the ordinary.

"I think we have everything we need right now," Meredith said as she handed Gertie a business card. "If you remember anything else, please call us. If we have any questions, we'll call you. Do you have a cell phone number?"

Gertie rattled off her number, and Meredith typed it into her phone. "Thank you. You've been really helpful."

"I won't leave Savannah until Ms. Terrance is found." Gertie put her hand over her heart. "You have my word."

The partners said their goodbyes and left Gertie's room.

"Let's see if we can find Allegra or Frederick," Julia suggested.

Neither one was hard to find. They were sitting together in a corner of the lobby Julia hadn't noticed earlier.

Allegra saw them first and went stiff. "I suppose Marcella ran to you and asked for your help."

"She did ask us for help," Julia said. "Do you mind if we ask you a few questions?"

"Me?" Allegra stood. "Am I under investigation?"

"No." Meredith shook her head. "We're just trying to help find Regina."

Allegra seemed to wilt, and she folded back into the chair. "I'll lose my job. I just know it. I had one responsibility, and I failed."

"Won't you join us?" Frederick extended his hand to Julia and then to Meredith. "I'm Frederick Hayes."

"It's nice to meet you," Julia said. She and Meredith introduced themselves and took seats across from them. "Do you mind if we ask some questions?"

"Of course not," Frederick said. "Ask away. We've already spoken to the police."

Julia shifted positions to get more comfortable. "Did they ask you where you were last night?"

"Yes. I was in my room all night." Frederick looked at Allegra. "Allegra said she was in her room also."

"What time did you get to your room?" Julia asked.

"I went right to my room after leaving Regina, around nine." Allegra straightened her shoulders. "I didn't leave again until this morning when I was supposed to meet her in the lobby."

"And I was in the hotel bar until about ten or so," Frederick said, "and then I stopped by Regina's room to ask her a question concerning today's filming schedule. We talked for about fifteen or twenty minutes and then I went to my room on the third floor and didn't come down until eight o'clock this morning, when I left with my production crew to get the site ready for filming. I came back here about two hours ago when I heard the news."

Was he telling the truth about why he'd been to Regina's room the night before? Given Gertie's report, they'd been fighting, not talking about filming.

"May I ask what kind of a relationship you have with Regina?" Meredith asked him.

He pulled back, surprise on his face. "Purely professional, of course."

"If you want to be helpful," Allegra said to Julia and Meredith, "you should be questioning Marcella Martus. She's the one who threatened Regina. And her lie about the diary has caused Regina's reputation to be questioned. Book sales fell over the weekend because of this mess. She's the one who has much to gain by abducting Regina."

"What would Marcella gain in abducting her?" Julia asked. "I can't think of any motive."

"Revenge?" Allegra pursed her lips. "Anger, hatred, maliciousness. I can think of several motives she might have."

"At this point," Julia said, "we're just trying to gather evidence, not point fingers."

Allegra scowled. "I'd advise you to start pointing fingers, and the sooner the better."

"What about that young woman Regina was worried about?" Frederick asked. "That gal from Wisconsin."

"Gertie Hanson," Meredith supplied.

"She's been stalking Regina's every move."

"What would be her motive?" Meredith asked.

"Obsession?" Frederick shrugged. "Psychosis. I don't know. She's a little off, if you ask me, and she knew every move Regina made. That's who I'd be looking at."

"I really don't have time for this." Allegra stood. "I'm already in hot water with my boss over book sales. I need to go deal with the press."

She left them, and Frederick also stood. "If you'll excuse me." He cleared his throat. "I should be going as well."

"Thank you for speaking to us." Meredith rose and shook his hand.

Julia did the same.

"Goodbye." Frederick went to the elevator, and Julia and Meredith left the lobby and walked back to the parking lot.

Something didn't sit well in Julia's gut, but she couldn't place her finger on what it was. Someone was lying—she just didn't know who.

***

They were just pulling out of the parking lot when Meredith asked, "Do you have any ideas?"

Julia turned right onto West Bay Street and was forced to stop as the traffic backed up behind a red light. "I have no idea what's happened to Regina Terrance, but it's clear that someone is lying."

"The three people to see her last—that we know of—are Allegra Timmons, Frederick Hayes, and Gertie Hanson." Meredith looked out her window. "Do you think it was one of them?"

"Don't forget Marcella Martus and her threat." Even though they were representing Marcella, that didn't rule her out as a suspect.

"Regina isn't a big woman," Meredith said, "but I find it hard to believe that Allegra, Gertie, or Marcella could have overpowered her to get her out of the hotel window."

"If she was drugged, they could. Or"—Julia glanced at Meredith—"they could have had help."

"True." Meredith put her chin in her hand. "And Gertie could be lying about Frederick and Regina fighting. Maybe he really did just go to Regina's room to talk about filming."

"Perhaps." Julia thought about everything they'd learned. "Can you google Frederick Hayes? Where does he live? Is he married?"

Meredith pulled out her smartphone. She was quiet as she typed.

At the stoplight, Julia turned left onto Jefferson Street and waited while Meredith searched.

"What in the world?" Meredith spun to Julia. "Look what I found." She lifted the phone up, and Julia glanced at it quickly.

"It's a picture of Frederick and Regina," Meredith said, pulling the phone back so Julia could concentrate on the road. "At a restaurant in Manhattan a year ago! A gossip magazine snapped a picture of them having a romantic dinner."

"A year ago?" Julia frowned. "But didn't they just meet?"

Meredith shrugged. "I thought so."

"At the press conference, when we first saw Regina and Frederick, she mispronounced his name, remember? She called him Frederick *Haynes*, with an *n*. He had to correct her. If they'd been dating a year ago, you'd think she could pronounce his name correctly."

"Unless it was an act," Meredith said.

"But for what purpose? Why would they want people to think they just met?"

"Who knows? And remember the rendezvous in the alcove at the Mansion. You said they were fighting—so maybe Gertie was telling the truth. Maybe Frederick was lying to us when he said they were just talking about filming and their relationship is purely professional."

"But why would he want to abduct Regina?"

"Jealousy? You saw how he reacted to Regina flirting with that board member at the fundraiser. Maybe their fighting turned into something more."

A shiver ran up Julia's spine. "I sure hope not." She took another left onto West Oglethorpe. The traffic was thick for a Monday.

"I think we should have Carmen do an online search for Allegra and Gertie too." Meredith locked her phone and put it back in her purse. "We might be surprised at what we find about them."

"Add Marcella Martus to the list." Julia sighed. "I think it's a bit premature to rule out anyone."

"I just hope Regina's okay." Meredith clasped her hands over her purse. "I'd hate to think something bad happened to her, or that she's suffering right now."

"I agree." Julia turned right onto Whitaker Street.

A few minutes later, they arrived at the agency and quickly put Carmen to work looking for information on their four suspects.

Any little clue would help.

Chapter Fourteen

JULIA RARELY STOOD AT CARMEN's desk, just waiting. She usually had a dozen things to keep her occupied while she waited for Carmen's reports—but this afternoon was different. Even though they had other cases to attend to, both Julia and Meredith stood at the receptionist's desk, watching both Carmen and her computer screen. A missing person's case trumped any other case they were currently investigating.

"Have you found *anything*?" Julia asked. "Any Gertie, Gertrude, or even Gretchen Hanson from Sheboygan, Wisconsin?"

Carmen shook her head. "It's no *bueno*. I can't find any Gertrude Hanson. There are other Hansons, many of them from Sheboygan and other parts of Wisconsin—it's one of the top five most popular surnames in the state—but no Gertrude—at least not one that matches the approximate age of the one you know."

"What about from somewhere else?" Meredith suggested. "How many Gertrude Hansons are there in the rest of the United States?"

A moment later Carmen had the answer. "There are sixty-nine Gertrude Hansons in the USA." She typed a little more and moved her mouse. "And three of the approximate age."

"Where do they live?" Julia asked.

"One lives in Washington State and is married, one lives in South Dakota with her two children, and one is a college student in Arizona."

"Can you find a picture of the college student?" Meredith asked.

"You think I'm a wizard with this computer?" Carmen teased.

"Yes," Julia and Meredith said at the same time with smiles on their faces.

Carmen laughed and did a little more searching. "Okay, here she is." She positioned the screen so Julia and Meredith could get a good look at the picture of Gertie Hanson from the University of Arizona. The young woman was tall and sleek with bright blond hair.

"That's not our Gertie Hanson." Disappointment tinted Julia's words.

"Maybe your *chica* isn't really named Gertie Hanson." Carmen leaned back in her chair and crossed her arms. "Maybe it's an alias."

"Why would she need an alias?" Meredith asked. "She's a sweet, albeit a little passionate, fan."

"Or is she?" Carmen lifted her eyebrows. "You're much too nice, Meredith. After all these cases, I'm surprised you still think people are who they say they are."

"And you're too jaded, Carmen." Meredith chuckled.

"You assume everyone is just as sweet and innocent as you." Carmen rubbed her hands together. "Maybe she came to Savannah to kidnap her favorite author and was waiting for the right time."

"It seems a little far-fetched, if you ask me. What would be the point in abducting her favorite author?" Julia crossed her arms on the raised portion of Carmen's desk. "But you're right, if Gertie is from Sheboygan, or if her name is really Gertie Hanson, as she claims, then we should be able to find her."

"What do you think?" Meredith asked Julia.

"I'm thinking we should go back to the hotel and find out more about Regina Terrance's number-one fan. We asked her a lot of questions about what happened last night, but we didn't bother to ask much about her."

Meredith nodded.

"And what about Allegra Timmons?" Julia asked Carmen.

Carmen pulled up a page on her computer. "She checks out. She's employed by Falcon Publishing House in NYC. Here's her home address, her alma mater, and her parents' names. And, as far as I can tell, she's the only Allegra Timmons in America."

"That's convenient." Meredith smiled. "Thanks for your help, Carmen."

"*De nada.*"

Julia and Meredith went back out to Julia's car. They were soon on Whitaker Street, heading back to the Bohemian Hotel.

"Do you think Gertie Hanson is an alias?" Julia asked Meredith.

"Carmen might have missed something in her search." Meredith was ever the optimist. "I'd like to believe Gertie, unless proven wrong."

"Same here."

"But we can't rule out the possibility."

The traffic was so heavy, Julia decided not to take the same route they'd used previously. Instead, she took a right and eventually found herself on East Broad Street. There wasn't as much tourist traffic, and it would give them an easy right-hand turn into the Bohemian Hotel when they took a left onto East Bay Street.

"Does that look like Marcella Martus to you?" Meredith pointed out the passenger side window to a woman getting out of a red compact car.

"That does look like Marcella." Julia frowned. "I wonder what she's doing on this side of town."

"Maybe she stopped to see a lawyer before going home."

Marcella pulled a white plastic bag from her car and then looked right and left before closing the door and walking toward an abandoned building.

"What is she doing?" Meredith asked as she strained to see. "Can you pull over?"

Julia found a space to park the car a little ways away from the ramshackle building. Marcella's black-and-white striped shirt was barely discernable as she pushed aside a broken piece of fencing and disappeared.

"What in the world?" Julia turned off the engine. "What could she be doing here?"

Meredith didn't speak for a moment as she surveyed the property from the safety of the vehicle. "What if she's holding Regina captive in there? It looks abandoned."

"Are you serious?" Julia asked.

"Well, look at it. What better place to hide someone than in plain sight? It's not too far from the hotel, so it would have been easy to get her here in the middle of the night before anyone knew she was missing."

Julia couldn't deny it would be a good location to keep someone hidden. "I wish we could go and look for ourselves, but we'll need permission from the owner."

"I wonder who owns the building."

Julia had both of her hands on the wheel even though the vehicle wasn't moving. "Can you call Carmen and ask her to find out?"

Meredith took out her phone and called Carmen. She gave her the address and asked her to locate the owner. Before she hung up, she said, "Ask him or her if we can have permission to enter the property. Thanks, Carmen."

"Should we wait until Marcella comes back out?" Julia asked.

"Why not?" Meredith put her phone back in her purse. "I don't think Gertie Hanson is going anywhere soon. Remember how she promised us she wouldn't leave Savannah until Regina was found?"

"That could all be part of her act. She might be gone already."

Meredith shrugged. "I hope Marcella doesn't notice us sitting here. How would we explain our stakeout?"

Julia grinned. "If this was a real stakeout, we'd need some binoculars and snack food, and you'd be my comic sidekick."

Meredith laughed. "I'd make for pretty poor comic relief."

They waited for about ten minutes before Marcella reappeared. She had to push the fence out of place again, and then looked cautiously from side to side before returning to the sidewalk. Thankfully, Julia and Meredith were far enough away that she didn't notice them.

"She still has the white bag," Meredith said a moment before Marcella dropped the bag and whatever it contained in a public garbage can near the building.

Meredith glanced at Julia, her eyebrows raised. "Are we going to have to go garbage diving now?"

Julia smiled. "You read my mind."

"This job definitely keeps us on our toes."

Marcella got into her car and pulled onto East Broad Street. At the corner, she turned right and was soon out of sight.

"I really wish we could get into that building," Julia said. "But I don't want to risk getting charged with trespassing."

"Let's go take a look in the garbage to see if something's in that bag. We'll decide if trespassing is worth the risk depending on what we find."

They waited a couple more minutes, to make sure Marcella didn't return, and then got out of Julia's car.

"Are you going to dig in the trash?" Meredith asked Julia.

"Not if you want to."

Meredith wrinkled her nose. "I wouldn't say I *want* to dig in the trash, but I will."

"Okay." Julia crossed her arms. "I won't fight you for the honor."

Thankfully, it was an open can and the bag was sitting on top of the pile.

Meredith gingerly reached in and grasped the bag. It crinkled from her touch, and when she pulled it out, Julia couldn't see any business logo on it.

"What's in it?" she asked Meredith.

Meredith frowned. "It's a to-go container." She opened the bag wider so Julia could see. A white Styrofoam container was in the bottom. It was open, and whatever had been inside was now gone, though there was a little food residue. It looked like some kind of brown sauce or gravy. A used napkin and a plastic fork were also in the bag.

"If she has Regina in there," Julia said, "at least she's feeding her."

"But why would she be holding Regina hostage?" Meredith closed the bag and put it back in the trash can.

"Maybe she's holding her hostage until Regina agrees to reveal the letters."

"Do you think we should call the police and have them come and search?"

"I don't think this is enough evidence to warrant a search. Maybe Marcella ate the meal herself."

"Why would she go into an abandoned building to eat her lunch?" Meredith asked.

"I don't know. Maybe Carmen will find out that Marcella owns the building—and then won't we look foolish if we have it searched, only to discover that she eats her lunch here every day?"

"I suppose you're right." Meredith looked at the building again. All the windows had been boarded up, long ago. There was nothing special to mark its use or purpose. No signage or any other indicators. "But if we find any other evidence that Marcella abducted Regina, we're calling the police and having them search this property."

"Agreed."

They walked back to the car and got inside then drove to the Bohemian Hotel. After they parked, Meredith asked Julia, "Ready to interview Gertie Hanson again?"

Julia took out her notepad and pen. "More than ready."

Hopefully they could learn Gertie's real name—if, in fact, she wasn't who she said she was.

***

There were no more police cars, journalists, or television reporters at the Bohemian Hotel when Julia and Meredith arrived for the second time that day. Police tape was still set up around the window outside Regina's room, and a pair of tourists stood there taking a picture.

"Should I call Gertie and ask her to meet us in the hotel lobby?" Meredith asked, holding up her cell phone. "I have her number."

Julia shook her head. "Let's ask the front desk to call her room. She just has the agency number from the business card you gave her. Let's not give her your cell phone number."

"Good thinking."

They got out of the car and walked into the lobby. It had quieted down quite a bit since they'd been there a couple of hours before. Two receptionists worked at the front desk, and there was a man sitting in a chair reading a newspaper. A woman walked through with two little kids. Julia smiled politely at them and directed her steps to the front desk.

"Hello," Meredith said to one of the staff members working behind the long counter. "Could you please dial Gertie Hanson's room?"

"It would be my pleasure to help you," the receptionist said with a pleasant smile. Her name tag read MONIQUE. "Let me go ahead and look up her room number for you."

Julia took the time to glance around the lobby. It was a lovely hotel, with a dark and modern motif. Very upscale.

"I'm sorry," Monique said a moment later. "I'm not finding a guest here by the name of Gertie Hanson. Is there another name I can check?"

Julia frowned. "No Gertie Hanson?"

"I'm afraid not, ma'am."

"Her room is on this floor," Meredith said. "Um, let me think of the number."

Julia said, "I believe it's room number 113. It's right next door to where Regina Terrance was staying."

Monique's eyes grew a little wider. "I just came on shift, but I heard there was quite a bit of activity here this morning."

Julia nodded.

"I'll go ahead and look up room 113 for you." Monique smiled and typed on her keyboard, but the smile soon slipped, and she shook her head. "Room 113 is occupied but not by a Gertie Hanson."

"Really?" Meredith frowned and glanced at Julia.

Maybe this was proof that Gertie *had* been lying about her name all along.

"Can you tell us the name of the guest in room 113?" Julia asked.

"I'm sorry, ma'am, but that's private information. I am not allowed to give out the name of any guest in our hotel."

"Of course not." Julia nodded in understanding. "Can you tell me if the room has been recently vacated and rented by someone else?"

Monique glanced at her screen. "It appears that the guest in number 113 has occupied that room for two days."

So it had to be Gertie—or whatever her name was.

"I know you can't tell us who is renting the room," Meredith said, "but could you ring up the room for us?"

"I would be happy to assist you." Monique nodded, clearly pleased to help. "One moment."

Just then a young woman entered the lobby and caught Julia's attention—but she had to look twice.

Gertie Hanson paused in her tracks. She was wearing a pair of cropped black pants and a flowing blouse, so different than her other outfits. Her hair, which was usually in a ponytail, was now loose and around her shoulders, and her ever-present glasses were nowhere to be found.

"What are you two doing back here?" Gertie asked.

Meredith was staring at Gertie, probably just as surprised as Julia. "We were just trying to call your room."

"Why?" Gertie frowned. "I gave you my cell phone number."

"We, uh, just thought it would be easier to have the front desk ring you."

Gertie studied Meredith and then turned her probing gaze on Julia. She looked skeptical. Her eyes were a dark brown, fringed with beautiful long lashes. How had Julia not noticed her lashes before? She wore mascara now. Had she been wearing makeup the last few times they saw her?

"Did you need something?" Gertie asked.

"We came to ask you a few more questions." Julia turned her attention back to Monique. "Thank you for your help."

Monique smiled. "Please let me know if I can be of more service to you."

"Thank you," Meredith said.

Gertie crossed her arms over her chest, rooted to the spot where she had been standing since Julia saw her. She was no longer smiling and didn't appear to want to be as helpful as she'd been earlier. "What do you need to know that I didn't tell you?"

"Can we go somewhere private to talk?" Meredith asked. "Like back to your room?"

Gertie studied them for another moment and then shook her head. "We can talk here in the lobby."

"All right." Julia didn't want Gertie to get too suspicious and shut down. "Where would you like to sit?"

Gertie led them to the corner where they'd spoken to Allegra and Frederick earlier. "Here's fine."

They each took a seat.

Meredith glanced at Julia, as if asking her who should start.

"Gertie," Julia began, "in all the excitement this morning, we forgot to ask you a few questions about yourself."

"Me?" Gertie pointed to her chest. "Why would you need to know more about me?" She squinted. "Am I on trial? Do you think I took Regina?"

Regina? When had Gertie started to call her Regina, and not Ms. Terrance?

"No, of course not." Meredith smiled. "But we want to be thorough, and since you were one of the last people to see Ms. Terrance, we thought we should ask a few more questions."

"But what does her disappearance have to do with me?"

"We don't think it does," Julia assured her. "We just want to know more about you." The first thing she wanted to know was if Gertie was her real name. But if she was using an alias, would she actually tell them her real name? It wasn't likely, though it didn't hurt to ask. "I'm curious about your name. We did a little search today and couldn't find a Gertrude Hanson from Sheboygan, Wisconsin."

"You did a search on me?" Gertie stood suddenly, her eyes huge. "You don't trust me."

"We don't know you," Meredith amended, putting her hand up to steady Gertie. "It's our job to be thorough."

Gertie removed her arm from Meredith's touch. "You said Regina's disappearance doesn't have anything to do with me."

"That doesn't mean we won't try to uncover all the facts about the people who have been in contact with Ms. Terrance." Julia motioned to the seat. "You don't have to be worried. Please stay and talk to us."

Gertie slowly took her seat again. "I don't know why you couldn't find a Gertrude Hanson. I've lived in Sheboygan my whole life."

"We asked the woman at the front desk if there's a guest here by the name of Gertie Hanson, and she didn't have your name listed." Julia spoke softly and gently, hoping she didn't upset Gertie again. "Can you tell me why?"

Gertie licked her lips. "I don't want my boyfriend finding me here, so I put my room under an alias."

Meredith frowned. "Why don't you want him to find you?"

"He's overbearing and controlling. He didn't want me to come here, and I wouldn't put it past him to try to find me and tell me to come home. So I blocked his calls and didn't give the hotel my real name." She shrugged. "This is my life and my adventure. No one has the right to tell me what to do."

Meredith glanced at Julia, more questions in her eyes. "May I ask what you do for a living?"

Gertie opened her mouth and then closed it again. She readjusted her position on the chair and lifted her chin, just a notch. "I work at a grocery store."

Julia didn't bother to take out her pad and pencil since she didn't want Gertie to become defensive again. "It's nice that your employer doesn't mind you being gone so long."

Gertie just shrugged.

It was clear she had no intention of opening up about herself any more than necessary. Did it even pay to continue questioning her?

"Have you been a fan of Regina Terrance's books for long?" Meredith tried another approach.

"Since I was a teenager."

"Had you met her before coming to Savannah?" Julia asked.

Gertie's arms were still crossed over her chest. "I really don't like being questioned. I would never do anything to hurt Ms. Terrance." She was back to referring to the author in a more formal tone. "I told you everything I know. I don't see how questioning me about where I work or how long I've been a fan has anything to do with her disappearance."

"We didn't say it did." Julia tried to keep her voice smooth and calm. "We're just curious about you."

Gertie stood up again. "Look. I said I'd help you, and I will. But call my cell phone the next time you want to talk. Okay? Don't come here to take me by surprise again. I don't like that. It feels dirty and underhanded."

Julia and Meredith also stood.

"I'm sorry," Meredith said. "We didn't mean to upset you."

"You have my cell number." Gertie pushed between them and walked across the lobby and down the hall toward her room. She didn't look back.

"That was a bit unexpected, don't you think?" Julia said to Meredith. "That was not the same Gertie Hanson we've seen the past couple of weeks."

"Most definitely not."

"Do you really think she's using an alias here at the hotel to protect herself from her boyfriend?"

"I don't have any reason not to believe her."

"But that doesn't explain why we can't find any record of Gertie Hanson from Sheboygan." Julia hiked her purse higher on her shoulder. "I have an idea how we can find out what her real name is—but I think we need to let her cool off a bit. Let's call her tomorrow morning and ask her to meet us for lunch at the Downhome Diner."

"What do you have in mind?" Meredith's eyes shone with interest.

Julia laid out her idea, and Meredith nodded her agreement.

Hopefully, by this time tomorrow, they would know Gertie Hanson's real identity. And when they did, they just might know whether or not she had something to do with Regina Terrance's abduction.

Chapter Fifteen

A GENTLE BREEZE BLEW THROUGH the lawn and onto the back deck where Julia sat with Beau, enjoying the supper he had made for her before she came home from work. The aroma of barbecued chicken mingled with the smell of freshly cut grass. Children played in the neighboring yard, and a couple of birds trilled their songs in the tops of the magnolia trees nearby.

Julia took a long, cool sip of Diet Dr Pepper and let out a contented sigh. "This is exactly what I needed after today."

"I heard the news reports about Regina Terrance." Beau held up the bowl of potato salad and offered it to Julia. "Do you have any leads?"

Julia took the salad and placed a small scoop on her plate. Even though she had already had two servings, she could never turn down Beau's famous potato salad. He had made it for their first picnic when they were dating, and each time she ate it, she was brought back to that magical time in their relationship. His triple-bypass surgery a while back had caused both of them to reexamine their diets, but he'd found a way to substitute some of the ingredients with heart-healthy choices and still retain its flavor. She liked it even better now.

"We have a few leads," she said. "But nothing solid yet. We've spoken to the last three people who saw her the night before she went missing."

"And you're doing this investigation on behalf of Marcella Martus, right?" Beau took a bite of his salad and watched her. His blue eyes were still capable of holding her captive, especially when he studied her so intently.

"Yes." Julia lifted her fork. "She's also a suspect, at least, in some people's opinions, because she threatened Regina at her book signing."

"What did she threaten to do?"

"Nothing specific. It was more of a general threat."

"Do you think she did it?"

Julia shook her head. "I don't think she's capable. I think her threat had more to do with claiming she found a diary that belonged to Florence Martus."

"But the diary doesn't exist?"

"No. It was a bluff to see if she could get Regina to share her letters."

Beau took another bite of his salad and nodded slowly, as if he was mulling all the information over in his mind.

A chickadee flew low and close to the deck before it landed on a branch close by. Lazy clouds passed overhead, and a jazzy tune from a neighbor's house drifted into the yard on the breeze.

Julia almost felt guilty for enjoying these simple pleasures while Regina's whereabouts were still unknown. What if she was suffering, tied up and held captive somewhere? The police were doing an investigation, but Julia wished they could all do more. She hoped and prayed that Gertie would meet with her and Meredith the next day, and that her idea would work to learn her real identity. After seeing Gertie at the hotel the second time, Julia was more convinced than ever that Gertie was lying about her identity—both her name and the persona she'd exhibited while in Savannah.

The question remained: Why?

"Have you finished reading *The Waving Girl*?" Beau asked.

"Not yet." Julia took a bite of her potato salad and savored the taste on her tongue. It was cold and tangy, just like she liked it. After she swallowed she said, "I just can't bring myself to keep reading. It feels wrong. Like I'm gossiping and spreading rumors about Florence Martus, even though she's long gone."

"All anyone could talk about today was Regina Terrance." Beau took a sip of his sweet tea. "Her disappearance will probably make front page news in a lot of newspapers. Book sales will probably skyrocket."

Julia nodded. "And the little I know about Allegra, she'll probably make the most of the publicity."

"It's all sad. If there's anything I can do to help you and Meredith, just let me know."

A smile lifted Julia's lips. "I will."

She had always known she had Beau's full support. Even after they both retired, and she suggested that she join Meredith in opening Magnolia Investigations, Beau didn't hinder her dreams. He often had supper waiting for her when she came home, and he was always quick to ask her about her work.

They finished eating and just sat to enjoy the evening. Over the years, Beau had done a lot of work on the yard and loved tending the beautifully landscaped flower beds. For a long time, he had talked about adding a patio off the deck, but the plans were still in the beginning stages.

"How is everything coming along with the fundraising?" he asked.

In all the excitement and activity that day, Julia had almost forgotten about the news from Pastor Jay.

"We made our goal and exceeded it! Pastor Jay received a donation today and emailed me to tell me we're all set to go. He said the donor wanted to remain anonymous, but he could tell me the man doesn't attend our church, and he's a friend of ours and Meredith."

Beau lifted his eyebrows. "Do you think it was Quin?"

She shrugged. "That's my best guess. He's the only person I can think of who knew we needed money and showed an interest in supporting our efforts. I'll have to ask Meredith if she can get the truth out of him, so I know who to thank. We have enough money now to take along a few extra students, if there should happen to be some latecomers. We won't have any trouble saying yes."

"That's wonderful, Julie-bean. I knew all your hard work would pay off."

"I can't take all the credit. Everyone rallied and did a fantastic job the past few weeks. I'm just so happy we won't have to turn away anyone who wants to come."

"I ran into Russ Harold at the clubhouse today." Beau leaned back in his chair and laced his fingers together as he laid them on his trim stomach. Russ Harold was Olivia's dad. He and Beau often golfed together. "He mentioned that Olivia had a new friend at school who was interested in joining the youth group. He asked if there was still room for the friend to attend the youth convention too."

Julia sat up straighter. "Olivia has a new friend? That's wonderful."

Beau grinned. "I thought you'd like to hear that."

"I'll email her mom tonight and tell her to extend the invitation. Of course we have room!"

"Russ also mentioned to me how much he and his wife appreciate all you've done to help Olivia." Pride shone from Beau's eyes. "He told me they've seen a real change in Olivia this past week, and they know a lot of it is due to you."

"It's due to Olivia. She's a good kid."

Beau reached across the table and took Julia's hand in his. He rubbed the top with his thumb. "It felt good to run into someone who thinks so highly of my wife. Made me even more proud of you, if that's possible."

Julia felt a blush creep up her neck and into her cheeks, and she laughed. "Even after almost forty-four years of marriage, you still make me blush, Beauregard Eugene Foley."

"That's my goal." He lifted her hand to his lips and placed a soft kiss there. "I plan to make you blush until you're a hundred years old."

She laughed. "I'll hold you to that."

"Please do." He lowered her hand but didn't let it go.

Julia was thankful for moments like these, amid the chaos and difficulty of her work, that reminded her of what was most important.

***

The smell of fried onions wafted on the air as Julia arrived at the Downhome Diner and took a seat in the booth next to Meredith the next afternoon.

"Have you seen Gertie yet?" she asked.

"No, but I only just arrived." Meredith hadn't been served her coffee yet, but Charlene was already on her way to the table with a steaming pot in hand.

"Hello, Julia, Meredith."

"Hello, Charlene." Julia flipped up her coffee cup and smiled. "Fill her up, please. We have a long day ahead of us."

Charlene grinned. "Mama stopped by here earlier today. Said she's been wanting to talk with you two about Marcella Martus, but that the ladies' aid society has got her running in circles. They're planning a bazaar, and Mama's the head of the committee." She shook her head. "She has more energy than I do, most days."

"We'd love to talk to her." Meredith turned her cup right side up to receive some coffee. "Tell her to stop by the office when she gets a free moment, or we can meet her here, if she'd like."

"I think she's planning on stopping in to see you later today, if that's okay."

"Sure is," Julia said. "Our coffee's not quite as good as yours, but we'll have a pot ready for her when she comes."

Charlene finished filling up their coffee cups and then nodded at the empty bench seat across from them. "Expecting someone else?"

"Yes." Meredith glanced toward the window. "Hopefully she'll be along soon."

"I'll wait until she arrives to take your order." Charlene set her hand on the back of the opposite bench. "Settle in and make yourselves comfortable. No hurry."

"Thank you."

As Charlene walked away, Julia took her first sip and sighed. "I love Charlene's coffee."

Meredith smiled and also took a sip. The appreciation on her face mirrored what Julia felt about the strong, dark brew.

"I'm starving," Julia mused as she looked at the daily special on the menu board. "What do you think you'll have?"

Meredith toyed with the handle on her mug. "I'll probably get a small salad."

"Aren't you hungry?"

"Quin asked me out to supper tonight, and I want to have a full appetite." She still didn't meet Julia's gaze.

"Any special reason you're going out?"

Meredith shrugged. "Just to catch up."

"You didn't have enough time here on Saturday, after your cars were washed?"

When Meredith didn't answer, Julia smiled and said, "The youth group received an anonymous donation, and I have reason to believe Quin was the donor."

That piqued Meredith's interest. "Really?"

"If you have a chance to ask him, I'd love to know where to send the thank-you card."

The door opened, and Gertie Hanson appeared. Her hair was back in its high pony, and her oversized glasses were in place. She wore a pair of jeans, a T-shirt, and a jean jacket. The only thing missing was the digital camera she usually wore around her neck.

Meredith looked relieved to stop talking about Quin.

"Hello, you guys." Gertie's mood and attitude had much improved since the last time they saw her. "Thanks for inviting me to lunch. I haven't been to this restaurant yet."

"Have a seat." Julia motioned to the bench across from them. "We've waited to order."

"Thanks." Gertie plopped into the seat and scooted to the center. She was bright and bubbly again today. "What do you recommend—and please don't say shrimp and grits." She made a face. "I've had it and I'm not a fan."

Julia smiled. "Have you had biscuits and gravy?"

"Oh sure. We have biscuits and gravy back home."

"Southern biscuits and gravy?" Meredith asked.

"Aren't they all the same?" Gertie wasn't wearing makeup today, and her pretty brown eyes were almost hidden behind her glasses. As soon as she pushed them up the brim of her nose, they slipped down again.

"Why don't you order them and let us know," Julia suggested.

Gertie grinned. "Sounds good to me." She set down the menu and gave Julia and Meredith her full attention. "I was happy you called me to help. I was serious when I said I want to do my part to find Ms. Terrance. What can I do for you?"

"Something you said the other day struck me." Julia wrapped her hands around her warm coffee cup. "You mentioned that you came to Savannah to keep an eye on Regina because of all the bad reviews she's received."

Gertie nodded, her lips pressed together. "Not everyone loves Ms. Terrance's writing like I do."

"We thought it would be helpful to have a list of those people who wrote negative reviews," Meredith said. "Perhaps, like you feared, one of them wanted to harm Regina. If we have their names, we could investigate them to see if they had any motive or opportunity."

Gertie's eyebrows rose over the rims of her glasses. "That would be a long list. She has thousands of reviews."

"Perhaps," Julia said, "you could give us a list of the top ten most alarming ones."

"I suppose I could do that." Gertie put her chin in her hand, disappointment written all over her face. "But I was hoping I could do something a little more exciting to help out."

Julia glanced at Meredith. They hadn't really called Gertie to meet with them to get her help with the negative reviews. Julia didn't think any of them were worth their time. In her experience, people were unkind online because they didn't have to look the other person in the eye and say all the mean, hurtful things. It made people feel a lot braver to write harsh words anonymously.

Her idea to learn Gertie's real name would have to wait until the end of the meal, and it depended solely on Gertie's method of payment.

Charlene returned and took their orders. Gertie asked for the biscuits and gravy, and Julia ordered the shrimp and grits. Meredith ordered a simple salad, just as she planned.

Once Charlene left to give their order to the cook, Julia turned her attention back to Gertie. "I've never been to Wisconsin. What's it like?"

"Oh, you'd love it." Gertie grinned. "Sheboygan is right on the shores of Lake Michigan. It's sometimes called the Bratwurst Capital of the World. It was settled in the 1780s and now has a population of almost fifty thousand people." She went on to list several more facts about Sheboygan, but all of them were things a person could find on Wikipedia.

"Your name is fairly common," Meredith mused. "Hanson. That's Scandinavian, isn't it?"

Gertie nodded.

"Were both your parents of Scandinavian descent?"

"Yes."

"Was your mother's maiden name just as common? Must get confusing with all those Hansons, Johnsons, and Andersons in Wisconsin."

Gertie laughed and put up her hands, like she was caught. "Mom's maiden name was Johnson."

"Really?" Julia asked.

"Yep. John Hanson married Hannah Johnson, and they had me." She smiled and pushed her glasses up her nose. "Crazy, huh?"

John Hanson and Hannah Johnson? Did she seriously think they'd believe her?

"Any brothers and sisters?" Julia asked.

"Nope. Just me." She waved her hand, as if to push aside the conversation, and then said, "What about the two of you? Are you married, are you from around here?"

Gertie spent the rest of the meal directing questions their way, and no matter how hard Julia and Meredith tried, they could not return the conversation to Gertie. She was a master at evasion and deflection.

Finally, after Gertie proclaimed the biscuits and gravy were better than back home, Charlene cleared away the plates and dropped off the bills. One for each of them.

Julia picked up her bill, Meredith picked up hers, but Gertie just stared at hers, as if she was waiting for Julia or Meredith to offer to pay.

Neither one did.

When Charlene returned to the table to take their debit cards, Gertie scrambled for her purse. She licked her lips and then reached into a slot in her wallet and pulled out a card.

Which was exactly what Julia had hoped she would do.

"Thank you." Charlene took the cards and went to the register.

Gertie watched her walk away and then looked back at Julia and Meredith with apprehension. Several times, she glanced over her shoulder to look toward Charlene.

"Will you excuse me?" Julia asked. "I need to use the ladies' room."

She slipped out of the booth and walked around the long counter to the back corner of the diner where the restrooms were located—walking right past Charlene. She stopped near her and said with a pleasant smile on her face, in case Gertie was watching, "Can you please write down the name on the credit card of our friend and give it to me when she leaves?"

"Sure thing, honey." Charlene didn't even bat an eye or look up at Julia.

Julia kept on walking toward the restroom as if nothing was out of the ordinary.

A few minutes later, when she returned to their booth, Gertie was gone.

"What happened to our sleuth-in-training?" Julia asked.

"As soon as Charlene returned our cards, Gertie grabbed hers and said she had a headache and needed to go back to the hotel to lie down."

Julia's card was still lying on the table with a receipt. She put it back in her wallet just as Charlene arrived with a slip of paper.

"Here's the name on the card your friend gave me." She handed the slip of paper to Julia. "It said Jasmine Terrance."

"Jasmine Terrance?" Julia looked down at the name. "Who in the world is Jasmine Terrance?"

Meredith crowded next to Julia and looked at the name on the paper. "I wonder if she's related to Regina—and if she is, what's the game they're playing?"

"I don't know." Julia shook her head. "But let's get back to the office and see what Carmen can find out about her."

Meredith gathered her purse and waited for Julia to scoot off the bench.

"Thank you, Charlene," Julia said. "We have to run."

"Anytime, ladies."

Julia couldn't wait to get back to the office. She had a strong suspicion that they would soon know a lot more about Jasmine Terrance than they did about Gertie Hanson.

Chapter Sixteen

THE TRAFFIC WAS THICK AS Julia drove to Magnolia Investigations. She had called Carmen on the way and asked her to do a search on Jasmine Terrance, hoping that by the time she and Meredith arrived at the office, Carmen would have a report ready for them.

Sunshine spilled over the car and warmed the inside as Julia pulled into the parking space behind the agency. Thankfully, Meredith was just behind Julia, because Julia wasn't sure if she would have had the patience to wait for her partner to get to the office before bombarding Carmen with questions.

Meredith pulled her vehicle to a stop, and she and Julia exited their cars at the same time. Nervous energy pushed Julia toward the back door, and Meredith was right on her heels.

"If Gertie—or should I say Jasmine?—is related to Regina," Julia said to Meredith, "why all the lies? Why go to all the trouble to have Jasmine pretend?"

"Maybe we'll find out when Carmen tells us who this woman really is."

"Hola," Carmen called out to them. "I'm at my desk—and, wow, do I have some juicy *información* for you."

Julia bypassed the coffeepot in the hall and went directly to Carmen's desk in the reception area. The room used to be a formal parlor when the house was still a residential property.

"Tell us," Julia said to Carmen. "I'm about ready to burst with anticipation."

Carmen turned the monitor on her computer so they could see. There were several pictures of Jasmine Terrance in various costumes from Shakespeare to *Grease*. "Your Miss Jasmine Terrance is an actress in New York City. She's been in dozens of plays both on and off Broadway, but more recently, she's been unemployed." Carmen pulled up another tab on her computer. It was Jasmine's website with some of her headshots. She was a beautiful woman, and it was clear that her Gertie Hanson persona was just another act. "She was born and raised in New York City," Carmen said. "And I learned an even more interesting fact. She's Regina Terrance's first cousin. Their fathers are brothers."

"They're cousins?" Julia couldn't stand any longer. She took a seat. "Surely Regina has to know Gertie is her cousin."

"There are pictures of them together at fundraisers and events in New York," Carmen said, pulling up even more tabs. "So yes, they know each other."

"Then why?" Meredith asked as she sat next to Julia. "Why the act? Do you think Allegra knows?"

"There's a picture of Allegra with them too," Carmen piped up. "At a fundraiser gala last Christmas."

Julia thought back to all the interactions she'd witnessed with Gertie/Jasmine, Regina, and Allegra. Not only had they appeared as if Jasmine was being a nuisance, they'd even called the police to complain about Jasmine's attention, claiming she was stalking Regina. And the day Regina went missing, instead of telling them the truth about who she really was, Jasmine had continued to lie and say she was Gertie Hanson. But when they arrived at the hotel a second time that day, when the police and reporters were all gone, Jasmine wasn't expecting them. Her guard had been down, and she had been uncomfortable. Today, though, Jasmine had returned to her Gertie character, continuing the ruse.

"What is she hiding?" Meredith asked. "And why is Allegra allowing it to continue?"

"Oh, look at this picture I found," Carmen said.

Julia and Meredith went to stand behind her, and Carmen showed them a picture of Regina, Allegra, Jasmine, and Frederick together at a New Year's Eve ball, just four months ago. There were other people in the picture, but it was clear all four of them knew each other.

"This whole time," Julia said, "they knew each other and were trying to trick us all."

"But for what purpose?" Meredith asked. "None of this makes any sense. Regina said she was in town to film a documentary. I can see why she might be hiding her relationship with Frederick, since he's employed to make the film. But why lie about her cousin—and create a whole different persona for her?"

"I think it's time we get Allegra, Jasmine, and Frederick together and confront them." Julia leaned against the counter. "We don't even need to tell them that we're pulling them together. We don't want to give them time to talk to each other."

"Surprise them with a group meeting?" Meredith asked.

"Exactly. Catch them off guard and tell them we know who they are. Maybe we can get more information out of them that way."

"It's a good idea." Meredith nodded.

The front door opened, and Maggie Lu entered the reception area. She glanced at the three women and said, "Is this a good time? Y'all look like you were just given some bad news."

"It's always a good time when you come." Meredith smiled. "We just discovered something about a case we're working on. Come on in and make yourself comfortable, Maggie Lu."

"Would you like some coffee?" Julia asked.

"No, thanks, honey. I can't stay long, but I wanted to talk to you about Marcella Martus."

"We saw Charlene earlier." Julia indicated one of the chairs near the front window in the reception area, and Maggie Lu took a seat. "She said you had something to tell us."

Julia and Meredith took seats near Maggie Lu, and Carmen went back to her computer, where she would probably keep looking up information on Jasmine.

"What did you want to tell us?" Julia asked.

"Well," Maggie Lu began, "I got to thinking some more about Marcella Martus, and then I remembered something from a while back. Did I tell you I first met her when she was volunteering at Rutgers Nursing Home, where Delyse lives?"

Julia shook her head. "No, you didn't."

"I only saw her there a few times, but whenever I did, she was always so kind to Delyse and the other folks." Maggie Lu chuckled. "Marcella could be a bit gruff and heavy-handed with the staff but only when she thought they weren't doing their job right."

That sounded a bit like the Marcella Martus Julia had come to know.

"But when it came to the residents in the nursing home, there was a soft spot Marcella had that made me like her a great deal. She was a champion of the underdog. She stood up for those who couldn't stand up for themselves. And when she saw injustice, she would charge like a bull."

Julia smiled. "That's been our experience with her as well."

"I know this information doesn't help your investigation," Maggie Lu continued, "but I thought a good character witness might help you. Sometimes it's hard to fight for someone like Marcella who's so hard to understand. I just wanted to encourage you to keep trying. She's spent so much of her time fighting for people who needed her help. Now she needs your help."

"Thank you," Meredith said to Maggie Lu. "You know, your opinion always carries a lot of weight with Julia and me."

"Good." Maggie Lu patted Meredith's knee.

"Are you sure you don't want some coffee?" Julia asked. "Carmen has a fresh pot brewing."

"I wish I could, but I need to run. We're raffling off a quilt for the ladies' aid society, and I'm supposed to be at the church to draw the winner's name."

They all rose and Maggie Lu moved toward the door. "We need to get together real soon and have a proper visit. Y'all take care."

"Goodbye," Julia and Meredith called out.

When Maggie Lu was out the door, Julia walked back to Carmen's desk, remembering the warehouse they had seen Marcella enter a couple of days ago. "Any luck finding the owner of the warehouse on East Broad Street?"

"Oh, sí! How could I forget?" Carmen looked through the piles of notes on her desk. "I got a call from the owner right before you called me about Jasmine Terrance."

"You located the owner?"

"Sí." She found the paper and held it up as she read. "His name is Howard Houston. He lives in Florida. He said you can go onto his property, especially if you think someone's trespassing, and if they are, to please let him know, so he can call the police."

"Excellent work," Julia said.

"Should we go now?" Meredith asked.

"Absolutely." If Regina was being held captive, they shouldn't waste another minute.

"I'll keep looking for more information on Jasmine," Carmen said.

"While you're at it," Meredith added, "please see if you can find anything more on Allegra or Frederick as well. Who knows what they might be hiding?"

"Sí, señora. You got it."

Julia and Meredith didn't wait another minute, but immediately left for the warehouse.

***

Back behind the steering wheel, Julia tried to catalog all the information they'd been given about Marcella and Jasmine in the past few hours. What was hard for Julia to understand was why Jasmine was portraying a rabid fan from Wisconsin. What was the plan?

And why was she still carrying on with her character after Regina was abducted?

"How will we get Jasmine, Allegra, and Frederick together without all of them knowing?" Meredith asked Julia as they turned onto East Broad Street. The warehouse was a few blocks ahead.

"The film crew is still working, right?" Julia asked.

"As far as I know."

"Then we need to figure out when and where Frederick will be working. We can call Jasmine to tell her we need her help and plan on meeting her wherever he's filming."

"What about Allegra?"

"I'll ask her to meet with me to discuss Marcella. She'll think we've finally come to her side. I'll tell her to meet us at the same place we meet Frederick and Jasmine."

Meredith took a deep breath and let it out on a sigh. "I hope it works. I have a feeling if we can get the three of them to come clean, we'll have a better chance of finding Regina."

"Agreed."

The warehouse was now visible—and just like last time, they approached it right as Marcella was getting out of her little red car. She held another white plastic bag in her hand.

"I'd say this is perfect timing," Meredith said to Julia.

Julia parked about a block away from the warehouse. As she and Meredith exited the car, Marcella ducked under the loose fencing and disappeared into the abandoned yard.

Meredith moved toward the warehouse, but Julia put her hand on Meredith's arm. "How will we explain to Marcella what we're doing here? She's going to be surprised to find us—and she'll know we're spying on her."

Meredith shrugged. "We'll have to tell her the truth. She hired us to uncover the whereabouts of Regina Terrance, and we're investigating every possibility. Besides"—Meredith tilted her head toward the building—"what if we find Regina inside?"

"Then I guess Marcella will be the one explaining things to us."

"Exactly. Come on." Meredith led the way as Julia glanced up and down the street, looking for anyone who might be helping Marcella or keeping watch.

Traffic rushed by on East Broad Street, and a few pedestrians walked on the opposite sidewalk. The Pirates' House, a famous restaurant and old haunt for pirates in the 1700s, was up the street, closer to the river. More than one person glanced at Julia and Meredith as they approached the warehouse, though no one was paying too much attention.

Meredith didn't even wait for Julia but lifted the loose fence board and walked into the yard. She held it for Julia to follow her.

The yard was full of junk. Everything from a rusted old car to a broken baby carriage. Tall weeds grew up between the garbage, and the fence surrounding the property was rotting and falling apart in places. To the left was the old warehouse, also in a complete state of disrepair. Only one window, high up on the building, was unbroken and uncovered. The tin siding was rusted in places with holes large enough for Julia to stick her hand through.

The only visible door leading into the warehouse was propped open with a rock.

Meredith motioned toward it, a question in her eyes.

Julia nodded. It was now or never.

They pushed the door open a little wider, but the darkness inside was almost impenetrable. Sunlight spilled in from the open door, the single window, and the random, rusted holes in the siding. Cobwebs crisscrossed the doorway, and Julia had to duck or walk right through them.

A movement in the corner drew her attention, and as her eyes adjusted, she saw a figure hunched over something in the corner.

It was Marcella.

"What are you two doing here?" she asked as she straightened to her full height. There was surprise, anger, and accusation in her voice.

More cars filled the inside of the warehouse, though they were in better shape than the one outside. There were other items as well, most of them tools. Some under tarps. But it looked as if the space hadn't been used in years—maybe even a decade.

"We were wondering the same thing about you," Meredith said. "We saw you come in here the day Regina went missing."

"You think I abducted her, don't you?" There was disbelief in Marcella's voice. "If I don't have you on my side, who do I have?"

"We're just being responsible investigators." Julia tried to assure Marcella. "We want to believe you, but we wouldn't be any good at our job if we didn't investigate every suspicious activity."

"You think what I'm doing is suspicious?"

"You're trespassing in an old warehouse," Julia pointed out. "With food. That seems a little suspicious to me."

"Feeding a new mama so she can take care of her babies is a crime now?"

"A new mama?" Julia asked, a frown on her face.

"Come look for yourself." Marcella moved to the side.

Julia's eyes had completely adjusted to the dark interior now, and she could see what was behind Marcella in the corner of the warehouse.

"I've been feeding her for about a week now," Marcella said, "trying to get her to trust me."

A beautiful, though emaciated, Dalmatian lay on an old blanket. Seven tiny puppies suckled her as she looked up at Julia with big, sad eyes.

"She wouldn't come home with me before she had her puppies," Marcella continued, "so I come to her."

Julia and Meredith just stared at the dog.

"So, you see," Marcella said in a sarcastic tone, "I'm not holding Regina Terrance hostage."

"We can see that," Julia said to Marcella. "When we saw you come in here with food, we didn't know what to think."

"How'd you know I was bringing food here?"

Julia glanced at Meredith, who looked a little sheepish. "We dug out the food container from the garbage after you left. If you were feeding it to the dog, then why was there a plastic fork in there? And why not dog food?"

Marcella rolled her eyes, clearly impatient and annoyed at them. "The fork comes with the meal." She took a water bottle out of her bag and filled a dish. She also opened up the container of food, which contained carved roast beef and gravy, and put it in a second dish. "And the roast beef and gravy are a treat. She needs to put on weight as quickly as possible."

The mama Dalmatian stood, and all the puppies dropped off of her. They wiggled and whined in a little pile on the blanket, but the mama was hungry and she went right to the food. Marcella lovingly petted her dirty fur while speaking soothing words to her.

"I'd like to see her at the humane society, so she can get adopted," Marcella said. "But these puppies are only a few days old, and I'm waiting to move them."

"Do you help other animals?" Meredith asked, bending down to pet a puppy.

The mama Dalmatian looked up from her food bowl to eye Meredith carefully.

"Whenever I can." Marcella squatted down to pick up one of the other puppies. "I've worked with animal rescue organizations for years. I hate seeing anything suffer, especially helpless animals who've been abandoned."

"How do you know this one has been abandoned?" Julia asked.

"I saw her roaming the streets without a collar. She's sweet and comfortable with me, so I know she's had human interaction."

Meredith picked up the puppy she had been petting. "They're so soft."

Julia wasn't much of a dog person, had only just recently acclimated to having a cat in the house, but she couldn't resist the urge to hold one of the puppies too. She bent down and took the littlest one into her hands. It fit almost perfectly in her palm.

The puppy's eyes were still closed, and the umbilical cord was still attached to its belly. It whimpered and nuzzled into her hand as it rooted for its mama's milk. Julia's heart warmed and she gently ran her fingers over the soft, silklike fur. "When will you move them?"

"In a couple of weeks."

"We found the owner of the warehouse," Meredith told Marcella. "We'll let him know about the abandoned dog and tell him you're coming to take care of it. If he wants you off his property, we'll come back and help you move them sooner."

Marcella nodded. "I'd appreciate that. Hopefully he won't mind me being here. I don't make it a habit to trespass on people's property, but when I see an animal in need, I don't usually stand on formality."

"I'm finding you don't worry too much about formality when anyone is in need," Meredith mused. "Much like Florence Martus."

Marcella scowled. "Don't even get me started."

Julia smiled at Marcella's fervor. "We're doing all we can to help find Regina and clear Florence's name."

"I appreciate your help." Marcella nodded. "But you're not getting anything done sitting around here. I've got this covered. Why don't you go out and find Regina's kidnapper?"

Meredith chuckled and set the puppy back on the blanket. "We're on our way."

Julia also set her puppy back down. "Let us know if you need any help with these puppies. We're happy to lend a hand."

"I will. And you let me know the minute you hear something about Regina."

"We're working on the case." Julia stood straight. "Hopefully we'll have something for you soon."

As Julia left the warehouse, she felt a little bit lighter on her feet. She was happy Marcella wasn't holding Regina hostage. She liked to think that people like Marcella were truly good, doing what they could for "the least of these."

But it didn't answer the most pressing questions: Where was Regina, and who took her?

Chapter Seventeen

September 15, 1931

Dear Lavinia,

*It does my heart good to know my story has encouraged
you. I pray it did not come as a complete shock, though your
letter assured me it did not. I know all of it happened
decades ago, but every once in a while, it feels like it was just
yesterday.*

*Your last letter was full of questions that I will gladly
answer. The first is yes, I have found happiness, despite the
heartache. In the beginning, I waved to gain Hai Ching's
attention, but eventually, the waving became so much more.
I realized I was offering the sailors something to look forward
to on their long voyage to Savannah—or something to hold
on to as they left. I received letters and telegrams from people
all over the world, telling me how much it meant to them.
Though my heart was broken and I struggled to face each
day, I had a purpose—even if it was a simple gesture like
waving. I loved seeing the men wave back or blast their horns.
I loved knowing that even if I never met any of them, we were*

connected by kindness. Theirs and mine. This has made me extremely happy.

You also asked if I ever fell in love again, and the answer is no. I have never stopped loving Hai Ching. Even if I had, I never met another man who captured my heart and soul the way he did, though there were a few who tried. Some came to the lighthouse, knowing me only as the Waving Girl, and asked if I'd marry them. I didn't take them seriously, though I think some of them were very serious. I received a few letters of proposal as well and never gave any of them a second thought. One man appealed to George, and George had a mind to send me off with him, but I refused.

When I finally accepted the fact that Hai Ching would not come back to me, I decided to dedicate my life to my brother's work as a lightkeeper. It was a noble calling, and I felt that God had called both of us. We have been companions since childhood, and we work well together. If I had married and moved away, I shudder to think of how George would have managed. We are a good pair. I'm very thankful for his friendship and care. He has provided well for me and, in turn, I have taken care of his home. Had Hai Ching ever returned and we'd found a way to move past my father's death, I would have considered leaving with him. But my father was right, and it would have been a difficult life. Perhaps Hai Ching came to accept that, and he honored my father's last wishes and left me alone. It is the only explanation my heart will accept.

You also asked me how I am doing now that we are retired and no longer on the river. You asked if I miss waving.

The simple answer is yes, I do miss it. The longer answer is that it was time to stop. Like all good things, it couldn't last forever. I looked at the waving as part of my job, and just as George had to give up his job, so too have I. We are trying to find purpose in our new home, with our new lives. We volunteer at church, we meet the needs of our friends and neighbors, and I still receive an occasional letter or visit from retired sailors who want to pay their respects. I've written to a few of them, and I've entertained them in my front parlor. I've even spoken to a few reporters and dignitaries. In truth, I feel like I've done very little to earn their accolades, but I have to remind myself that the waving meant something different to everyone.

As to your last statement, I must wholeheartedly agree. I have had a life well lived. I am thankful and grateful for every single day God has given me on earth. Yes, I'm disappointed and heartbroken that my one true love was only a part of my life for five short weeks, but I have so many blessings, I cannot begin to count them. And, as the old saying goes, it is better to have loved and lost than to never have loved at all. There were days when I was so crushed and heartbroken, I wished Hai Ching had never come. But, as the years have moved onward, I have come to cherish those few golden hours in his loving embrace and count myself fortunate to have experienced a love so pure. Unlike many people who go on to spend a lifetime together and possibly grow bitter and resentful in time, my love for Hai Ching will never tarnish.

And, had I not met Hai Ching, I might never have started to wave. Think of all the lives that were impacted over the years. Something that began in heartbreak ended in joy. How like our God to orchestrate such a miracle.

Instead of waving, my days are now spent sewing, quilting, and knitting for charity. Now the work of my hands is more tangible and brings warmth and comfort to those who suffer. I tend to my gardens, prepare meals for George, and care for our home. I volunteer where I'm needed and look for those who are less fortunate.

If truth be told, I still hold on to hope, and every time I'm in public, I scan the crowd for a glimpse of Hai Ching's tender face. If he is still alive, which I believe in my heart he is, then I pray for one final moment with him. One last opportunity to look upon his face. All I would ask is for the chance to see his smile. To know that he has had a good life, even if it meant he could not have it with me. That is my prayer.

Thank you for humoring an old woman, Lavinia. Thank you for listening and understanding, for allowing me to relive a short chapter in my life. And thank you for the assurance that you've taken care of the letters. I shudder to think of what might happen if they fell into the wrong hands.

If you have the opportunity to visit me in Savannah, I hope you come. I would love to sit with you and have a nice long visit over a glass of sweet tea. It has been too long since I've seen you. Do you remember when you visited George and me at the lighthouse before you left Georgia? I do, and it was a wonderful week. Sadly, I do not leave home much and cannot foresee a reason to travel to New York City, but if the opportunity arises, you know I will come.

I look forward to your next letter. Even though we are miles apart, your words make me feel close to you once again. Please say hello to all the family with you and know that I will convey your love to George. We are both so proud of you and all your charity work in the city. The Great Depression has reached its long fingers into our community as well, and there are many in need. You have gone where most people would not dare go in the tenements, and you have carried hope and compassion with you. Well done, Lavinia.

I send you all my love,

Florence

The youth room was louder than usual that Wednesday night as Julia opened the snack shop. Kids were already waiting to get their sugar high for the evening, their money clasped in their sweaty palms. Thankfully, the dad scheduled to volunteer was already there to help and Julia was able to hand the job over to him.

The scent of fresh popcorn and warm bodies filled the air, but no one seemed to notice or care. With the youth convention a little over a week away, the kids had an excited energy about them that was usually only present around holidays and summer breaks. Everywhere she turned, she heard them talking about the weekend: the four-hour bus ride to Atlanta, the two nights in a hotel, and the popular band scheduled to lead worship music. There was also an awesome lineup of speakers, including a reality television star that the kids were excited to meet.

As for Julia, she was looking forward to the service projects the convention organizers had planned. Dozens of groups of students would be serving in Atlanta. They would volunteer at a homeless shelter, help clean up an inner-city park, and even sort donations at a Goodwill. Not only would the students have the opportunity to give back to the city hosting them, but they would have a chance to do something good.

Julia went to the thermostat on the wall to make sure the air-conditioning was working. The room was too hot and stuffy for her comfort. Several fans were blowing and the air conditioner was on, but the sheer number of kids had raised the temperature. Julia fanned her face, deciding to be thankful for the surge in numbers that brought about the discomforting heat. She'd rather be too hot with a bunch of kids than just right with only a few.

She smiled at the kids, stopping to say hello to several. She made sure to ask how they were doing and chat about the convention. Not all the kids would be going on the trip, but there were other events coming up in the next couple of months, and she was always recruiting.

Ebony, Sally, and Elena stood in one corner of the room in a tight knot. Julia thought back and realized that the three girls never welcomed anyone else into their small group. It was rare to see them talking to the other kids, though most of the students moved freely from one person to another.

Olivia walked into the youth room with two new girls. She was animated and laughing, and her friends were smiling. Julia's heart warmed to see their happiness.

Immediately, Olivia began to introduce the new girls to some of the other kids. She was a completely different person than two weeks ago. She didn't even glance in Ebony's direction, though Ebony, Sally, and Elena had their eyes on Olivia.

Eventually, Olivia made her way to Julia, her smile still wide and inviting.

"Hello, Miss Julia."

"Hi, Olivia."

"This is Courtney Fjeld and Aubrihannah Henry."

Julia gave the girls a warm smile. "Welcome to New Beginnings Youth Group. I hope you'll make yourselves at home. If you have any questions, I'm sure Olivia will be happy to answer them. If she isn't, you can ask me or Pastor Jay." She nodded at Aubrihannah. "I recognize your name. We have you signed up for the youth convention."

"Thank you for letting me come." Aubrihannah was tall, with rich brown eyes and skin. Her long black hair was a mass of tight spiral curls. "I've never been to a youth convention—or even youth group." She smiled nervously as she looked around the room. "I really don't know what to do here."

"Just be yourself," Julia assured her. "That's the beautiful thing about church. Each one of us comes with unique strengths and weaknesses, and through the grace of God, we all work well together. You don't need to be anyone you're not." She leaned forward. "A lot of people are afraid they have to be perfect to come to church—but the reverse is true. Jesus came to save the sinners, just like me and you."

"Olivia already said that." Aubrihannah smiled at her friend. "She said coming to church is like going to school for the first time. There are kids in older grades who know more, but there are also new kids too, who are just starting. I shouldn't expect to know everything the first day."

Julia put her arm around Olivia. "That's a great analogy." She looked at Courtney. "We still have room if you'd like to join us for the youth convention."

Courtney wore stylish clothes and stood with quiet confidence. She studied everything and everyone from behind dark-rimmed glasses. "Thanks, but I'm just here to check things out."

"I told her she'll love it here," Olivia said with a smile. "Maybe she'll come to the next event."

"I hope all of you will enjoy yourselves." Julia didn't want to overstay her welcome with the girls and make them feel uncomfortable.

She left them to mingle with the other students and found her way to Ebony, Sally, and Elena.

"Hi, girls."

"Hi," they each echoed, their gazes still locked on Olivia and her new friends.

"Have you had a chance to meet Aubrihannah and Courtney?" Julia asked them.

"We don't have to meet them," Ebony said a bit sarcastically. "Everyone knows who they are."

Julia glanced back at the new girls. "Really? Why? Who are they?"

"Courtney is into the plays at school and Aubrihannah is a really good basketball player," Sally said. She glanced at Ebony out of the corner of her eye and then said to Julia, "They're really nice and friendly with everyone."

"Courtney dated Tyler Toby before Olivia," Elena said. "But she broke up with him, so he made a music video using her old texts and put it on TikTok."

"Really?" Julia couldn't imagine dating in the modern age of social media. It seemed so destructive. "How awful."

Sally crossed her arms. "I heard that Olivia and Courtney became friends because of the rumors Tyler spread about Courtney after they broke up."

Had Sally accepted that the gossip spread about Olivia was, in fact, a bunch of lies?

"They bonded over what a jerk Tyler is," Ebony said dryly. "How nice."

"If we had believed her," Sally said quietly, but with conviction, "maybe she wouldn't have needed to turn to Courtney." She continued to watch the new girls. "I wonder if Olivia will introduce us to them."

"I have a feeling she would," Julia offered. "She's introducing them to everyone tonight. No time like the present to find out."

Sally looked at Ebony with uncertainty. Was she trying to weigh the consequences of making Ebony angry? It was sad that Ebony had so much power over her friends.

"Go ahead," Ebony said. "But I'm not coming. I'm not in the plays or in basketball, so those girls have never even talked to me. Why would I make them feel welcome at my church?"

Julia's heart broke at Ebony's words. "This church doesn't belong to us, Ebony. It's the House of God. We're all guests here—just like Courtney and Aubrihannah."

Sally glanced at Elena, hope in her eyes. "Want to meet them?"

Elena nodded. "Sure."

"Excuse us, Miss Julia," Sally said.

"Of course. Go ahead."

Elena and Sally started to walk away.

Ebony's mouth fell open, as if she was surprised that her friends would actually walk away from her. "Wait for me," she said as she trailed after them.

Holding her breath, Julia watched as the three girls joined Olivia and her new friends. She hoped and prayed that Olivia would take the high road and not snub her old friends.

When Olivia caught sight of Ebony, Sally, and Elena, she didn't smile, but she did nod at them and welcome them into her circle. She also introduced them to Courtney and Aubrihannah, who had pleasant smiles on their faces.

Julia breathed a sigh of relief and thanked God that things appeared to be on the mend. She hated to see any strife within the youth group—especially among kids that had been friends for so long.

Now, if only she could find Regina and discover why Jasmine had been lying about her identity, then she would be able to go on the trip to Atlanta without anything hanging over her head.

Chapter Eighteen

IT TOOK A LITTLE BIT of work on Carmen's part, but she was able to find out where Frederick Hayes would be working on Thursday afternoon. He and his production crew would be on Cockspur Island, filming Fort Pulaski and the lighthouse Florence Martus's father had manned nearby.

The day was gray and dreary as Julia and Meredith drove out to the fort in Meredith's car with Jasmine Terrance in the back seat. Cockspur Island, like so many other islands on the Georgia coast, was flat and swampy, with few trees to mark the landscape. The drive felt a little barren and forlorn, with roads that were bumpy and wavy from settling into the spongy earth.

Jasmine, playing the part of Gertie, had not stopped talking since they'd left the outskirts of Savannah. Julia wondered if Jasmine had done more research on Wisconsin, because she had a plethora of new state facts she was sharing. Julia now knew the state bird, state flower, state tree, and even the state song, which Jasmine sang for them.

Meredith had suggested picking up Jasmine at the hotel and taking her out to the fort with them since she had no rental car and had been relying on public transportation. Meredith called Jasmine and told her they were going to the fort to do some investigative work. Jasmine had been very willing and eager to come along to help. She hadn't even asked many questions.

Getting Allegra to the fort had been a lot harder. Julia had called her earlier that morning and asked if they could meet. Allegra had been impatient and rude, claiming she was too busy managing the press to deal with Magnolia Investigations as well. When Julia told her that she had information that would benefit her, she was a little less impatient but said she wanted to meet at the hotel. Julia told her that what she needed to say could only be said at Fort Pulaski, and Allegra had finally agreed to come.

Julia just hoped that Allegra would show.

"I read all about Fort Pulaski after you invited me," Jasmine said from the back seat.

Julia glanced back and saw that Jasmine was on her phone. "I'll read it to you," she said. "'A system of coastal forts was established in America after the War of 1812, and Fort Pulaski was built to protect the Port of Savannah. It was named in honor of Kazimierz Pulaski'—I hope I said that right—'who was a soldier and military commander. He fought under the command of George Washington during the American Revolution.'"

"That's very interesting," Meredith said to Jasmine.

"There's more." Jasmine repositioned herself in the back seat, as if just getting started. "'The fort was built on pilings sunk seventy feet into the mud to support over twenty-five million bricks. It took over eighteen years of construction and nearly a million dollars.' That was a *lot* of money back then."

"It's still a lot of money," Julia mused.

"'The walls of the fort are eleven feet thick and were thought to be impenetrable by all but the largest land artillery. But it was put to the test after Georgia seceded from the Union and Confederate troops took over the fort. In April of 1862, the Union asked the fort to surrender, but the commander of the garrison rejected the offer. There was a new rifled canon and Parrott rifles that could fire more accurately than before, so within thirty hours, the wall of Fort Pulaski was breached by the Union, forcing the Confederate commander to surrender.'"

"The walls of the fort were rebuilt by Union soldiers," Meredith added, "and eventually the fort was used to house prisoners of war. It was also the last stop on the Underground Railroad, because the moment the enslaved people reached the island, they were freed."

"You can actually still see a lot of the damage from the artillery fire on one of the external walls," Julia said to Jasmine. "It's pretty powerful to see."

"I'm so happy you invited me to come with you." Jasmine folded her hands on her lap as if she had all the time in the world. "I was starting to get bored in my hotel room."

"Any more news about Regina?" Meredith asked.

"Nope. Nothing. And the police won't tell me a thing. They did question me again, but they seem satisfied that I'm not the one who took Ms. Terrance."

Julia glanced over her shoulder. "Won't you be missed back home? Doesn't the grocery store need you?"

Jasmine shrugged. "I took a leave of absence. No one will be missing me there."

"What about your boyfriend?" Meredith asked.

"I'm not too worried about him, either."

They came to the entrance of the Fort Pulaski Historical Monument and paid to be admitted onto the property. There was a long drive to the fort, but when they finally arrived, it was worth the effort. A fairly new visitor center greeted them, with lots of exhibits. Just beyond that, surrounded by a moat and mounded earthen works, was the redbrick fort.

"That's pretty cool," Jasmine said. "Didn't they have a birthday party celebration for Florence Martus here?"

"They did." Julia nodded. "Over three thousand people came out here to celebrate."

"Wow. I can't imagine having a birthday party with three thousand people." Jasmine got out of the car and opened her umbrella. The gray skies had begun to drizzle, which would make it a less enjoyable outing. "Where do we begin?" she asked.

Julia also opened an umbrella and grabbed her purse. She and Meredith led Jasmine toward the fort. "We're going to go right in. We're here to look for someone."

Again, Jasmine didn't seem to mind the evasive way Julia and Meredith were proceeding.

From what Carmen had gathered, Frederick would be filming inside the historic building and then going out to the lighthouse later in the day. Hopefully the dreary weather hadn't ruined his plans, or the trip out to Cockspur Island would be for naught.

"So," Jasmine said as she trudged along, "who are we looking for exactly?"

"We heard that there's someone here who knows quite a bit about Florence, so we thought we'd look for him." It wasn't a lie. One of the docents had written an article about Florence earlier that week in response to the new book. Carmen had found it to be the most factual article written about Florence and had encouraged Julia and Meredith to read it. Hopefully, though, if they were able to get enough information from Frederick, Allegra, and Jasmine, they wouldn't need to worry about locating the knowledgeable docent.

As they passed through the wide front gates, Julia immediately located Frederick and his crew in a corner, under a protective awning. There were a few other visitors, but most were moving in and out of the various rooms, and no one was standing in the open parade grounds.

Julia didn't want to join Frederick until Allegra was with them, so when she spotted a docent standing near an information kiosk, she approached him to pass the time. "Excuse me," she said, "do you know anyone by the name of Samuel Rothberg?"

"Sam? Sure." The man nodded. "He's one of the docents here."

"Is he working today?" Meredith asked. "He wrote an article we're interested in discussing."

"I don't think Sam's working today, sorry. He only works a few times a month." The man smiled, revealing a wide space between his front teeth. He was an older man with a shock of white hair. "Perhaps I could help you."

"We're looking for information about Florence Martus," Julia said.

"The Waving Girl?" The man's smile dimmed. "A shame what's happening to her good name. Sorry, though, I don't know much about her. I could get Sam's email address for you, and you could send him a message."

"Thank you," Julia said, "but I don't think that'll be necessary."

Allegra had just entered the fort gates. She looked around, and her gaze first landed on Frederick and his film crew and then on Julia, Meredith, and Jasmine.

Allegra did not look happy.

"Excuse us," Julia said to the docent.

"Any time, ma'am." He nodded at them and resumed his position near the information table.

"What's this about?" Allegra asked when Julia, Meredith, and Jasmine approached her. "What's *she* doing here?" She tilted her head with disdain toward Jasmine. "Is she stalking you too?"

Jasmine pushed her glasses up her nose and scowled at Allegra. "I was never stalking Ms. Terrance. I was keeping an eye on her."

"Little good that did." Allegra scoffed and crossed her arms. She looked from Julia to Meredith. "Seriously. What's this about?"

"We'd like to speak to you about Regina," Meredith said.

"Couldn't this have been done at the hotel?" Allegra's lips were pursed, even as she spoke. "Why drag me all the way out here in this terrible weather?"

"We wanted to speak to all of you. At the same time." Julia motioned toward Frederick.

Allegra frowned but didn't say anything.

Julia led the way toward Frederick, but he didn't wait for them to approach. He left the awning and met up with the women in one of the many arched alcoves in the side of the fort. He was wearing a pair of loose khaki pants, a white button-down shirt, and a khaki vest. On his head was a wide-brimmed leather hat, which was wet from the rain.

"What are all of you doing here?" he asked.

"I'd like to know the same thing." Allegra stared down her nose at Julia and Meredith. "You two have been nothing but trouble since we arrived."

"I'm sorry you feel that way," Meredith said. "We've only been trying to do our job."

"Which is what, exactly?" Allegra asked. "Interfere in matters that don't concern you?"

"Anything that has to do with Savannah history concerns us." Julia had no desire to play any more games. "We've brought the three of you here to tell you we know who you are."

Allegra, Jasmine, and Frederick looked at one another.

"Excuse me?" Allegra asked.

Julia looked at Jasmine first. "We know your name is not Gertie Hanson but Jasmine Terrance."

"We also know you're not a grocery store clerk, but an actress from New York City." Meredith spoke with a clear, confident voice. "We also know you and Regina are first cousins."

Jasmine's mouth fell open, and she blinked several times.

Julia turned to Frederick. "We're also aware that you and Regina didn't just meet here in Savannah, as you'd like us to believe but have been in a romantic relationship for quite a while."

"There, you're wrong," Frederick said, lifting his chin. "Regina and I no longer have anything to say to one another. She's cheated on me for the last time."

"But you didn't just meet here in Savannah." Meredith didn't back down. "As for you, Allegra—"

"I am exactly who I say I am," Allegra said with a smirk. "There's no dirty gossip to dredge up about me."

"No." Julia shook her head. "Perhaps not, but I have a feeling you're hiding something too."

Allegra looked as if she was going to speak, but then she snapped her mouth shut.

"I don't know why all the secrets or false identities," Julia said to the group, looking at each one in turn. "But I do know that something isn't right here. Allegra, you continued the ruse about Jasmine's fake identity, even now, when you first saw her in the fort. Why?"

"And the same goes for you, Jasmine," Meredith said. "Even after Regina went missing, you continued on with your charade, trying to convince us you're Gertie Hanson. It doesn't make any sense."

"I have a feeling the three of you—or four, including Regina for that matter—had a plan when you came to Savannah." Julia watched them carefully to see if they would offer any hints. "But something went wrong, and now you're all trying to grapple with the new situation."

Jasmine took off her glasses and shoved them in her pocket. "Now that you know who I am, I can get rid of these infernal glasses." She made a face at Allegra. "Which were too big for me to begin with."

Allegra rolled her eyes. "Whatever you think you know, you should know this: none of us have any idea where Regina is."

"I think it's safe to say we all want Regina back," Meredith said. "And Julia and I are willing to help."

Allegra sneered. "Go talk to Marcella Martus. She'll have—"

"No," Julia said. "Marcella isn't responsible for Regina's disappearance. If we keep looking in the wrong places, we'll never find her."

"Julia's right." Jasmine took her ponytail out and let her hair drop around her shoulders. "I'm tired of this role. I'm tired of all of it. The sooner—"

"Jasmine," Allegra said, "we don't owe these people any explanation. If you know what's good for you, you'll keep your mouth shut."

Jasmine's nostrils flared as she pressed her lips together.

"Same goes for you, Frederick." Allegra's arms fell to her sides, and she took a step closer to Julia and Meredith. "As for the two of you, we wouldn't be in this situation if it wasn't for you and Marcella Martus."

What situation were they in, and why was it Julia and Meredith's fault?

"Stay out of our way," Allegra said, "or you might just be sorry."

Julia couldn't believe her ears. "Are you threatening us?"

"I'll do whatever it takes to promote Regina and her books." Allegra took Jasmine by the arm and pulled her away from Julia and Meredith. "Don't get in my way again."

Jasmine tore her arm out of Allegra's grasp but followed her. The two of them stalked out of the fort.

Frederick stared after them and then shook his head in disgust. "I should have never agreed to any of this."

"What?" Julia asked him. "What did you agree to?"

"Never mind," he said, waving his hand in dismissal. "It was all Allegra's and Regina's idea. I just went along for the job. Now that it's all been compromised, this documentary will be a bust. There won't be a story to tell here after all."

"What was their idea?" Meredith asked. "Can you please tell us what's going on?"

Frederick continued to shake his head. "I'm washing my hands of all of it and going back to New York." He walked back to his film crew. Soon, everyone was packing up their things to leave.

"Well," Julia said to Meredith, "we didn't quite get the answers we were hoping for."

"No," Meredith agreed, "but I think we've weakened their defenses. One more push, and I think we'll penetrate their well-laid plans."

Julia grinned. "I don't think their plan was as strong as they had hoped—just like this fort."

"Apparently not."

***

Early the next morning, Julia's phone rang. Beau was in the kitchen, whistling a tune while he made egg white and vegetable omelets for their breakfast. Julia stood in front of her full-length mirror, looking over her appearance one more time before she left their bedroom. She had chosen to wear a pair of black trousers and a white blouse, tucked in at her waist. The cool fabric would be needed, since the day was already hot and humid.

Julia grabbed her ringing cell phone off her nightstand and saw Meredith's name and picture on the screen.

"Hello, Mere," Julia said.

"Julia, you'll never guess what's happening." Meredith's voice was high and excited. "I think the walls of Fort Allegra have come tumbling down."

Julia frowned. "What are you talking about?"

"Carmen just called me and said there's a press conference scheduled for ten o'clock at the Bohemian Hotel. Regina Terrance has miraculously reappeared."

"Regina's back?" Julia was happy she was standing near her bed, because she had to take a seat.

"Yes, and she's apologizing like mad to the press, claiming she wasn't abducted but had to leave town on urgent business. She says she didn't know everyone was looking for her."

"What?" Julia slipped her shoes on and stood again. It was already past nine. "That seems a bit far-fetched to me."

"Same here. Do you want to meet at the hotel?"

"Sure. I'll see you there." Julia ended the call and grabbed a sheer scarf to pair with the outfit. "Beau," she called as she left their room, "I might have to take the omelet to go."

"Really?" Disappointment lined Beau's voice. "What's going on?"

"Meredith just called. It appears that Regina has magically reappeared, and she's holding a press conference at the Bohemian Hotel in less than an hour."

"Interesting." Beau slipped an omelet on a plate. "It's all ready. Do you think you could take a couple of minutes and eat with me?"

Julia hated leaving Beau so suddenly, especially after he made her breakfast. "I guess I have a few minutes."

He smiled and set her plate on the kitchen table. Toast and orange juice were already there.

"This looks good enough to eat." Julia took a seat and inhaled the delicious aromas coming from her plate. "Thank you."

After Beau said grace, they dug into their meal. It tasted as good as it looked and smelled.

"Where do you think Regina has been this whole time?" Beau asked.

"I don't know." Julia took a sip of her orange juice. "But I hope we'll find out."

"Do you think Marcella will back down now that Regina's back?"

Julia groaned. "I hope Marcella doesn't come to the press conference this morning. She's done nothing but make trouble every time she's shown up."

"Maybe she's learned her lesson," Beau offered. "After being accused of kidnapping."

"We can only hope." Marcella had been scared, but now that the threat had passed, Julia was certain Marcella would continue her crusade to clear Florence's name.

Julia tried not to rush the meal, knowing Beau had put a lot of time and effort into it, but she didn't want to get to the hotel after the press conference started. "I'm sorry—"

"Go ahead," he said with a smile. "I know you don't want to be late."

"Thank you." Julia stood and placed a kiss on his forehead. "I love you."

"Love you too. Have a good day."

Julia grabbed her purse and keys and ran out to her car. It was about a twenty-minute drive to the hotel, if traffic cooperated. Hopefully, Meredith would get there first and save her a spot.

Twenty minutes later, Julia pulled into the parking lot. The hotel was swarming with news crews, just like it had been the day Regina went missing. Julia drove around the parking lot for a couple of minutes to find a spot to park, and then she rushed across the pavement and into the hotel.

The meeting room was packed, with standing room only. Thankfully, Meredith had a seat near the front, and when Julia appeared, relief was written all over Meredith's face.

"You have no idea how hard it was to save this spot. One of the reporters looked like he was going to take it by force about two minutes ago. I don't think I could have fended him off."

"Thanks for saving it for me. Beau had just finished making breakfast, and I didn't want to disappoint him by leaving before we could eat."

"It's okay." Meredith smiled. "I would have done the same for Ron."

Julia squeezed Meredith's hand and smiled.

Allegra and Regina entered the room, and the noise level increased. Regina looked radiant in a blue dress suit, her hair twisted up in a stylish knot. Allegra didn't look quite so rested. For the first time since Julia had met her, Allegra looked frazzled and sleep deprived. Her hair, which was usually just as immaculate as Regina's, was frizzy and disheveled. Her clothes were wrinkled, and she had bags under her eyes.

"I wonder where Frederick and Jasmine are," Julia mused as she looked around the room. Neither one was present.

"They probably went back to New York." Meredith spoke quietly, for Julia's ears alone. "We've probably seen the last of them."

"Can I have your attention, please?" Allegra called to the people who had gathered. "Quiet, please. Ms. Terrance has several interviews to give today, so we don't have a lot of time." She made eye contact with Julia, but otherwise ignored her and Meredith. "Ms. Terrance has a prepared statement to make, but she will not answer any questions. Thank you." Allegra nodded at Regina.

Regina was poised as she stood before the group. Then she dropped her gaze for a moment. "First," she said, "I'd like to apologize for all the confusion and misunderstanding of these past five days. I have already spoken with the Savannah Police Department and explained my absence. They have accepted my apology, and I hope everyone else will as well." She pressed her hands together and let out a long breath. "Last Sunday evening, someone visited me in my hotel room—a personal friend—and was very distraught. She asked me to help her with a private matter of the utmost importance. With the urgency of the situation, I left my personal belongings behind. I know it sounds silly and drastic, but we left through my window so we wouldn't attract any attention from the staff. My friend is well known and didn't want anyone spreading rumors about her. As a consequence, I didn't have my phone to get word to my publicist, and I hoped that she would understand." She gave a tremulous smile. "I hope and trust that you will not ask me more about this matter, since my friend has asked for complete privacy. If I told you where I was and what I was doing, it would deeply hurt and impact her life."

"Ms. Terrance!" one of the reporters called out. "Why didn't you get word to someone—anyone?"

"I will not be answering questions," Regina said. "I have fully cooperated with the police department and all investigations have ceased. As an adult, I am not obligated to give my whereabouts to anyone. Suffice it to say, I was safe, and I have returned to complete my work here in Savannah."

"About that work," another reporter called out. "I've heard Frederick Hayes has left town with his film crew. Are you done with your documentary?"

Regina glanced at Allegra, who shrugged her confusion.

"Thank you all for coming," Regina said. "That is all I have to say."

Allegra and Regina left the room, their heads bent close to each other in conversation.

The reporters quickly followed them out, leaving just a handful of people in the conference room.

"I don't buy it," Meredith said, shaking her head. "Who leaves through the window for five days without worrying about getting word to her friends and family? Regina Terrance doesn't come across as that irresponsible—even if she was trying to protect a friend."

"I agree." Julia glanced around the room. "I'm happy to see Marcella didn't make an appearance."

"You and me both." Meredith's phone buzzed, and she pulled open her purse. "We're still not any closer to finding out the truth behind Regina's book—" Her voice faltered as she looked at the text on her phone's screen. "It's from Jasmine."

Julia crowded closer to Meredith to read the text.

"She says she has something she wants to show us," Meredith said. "She wants to meet us at the statue of the Waving Girl on River Street tonight after dark."

Julia frowned. "I would have thought she'd left town by now."

"Apparently not." Meredith nibbled her bottom lip. "She says to come alone."

"After dark?"

"It's a generally well-lit area," Meredith said. "Close to shops and restaurants. It should be fairly safe."

"Should be," Julia said, "but I don't feel comfortable going alone."

"We can always ask Beau to drive us and stand by if there's any trouble."

It was a good idea. Knowing Beau would be there gave Julia a bit more confidence. "I'd like to know what she has to show us."

"Same here."

"I doubt she'd tell us if we texted and asked."

"I'll see." Meredith typed in her question.

Jasmine's response was almost immediate.

Meredith sighed. "She says the only way she'll tell us is if we meet her there. What do you think?"

"She seems fairly harmless." Julia pondered the risk. "And if Beau is nearby…"

"I'll tell her we'll see her there at nine."

A nervous chill ran up Julia's spine, but she nodded.

Hopefully, whatever Jasmine had to show them would make it worth the risk.

Chapter Nineteen

Darkness had settled over Savannah for nearly a half an hour when Beau drove Julia and Meredith on East Bay Street. The evening traffic had picked up, and the parking spaces were limited. River Street ran parallel with East Bay Street, but River Street was on a lower level, even with the river. The buildings between the two streets were two stories with the top floor facing East Bay Street and the bottom floors facing River Street. Both the upper and lower floors housed all sorts of restaurants, tourist shops, and boutiques. It was a popular destination for both tourists and locals, and there were several restaurants Julia and Beau enjoyed eating at together. The famous Praline Pecans, for which Savannah was well known, could be found here in several candy shops.

Tonight, however, food was far from Julia's thoughts as Beau finally found a place to park in front of the upper-floor businesses. The area was well lit and there were several people coming and going, but Julia couldn't shake the unease she felt about this rendezvous.

"Are you sure we should be doing this?" she asked Meredith. "What if something goes wrong?"

"What could go wrong?" Meredith countered. "Jasmine Terrance is harmless."

"This feels like a setup, though, doesn't it?" Julia rubbed her arms as she looked around at the shops and restaurants. She wasn't usually so anxious about situations like this, but something didn't sit right with her.

"I'll be waiting nearby at the Waving Girl landing," Beau said to reassure Julia for the dozenth time that evening. He swiped his debit card in the parking meter and then typed in their stall number. "Jasmine has never met me and won't know who I am, plus it's dark. She'll think I'm a tourist watching the traffic on the river. I'll keep an eye on you, and if something looks off, I'll intervene."

Julia put her hand on Beau's arm. "I feel safer knowing you're watching."

"You have nothing to worry about, Julie-Bean." He leaned over and kissed her cheek. "Just keep your wits about you, and hopefully this Jasmine gal has something valuable for you."

"That's what I keep telling myself," Meredith said. "If Jasmine has something important, I want to see it."

They were quiet for a moment as Beau finished the parking meter transaction.

"There," he said as he took a receipt from the machine. "I think we're all set. Ready to go?"

Julia took a deep breath and nodded.

"I see you came ready for action." Meredith chuckled as she pointed at Julia's feet.

Julia had opted to wear a pair of tennis shoes. She'd also worn comfortable jeans and a loose top. "One can never be too prepared to run away."

Meredith grinned and linked arms with Julia. "Have I ever told you that you're one of my favorite people?"

Julia squeezed Meredith's arm. "No, but I knew it anyway."

Beau laughed and shook his head. "You two are quite a pair."

A set of steep stairs descended from the parking lot and went under a bridge that connected to a shop overhead. It was dark and echoey, and Julia had to force herself not to shiver. The trio entered a sort of alleyway, which was made of cobblestones, and continued down the decline toward River Street.

Along the riverfront, music blared from Joe's Crab Shack and people were moving in and out of restaurants and waiting in lines to be seated at several of them.

"Here's where I'll go my separate way," Beau said to Julia and Meredith. "But I'll be just over there." He pointed to a cement landing where other people were sitting or standing and looking out at the river. A thousand lights sparkled and shifted across the river as waves rippled and swayed the boats still plying the water. The river was wide enough for ocean-going cargo ships to pass by, but there were other, smaller, private crafts on the water as well. Across the way, the impressive Westin Hotel rose up about twenty stories high. Ferries brought people back and forth from River Street to the resort complex at all hours of the day.

"I'll keep her safe," Meredith said to Beau with a wink. "I think we'll be just fine."

"I wish I shared your confidence right now." Julia smiled at Beau and then forced herself to straighten her shoulders. Why was she being such a coward about all this?

The Waving Girl statue wasn't far away, at the end of River Street, in a more secluded parklike setting. There were a few landscape lights to highlight the statue but no overhead lights to add extra security. Nearby, there were several overgrown bushes and trees, offering privacy for those who desired it.

As Julia and Meredith walked along River Street toward the statue, other people moved in the same direction and a few of them sat near the statue. Most were simply watching the passing water and enjoying the warm, gentle breeze off the Savannah River.

A lone figure stood on the outer edge of the platform where the Waving Girl stood. The woman was about the size of Jasmine, and she looked a little more agitated than the random tourist. When they were close enough, Julia was able to make out Jasmine's form a little better.

"There she is," Meredith said.

"I see her." Julia looked around to see if Jasmine was alone, though it was hard to tell with all the other people. She did look like she was there by herself.

"You came," Jasmine said when they were finally close enough to hear her. She no longer looked like the overeager fan she had portrayed the last couple of weeks. Her long brown hair was blowing in the wind, and she had on a pair of leggings, tall boots, and a few layered tops. At her side was a tote bag, which is what captured Julia's full attention. "Are you alone?"

"We are," Meredith said.

"Good." Jasmine let out a breath and then looked left and right, scanning the area.

"Are *you* alone?" Julia asked.

"Gee, I sure hope so." Jasmine reached for her bag. "I can't even tell you how angry they're going to be when they find out what I'm doing."

Meredith took a step closer to Jasmine. "What *are* you doing here?"

"Come on." Jasmine tilted her head toward the bushes nearby. It was completely dark there.

Julia shook her head. "You asked us to meet you here. We want to see what you have."

"I told you to meet me here, but I'm not about to show this to you right here in plain sight of everyone."

"Why not?" Meredith asked. "Is it illegal?"

"No," Jasmine said quickly. "It's nothing like that. I just can't take the chance that Regina or Allegra are looking for me."

Julia wanted to keep Jasmine talking. She didn't want to move to where Beau couldn't see them. "Why would they be looking for you?"

Leaning forward, Jasmine whispered, "I took the letters."

Julia couldn't believe it. "You have *the* letters? Florence's letters? The ones Regina used for the story?"

"Yes." Jasmine clutched the bag under her arm. "And they don't tell the same story Regina claims. I've read them myself."

"I thought they were in New York." Meredith took another step closer to Jasmine. "Did she have them with her in Savannah this whole time?"

"She went to New York while she was 'missing' and got them. She was getting worried that someone might go looking for them. She was going to take them somewhere else when Allegra contacted her and told her to get back to Savannah as soon as possible. She brought them with her for safekeeping." Jasmine laughed sardonically. "But they weren't safe, were they?"

"Why did Regina leave?" Julia asked, hoping Jasmine would open up about everything.

Jasmine looked toward River Street, clearly agitated. "Can we move to a quieter spot? I don't want anyone overhearing us."

"Are you ready to tell us what's been happening?" Meredith asked.

Nodding, Jasmine started moving toward the bushes. "Yes—but we can't stay here. Regina and Allegra will be looking for me, and if they find me, they'll take the letters, and none of us will ever see them again."

Julia glanced over her shoulder to see if Beau was watching, but it was hard to pick him out among all the dark figures on the landing. She hoped and prayed he had his eyes on them and would see where they were going.

Meredith was the first to follow Jasmine. She glanced back at Julia and gave her an encouraging nod. Julia wanted to know the whole story, and she wanted to see those letters, so she followed.

It wasn't more than twenty yards to the overgrown shrubs, but it was completely dark now, and Julia's eyes took a moment to adjust. Jasmine stopped behind the bush and waited for Meredith and Julia to join her.

"What can you tell us?" Meredith asked.

Jasmine still clutched her tote bag as she searched the area. Finally, seeing they were alone, she leaned toward Meredith and Julia.

"Regina approached me last year, before Christmas, and told me that she and her publicist had come up with a unique plan to promote her next book, *The Waving Girl*. They needed to hire me to play the part of a superfan, and since I was out of work, I agreed."

Julia crossed her arms as she listened intently. "What was the point of having you play a fan?"

"It was all part of the publicity stunt." Jasmine's voice was getting a little more agitated as she spoke. "We would come to Savannah, under the guise of creating a documentary—"

"So the documentary isn't real?" Meredith asked.

Jasmine nodded. "It's real—or, at least, it was until Freddy left yesterday. From the start, Freddy and Regina were having problems. Apparently, my cousin likes flirting—and Freddy doesn't like it. He thought he'd have more time with Regina, away from New York, but she started to avoid him as she put in appearances all over Savannah. They had a big fight, and he threatened to blow the whole thing. He said he was tired of chasing her all over town, only to find her with one man after the other."

"What was your part of the plan?" Julia asked Jasmine.

"I was hired to play a stalker—that's why the police were called in on the whole charade. Make it look like Regina was being threatened. Then, when she disappeared, I was supposed to disappear too—and Allegra and Freddy were going to stay in Savannah to deal with the publicity." Jasmine shook her head. "It was supposed to cause a sensation, which was supposed to bring attention to Regina's book."

"That seems a little complicated to me," Meredith said.

"Allegra and Regina were desperate. Regina's last two books haven't sold well, and they both knew their jobs were on the line if *The Waving Girl* was a flop."

A branch snapped nearby, and all three women jumped.

No one was there.

Jasmine took a few steadying breaths.

"What happened?" Julia asked. "Why didn't you leave when Regina left?"

"That's why Allegra and Regina are mad at you and Marcella Martus. You ruined all their plans. When Marcella came forward with the threat of a diary, Allegra and Regina needed to put their plan into action fast. They thought it would look more credible to lay the blame on Marcella's shoulders, especially after she made those threats in public." Jasmine wore a self-satisfied smile. "But the two of you wouldn't let up on them, and when you uncovered all our identities, you ruined their plans, again, so Regina came back."

"Where did Frederick go?" Meredith asked.

Jasmine shrugged. "Who knows? Maybe he's back in New York telling everyone the truth. All I know is Allegra and Regina are worried, and they're trying to hatch a new plan, even as we speak."

Julia thought for a moment. "Do you think they'll stay in Savannah?"

"I have no idea," Jasmine said. "But I do know they've tossed me aside and refuse to pay me what they promised." Her voice rose higher. "I put my reputation and name on the line for them—taking the chance that the police would come after me if they thought I abducted Regina. And what do I get in return? Nothing. Regina said I failed and that it's my fault the two of you figured out my identity."

Regina was right. Julia and Meredith had been able to piece everything together because of a few slips on Jasmine's part.

"So they won't pay you?" Julia asked.

"No, and I need money for rent this month." Jasmine placed her hand on her chest in a dramatic fashion. "It isn't easy pursuing a career on the stage. I poured my heart and soul into this role. I could have been back in the city auditioning and looking for a new part. But now I have nothing to show for all this work."

Julia wanted to tell her she was sorry for her, but how could she when Jasmine had agreed to be a part of this debacle?

"That's why I'm bringing the letters to you." Jasmine held the tote bag in front of her. "If I can't have the money owed to me, then at least I'll have the satisfaction in knowing that I helped to ruin Regina's floundering career. Once these letters go public, everyone will know that her story was fiction even though she tried to pass it off as the truth to sell more books."

"We're not in the business of ruining anyone's career," Meredith said. "I don't think it's right to take pleasure in something like that. It would be better to focus on justice being served and bringing the truth to light."

"Whatever," Jasmine said. "You can enjoy that while I enjoy seeing Regina's fall."

Meredith glanced at Julia, who shrugged.

"I need to hand these over to you before Allegra and Regina find out I took them." Jasmine extended the bag to Julia.

"It's too late, Jasmine." Allegra appeared from around the bush, her voice cool and calm. "If you didn't want to be found, you shouldn't have brought your cell phone with you. All Regina had to do was look at your Snapchat account, and she could see your location."

Julia almost had the bag in her grasp, but Jasmine pulled it back again, clutching it to her chest.

"I won't let you and Regina get away with this," Jasmine said. "Someone needs to stop you."

Allegra laughed. "You honestly think you have the power to stop us?"

Jasmine lifted her shoulders. "I'm the one holding the letters."

"Not for long." Allegra reached into her purse and pulled out a dark, shiny object and pointed it at Jasmine. "I told you I would do anything to sell Regina's books. I wasn't joking."

Chapter Twenty

THE SOUNDS OF THE RIVERFRONT faded as Julia stared at the pistol in Allegra Timmons's hand. All of her concerns and uneasiness about this evening came rushing back to her, fueled by the terror of seeing the gun. She should have listened to her intuition. They should have stayed by the statue where Beau could see them. They should have made Jasmine come to them.

But none of it mattered now. All Julia could do was face their current predicament and keep her wits about her, like Beau had said. But where was Beau? Had he noticed when they left? Had he watched them go behind this shrubbery? Would he come and help, and if he did, would he be in danger? If he startled Allegra, there was no telling what she might do.

Julia began to pray.

"Allegra," Meredith said calmly, though Julia imagined she was anything but calm. "There's no need to do anything drastic."

"Stop talking." Allegra turned the gun on Meredith.

Julia inhaled sharply, and Meredith jumped.

"I only came for the letters. I don't want to use this gun, but I will if I need to." She took a step toward Jasmine. "Those letters could be the end of Regina and me, and I won't let you have them. I should have forced Regina to burn them when I first learned about them, but she wouldn't listen." Allegra pulled a cigarette lighter from her back pocket. "I'll burn them now, before any of us leave this spot."

Jasmine pulled the bag tighter to her chest. "I won't let you touch them. You and Regina need to be stopped. If you get away with this, who knows what you'll try next."

"You need to stop talking too," Allegra said as she walked closer to Jasmine. She waved her gun to the side and said, "I want the three of you to stand together, so I can keep an eye on you while I burn those."

Jasmine walked across the space and stood beside Julia and Meredith, but she didn't relinquish the bag. "I've already told them the truth. They know what you planned to do, and they know what's in these letters."

Julia wasn't exactly sure what was in the letters, but it was clear they didn't tell the same story Regina said they did.

"You should have kept your mouth shut, Jasmine." Allegra shook her head. "I told Regina you weren't good enough to play this part, and I was right."

Jasmine scoffed. "I'm so much better than all this. The only thing I'm not good at is keeping your lies a secret."

"Just give me the letters, and let's get this over with."

"Maybe we can come to a different solution." Julia forced her voice to be reasonable and calm. She tried to remember the times she'd been in a stressful situation in court. How many times had she given a ruling that she hated to give? Her heart had hammered just like it did now, but she had been forced to appear confident and certain. She needed to appear that way now. "Why can't Regina just tell the press that the book was fictionalized? Why does it have to be fact?"

"You really don't understand, do you?" Allegra sighed, but her arm did not lower, and the gun was still pointed at Jasmine. "Haven't you ever read any of Regina's books?"

Julia shook her head. "I'm afraid not."

"Regina's breakout book told the story of a man who survived torture as a prisoner of war in 1943. It was made into a movie. Perhaps you saw it. *The Bridge to Forgiveness*?"

Julia nodded. "It was a remarkable story. I'm not surprised Regina wrote it. She's an amazing storyteller."

"The book did so well, Regina was given an astronomical advance for her second story and I was hired as her personal publicist. It was my dream job. I've worked my entire career to get to this position. That first book won several prestigious awards and has been acclaimed by historians all over the world." Allegra paused, as if wondering whether she should continue. Finally, she went on. "But her second book was a complete failure. It was laughable. People wondered if Regina had actually written the first book. No matter what I did, sales were abysmal, and it reflected poorly on both her and me." Her hand shook as she held the gun. "I've worked too long and too hard to get this position, and I refuse to let anything come between me and success. We both agreed the third book—and any subsequent books—had to be as good as the first, so Regina tells the story people *want* to read, not necessarily what happened." She shrugged. "So Regina embellishes her stories a little bit—who cares? They sell better if they're more interesting."

"But if people knew the truth, that her books aren't factual," Meredith said slowly, as if finally understanding Allegra's dilemma, "then it would cast suspicions on her first story."

"Which is still selling really well." Allegra took another step closer. "And has ensured my position with Falcon Publishing. If anything happened to Regina's reputation, and that book stopped selling, it would be over for both of us. No one would hire me, and Regina's writing career would come to an end."

Everything was becoming clear to Julia—yet justice needed to prevail. She felt bad for both Regina and Allegra, but she also felt bad for Florence and Marcella and all the other Savannahians who were proud of their native daughter. There was never a good reason to hurt one person's reputation to save another's—especially an innocent person like Florence.

"So now you understand why I need those letters." Allegra put her hand on the tote bag, but Jasmine refused to let it go. "These have to be destroyed."

"What do the letters say?" Julia asked, trying to stall for time.

"What does it matter?" Allegra tore the bag from Jasmine's hands. "They're going to be burned right now."

"They're letters written to Florence's cousin, Lavinia, in 1931," Jasmine said. "Lavinia lived in New York City and was a Red Cross nurse, serving people in the tenements during the Great Depression. Lavinia asked Florence why she started to wave, and Florence told her the story but made Lavinia promise to destroy the letters. Apparently, Lavinia decided not to."

"So now I will," Allegra said.

"Did she tell Lavinia why she started waving?" Julia asked, a little breathless, hoping to stall for time.

Allegra walked backward and set the tote bag on the ground, the entire time keeping her eyes on Jasmine, Meredith, and Julia.

Allegra opened the zipper on the bag and then dumped the letters onto the ground. "She did," she said in a sarcastic tone. "But who cares? Her reason wasn't as exciting as Regina's version."

"Florence would have cared," Julia said, "and so does Marcella Martus and everyone else in Savannah and around the world who remembers Florence." Julia's heart was still pumping hard as Allegra flipped the lighter open and a flame came to life. "Please don't destroy this information, Allegra. If we don't have the truth about the past, how will we have solid ground to stand on today?"

"What does the truth have to do with anything? People rewrite history every day. What will it matter if one woman's story gets rewritten?" Allegra lowered the flame, all the while keeping the gun on the three women standing by, helpless. "Besides, she didn't want these letters to survive."

"Keeping history and knowing the past matters," Meredith said. "How would you like it if your story was rewritten one day by people who had an agenda? We have to keep as many facts available for future generations as possible, so they can interpret history accurately. It's our responsibility—regardless of our personal feelings or beliefs."

"Stop and put your hands up!" A deep, unruffled voice called through the shadows. "Savannah PD."

A tall, broad-shouldered officer stood near the edge of the shrubs, his gun drawn, while a second officer came around the other side.

Allegra cried out in alarm and dropped the lighter. It hit the ground and sputtered out.

Julia let out a breath she didn't know she'd been holding.

"Put the gun down and step away from it, ma'am," the first officer said. "Don't do anything we'll all regret."

"B-but—" Allegra stuttered. "I wasn't going to use it."

"Listen to Officer Clemmons," the second officer said, "and no one will get hurt."

Allegra threw the gun on the ground and stepped away from it. "I didn't mean to—it's just a small pistol I carry for protection. I've never used it—I wouldn't use it—I just couldn't let Jasmine ruin everything."

"Ma'am," Officer Clemmons said as he took hold of her arm with one hand and put his gun away with the other, "you are under arrest. You have the right to remain silent. Anything you say can and will be used against you in a court of law. You have the right to an attorney. If you cannot afford an attorney, one will be provided for you. Do you understand the rights I have just read to you? With these rights in mind, do you wish to continue speaking to me?"

Allegra shook her head and began to cry.

As the officers were putting her in handcuffs, Beau appeared with two more police officers.

"Jules," he said on a breath. She ran into his arms. "Thank God you're all right."

Julia clung to her husband, unable to speak.

"As soon as I saw you leave the statue, I called the police," he said. "I didn't know what was happening, but I felt a strong urge in my gut to bring in some help."

"Jasmine was fine," Julia finally said. "She had honorable intentions." More or less. "It was Allegra who showed up with a gun that was the real threat."

What if Beau hadn't listened to his intuition? Allegra would have probably destroyed the letters, and then what would have happened? She'd told Meredith and her too much. What would Allegra have done when they came forward with their accusations and Jasmine as a witness?

Thankfully, now Julia and Meredith wouldn't need to make accusations. Everything would come to light on its own.

"Meredith," Julia said, pulling away from Beau, "are you okay?"

Meredith nodded and put her hands up to her cheeks. "I'm okay."

Julia put her arm around her friend. Meredith was shaking. "Are you sure?"

After taking a couple of deep breaths, Meredith nodded. "Yes."

The police officers taped off the scene of the crime and then they questioned Jasmine, Meredith, and Julia. The letters were retrieved and taken into custody. Since they rightfully belonged to Regina, they would be returned to her, but there was no way to keep their contents secret now. Hopefully, Regina would do the right thing and donate them to the Savannah Historical Society.

Julia couldn't wait to find out what the letters contained.

Within an hour, one of the officers told Julia and Meredith that they were free to go. They had already taken Allegra to jail, and Jasmine was going to be taken in for questioning because she'd given false testimony regarding Regina's disappearance. Law enforcement agents were already on their way to the hotel to detain Regina as well, and no doubt they'd soon be looking for Frederick Hayes. As more information came to light, it was likely that Regina's publishing house would be seeking legal actions against her and the books she'd written under the guise of factual history.

It was late when Julia and Meredith had a chance to speak directly to Jasmine once again. The majority of the foot traffic along the riverfront had died down for the night. Only a few people were walking along River Street, and no one was near the statue. The police officers were just about to lead her away when Julia said, "Jasmine, I appreciate all you did tonight. I know it couldn't have been easy."

Jasmine shrugged as she glanced at the officers. "I'm just happy Regina won't get away with all the lies anymore."

"I wish you the best," Julia said to her. "Regardless of what happened, you're a good actress. You had us fooled until the night Regina went missing and we surprised you at the hotel."

"We couldn't find your alias in any database or on any social media," Meredith said. "But other than that, you were really good at being Gertie Hanson."

Jasmine's smile lacked any real depth. "Thanks."

"But don't make a habit of impersonating people," Julia warned. "At least, when you're off stage."

"Don't worry. I'll stick to a scripted part and a willing audience."

"Good." Julia smiled. "Thanks again for helping us tonight. We know you didn't need to, so we're especially grateful."

She nodded at them as the police led her away.

Beau turned to the women. "Have you had enough excitement for one night?"

"More than enough," Meredith said. "I'm ready to head home and go to bed."

"Same here." Julia sighed. "I'm sure we'll have a lot of reporters to talk to tomorrow."

"But we'll get to call Marcella to give her the good news," Meredith added.

"I think you'll both feel better with a good night's sleep." Beau took Julia's hand in his. "Are you ready to go?"

Julia nodded. "Thank you for all your help tonight, Beau."

He tugged her close as the three of them started back toward their car. "I wouldn't have it any other way."

Neither would Julia.

Chapter Twenty-One

THE DAY WAS BRIGHT AND the air was pleasantly cool for the last week in April. Julia wore sunglasses to shade her eyes from the glare off the Savannah River. The Waving Girl statue was front and center, and the chair Julia had occupied was facing the back side of the statue with the river beyond. At least a hundred people had shown up for the important press conference Marcella had scheduled for today, six days after the police had taken custody of the letters.

"Thanks for saving me a seat," Meredith said as she slipped into the spot beside Julia.

"How is Quin?" Julia asked, a sly smile on her lips.

"Stop." Meredith smiled. "It was just brunch, and we're just friends."

"How long do you think he'll be willing to stay 'just friends'?" Julia didn't often press Meredith for answers concerning Quin. It had been a couple of years since Ron had passed away, but Meredith wasn't rushing toward another relationship.

"*If*," Meredith stressed the word, "we become more than 'just friends,' you'll be the first to know."

Julia grinned. "I don't think it's a matter of if, but *when*."

Meredith rolled her eyes, which was an uncommon thing for her to do.

"Why don't you ask him?" Julia suggested.

"We're not in junior high, Jules. I can't just pass him a note and ask him to circle yes or no."

"You're right. You're not in junior high. You're grown adults who've been down this path before. Why not be open and honest with him about your feelings?"

"I don't even know what my feelings are." Meredith took her sunglasses off the top of her head and set them on the bridge of her nose. "Besides, I have no desire to lose his friendship right now."

Marcella Martus appeared on the edge of the crowd with Beatrice Enterline close on her heels. Marcella was dressed in another outdated ensemble with stiff, padded shoulders and brass buttons. Beatrice was dressed in a shockingly bright yellow pantsuit with a matching floppy hat, which waved in the breeze.

Julia's eyes hurt to look at Beatrice's bright outfit, even with her sunglasses on.

"Why do you think you'd lose Quin's friendship?" Julia asked softly, since the crowd had quieted upon seeing Marcella and Beatrice.

Meredith watched Marcella and Beatrice as they spoke to a man at the front of the group. Someone was setting up the microphone and another was putting a small podium in place. Meredith sighed. "If I tell him I want more out of our relationship—which I'm not sure I do—what if he doesn't feel the same way? I would risk losing him all together."

"What if he does want more and you're both wasting your time?"

"I'm happy with my life, Jules. Besides, I'm old-fashioned and think the man should make the first move."

"I don't think that's fair." Julia frowned. "Why should men have to be the ones putting their hearts on the line all the time?"

"It doesn't matter." Meredith looked beyond the group toward the river. "I'm getting too old to look for love and romance."

"Nonsense." Julia put her hand on Meredith's arm. "You'll never be too old to be loved." She nudged Meredith. "What if he did approach you and tell you he liked you?"

Color tinted Meredith's cheeks, and a telltale smile tilted up her lips. "I don't think that'll happen."

"But what if it did?"

Meredith shrugged, but the smile grew brighter. "I suppose I'll know how to respond *if* that time should ever come." She paused and then said, "By the way, I asked him about the anonymous donation to the youth group. He didn't admit giving the money—but he also didn't deny it."

"It was a really nice gesture. We've had a couple of new kids take advantage of the extra funds." She nudged Meredith playfully. "I can't help but think he did it to impress you."

Meredith didn't answer—but her smile gave away her pleasure at the thought.

"Excuse me," Beatrice said into the microphone, interrupting their conversation. "Is this thing on?" She tapped it several times, and the loud pounding noise echoed through the speakers.

"Yes," several people called out.

"Good." Beatrice straightened and grinned at the group. "How y'all doing? Are you as excited to be here as I am?"

She waited as people in the group nodded.

"For those who don't know me," Beatrice said, "I'm Beatrice Enterline, president of the illustrious Savannah Historical Society, and I'm thrilled to welcome Marcella Martus here today. Marcella is the grandniece of our very own Florence Martus, known to everyone in these parts as the Waving Girl." Beatrice motioned to the over-sized statue of Florence just behind her. "Marcella first contacted me a few days ago to share some wonderful news, and I suggested she call together a press conference to make the announcement public. Thankfully, she agreed, and we're all here now."

The crowd clapped politely, though Julia wasn't quite sure what it was they were clapping for. She had a sneaky suspicion she knew what Marcella would have to tell them, but she wasn't 100 percent certain. She was just as curious as the rest of the audience.

"Without further ado," Beatrice said, "I'd like to introduce you to Marcella Martus."

Once again, everyone clapped. Marcella came to the microphone and smiled at Beatrice. She shaded her eyes as she looked out at the crowd. When she made eye contact with Julia, she offered a nod of recognition. "Thank you for coming today," she began as she pulled a folded piece of paper from a large pocket in her blazer. "I've prepared a statement, but I think I'm going to just shoot from the hip, as the saying goes."

Marcella cleared her throat, and it ricocheted through the microphone.

Julia smiled at Meredith, surprised to see Marcella uncomfortable. When she was on a mission, she was so confident and bold. Today, her nerves were showing.

"About a month ago, a book was released into the world that told a far different story of my great-aunt Florence Martus than the one we all knew. From the moment I read the book, I was enraged, as I know some of you were as well."

Many people nodded their agreement.

"Not only did the book portray Florence as a spy and an accomplice to murder, but it also painted her family—including my great-grandfather—in a poor light. I didn't think this was fair, or right, so I asked two of Savannah's finest detectives to help me prove the book was fake." Marcella gestured to Julia and Meredith. "Those women, who operate Magnolia Investigations, are here today. Julia and Meredith, would you please stand?"

Julia's cheeks warmed as she and Meredith rose from their seats.

"I would like to publicly thank Julia Foley and Meredith Bellefontaine for their help in clearing my great-aunt's name," Marcella said. "If it wasn't for these two, I wouldn't have Florence's letters in my possession today, and I wouldn't be able to prove, once and for all, that Regina Terrance's book is based on lies."

The crowd clapped for Julia and Meredith, who nodded and smiled and then quickly took their seats again. Julia had no wish to draw so much attention, and she was certain Meredith felt the same.

"Julia and Meredith are directly responsible for uncovering the publicity stunt Regina and her publicist, Allegra Timmons, were trying to pull over on us." Marcella's lips pursed together in disgust. Several local and national papers had carried the true story about their plans in Savannah. Almost everyone in town knew it had all been for publicity. Regina, Allegra, Jasmine, and Frederick were all facing punishment for lying and withholding information from law-enforcement agents, but it might be weeks or months before they received their convictions. "But," Marcella continued, "now that it's behind us, we can look forward to brighter days." She took a deep breath. "This past week, I spoke to Regina Terrance about the letters. Since she no longer has a need for them, and, quite frankly, wishes she'd never seen them, I asked if she would do the right thing and give them to me. In her defense, she did seem contrite about the whole thing and told me she never meant to hurt anyone. She said that if giving me the letters would make up for part of the trouble she caused, then she was happy to hand them over."

The crowd clapped once again.

Marcella nodded and smiled, waiting for the applause to die down. "I was able to retrieve the letters from the police department, and, that very same day, I contacted the Savannah Historical Society to make a donation."

"That's the exciting announcement," Beatrice said as she quickly darted to the microphone and then moved back again.

Marcella looked at her and made a face, clearly irritated at her interruption. She let out a breath and then continued. "I'm happy to say that my great-aunt's letters, which prove that Regina Terrance's book is a lie and tell the real story behind Florence's waving, are now safely stored at the Savannah Historical Society."

Again the audience clapped, but this time Marcella turned to face the statue and she, too, clapped in honor of Florence Martus.

Julia smiled, thankful she had played a part in restoring Florence's reputation and standing in Savannah. Justice had been served for Florence. It felt good.

"And to think," Meredith said to Julia, "if Florence's cousin had actually destroyed the letters, as Florence asked her to, there would be no way to know the real story."

"Why do you think Lavinia didn't destroy them, even though she told Florence she would?"

Meredith shrugged. "Maybe she knew better than Florence that someday a future generation would want to know the truth. And she probably hid them away, knowing Florence wouldn't want the news shared while she was still alive."

"God is always orchestrating our stories, isn't He?" Meredith asked.

"He is, indeed." Julia had seen the hand of God at work time and time again, making her wonder why she ever questioned Him.

***

The next afternoon was cloudy, but it didn't dampen anyone's enthusiasm as Julia stood by the tour bus with a clipboard in hand. Thirty-six teenagers—three more than originally planned—would be dropped off at the church's parking lot by their parents to take the four-hour drive to Atlanta for the youth convention. Julia wore her walking shoes and a comfortable outfit, knowing she'd be on duty until at least midnight overseeing all these kids. There would be five parent chaperones coming along, but Julia had coordinated the entire event, and she would be the one to make sure everything went off without a hitch.

She was also sharing a hotel room with three of the girls and knew that sleep would be at a minimum for the next two nights, but she was fine with that. She was rested and prepared. She had told Beau he didn't need to bother with seeing her off at the bus. They had said their goodbyes that morning over breakfast and he had packed her a healthy lunch, which she had quickly eaten before the bus arrived at the church.

"Hello, Miss Julia!" Ebony Lester left her parents' minivan and waved at them as they drove out of the parking lot.

"Hello, Ebony."

It was rare to see Ebony on her own without her sidekicks nearby. Julia was ever conscious of the fact that teenagers were most vulnerable or real when they were alone. If they were in a group of their peers, they were more likely to come across as bold and confrontational. Maybe now was a good time to talk to Ebony about the weekend's expectations.

"How are you?" Julia asked her.

"I'm good."

"Are you excited for the conference?"

"Sure." Ebony shrugged, though she looked excited and eager to be there.

"Did you hear that Olivia has a couple more friends who signed up to come this weekend? Both Courtney and Aubrihannah, as well as another friend named—"

"Sierra Tanner. I know."

"From what I've heard, the girls are new to church and are looking forward to getting to know everyone."

"They already know almost everyone in school."

"But not all the kids who come to New Beginnings go to your school. I'm hoping that all of us can put our best foot forward and make them feel welcome."

Ebony nodded. "I know."

"Do you know Sierra?"

"As well as I know Courtney and Aubrihannah. Sierra dated Tyler before Courtney or Olivia." She lifted a shoulder. "I think that's why Olivia became friends with her."

"This Tyler kid sounds like he's had a lot of girlfriends."

"Yeah, he has." She readjusted her backpack. "And now that all his old girlfriends are friends, telling their side of the story, people are starting to realize Tyler's not that great of a guy."

Julia studied Ebony for a moment, wondering if she finally believed Olivia. "How does that make you feel about all that's happened with Olivia these past few weeks?"

Ebony didn't meet Julia's gaze as she squinted toward the bus, where several of the kids were putting away their luggage. "I haven't been very nice to Olivia." She paused and looked at Julia, sadness in her eyes. "I'm sorry I didn't believe her."

"Have you talked to Olivia about it?" Julia asked softly. "I think she'd really like to hear what you have to say."

"I don't know if she'll want to talk to me. She has new friends now." She looked down toward her feet and moved a pebble with the toe of her shoe. "I messed things up with Olivia."

"You two have been friends for a long, long time. Maybe that'll be enough for you to mend what's been broken."

"Do you think so?" Ebony looked up at Julia, hope shining in her beautiful brown eyes.

"I do." Julia smiled. "And here she comes now, if you'd like to talk to her."

Olivia had just stepped out of her family's car and waved good-bye to her parents before turning to face Ebony and Julia.

At first, Olivia hesitated, but when Julia waved for her to come over, Olivia's face brightened. She had come alone, and her new friends were not there yet.

"Hello, Miss Julia."

Julia smiled at her. "Hi, Olivia."

"Hey," Ebony said to Olivia.

Olivia gave her a half smile.

"Would you like me to leave you alone?" Julia asked Ebony.

Ebony shook her head. "No. You can stay, Miss Julia."

Julia nodded and didn't leave, but she also didn't speak. What Ebony needed to say, she had to say on her own.

Olivia looked at Ebony expectantly, her carry-on at her side.

"I'm sorry I didn't believe you," Ebony said without any preamble. "I'm sorry I waited until other people said the same thing before I was ready to listen." Her bottom lip quivered. "But I'm especially sorry I hurt you. I should have trusted you and stood by you when you were hurting the worst. I'm sorry, Livy."

Olivia's mouth turned down, and she looked like she might cry too. "Oh, Eb." She left her suitcase and rushed in to hug Ebony. "I missed you."

"I missed you too." Ebony hugged Olivia tight and closed her eyes.

"And I forgive you," Olivia said. "Of course I forgive you."

"I was such an idiot." Ebony pulled back and wiped her eyes. "I was jealous of your relationship with Tyler last year, and then I was angry that if you had done the things he said, that you hadn't told me." She shook her head. "I'm just happy I finally saw the truth."

Olivia also wiped her eyes, but she smiled through the tears. "So much has happened, Eb. Aubrihannah and Courtney and Sierra are really nice and so much fun to hang out with. I know you'll love them."

"Do you think they'll want me to be their friend?" Ebony asked.

"Of course! Who wouldn't want to be your friend?" Olivia picked up her suitcase. "Want to sit together on the bus? We'll save seats for the others."

"Sure." The girls linked arms and left Julia, their old camaraderie returning as if nothing had come between them.

Julia stood for a moment, a smile on her lips.

The other students arrived, one after the other. Julia checked each of them off her list and was happy when everyone was there and accounted for by the appointed time. All the bags were tucked under the bus in the luggage area, and all the chaperones had checked in.

Julia climbed the steps and smiled at the bus driver.

"Are we all set?" he asked.

"We're all set."

"Then let's be off." He closed the door behind Julia.

The first thing she noticed was Ebony and Olivia. They were seated next to each other, but they were busy talking with Sally,

Elena, Aubrihannah, Courtney, and Sierra. The girls were visiting as if they'd all been friends for years.

Julia paused, for just a second as the bus started to pull out of the church parking lot on their adventure, and offered up a prayer of thanksgiving. She was so grateful for new beginnings, old friends, and unconditional forgiveness. They were all gifts from God, and she would not take them for granted ever again.

Dear Reader,

In 2019, my husband and I took a trip to Savannah, Georgia, for the first time. We did all the tours, walked through almost all the unique squares, dined in some of the fabulous restaurants, and went to more museums and historic sites than I can recall. One thing that stood out to me after I left Savannah, and continues to stay with me, is the genuine kindness and hospitality of this beautiful Southern city. Savannah is affectionately known as the Hostess City, and for good reason. They excel at making anyone and everyone feel at home there.

Florence Martus, known to locals and to seamen around the world as the Waving Girl, has often been referred to as the first hostess of Savannah. In the forty-four years she waved at ships coming into and leaving the Port of Savannah, she never missed a single one. There are estimates that she waved at between fifty to a hundred thousand ships. Whether by day or by night, no matter the weather or her health, she was on her front porch, demonstrating that hospitality for which she, and her city, are famous.

From the moment I heard Florence's story, my mind began to wander with all the possibilities that led to her waving. We may never know for sure, but it was still fun to imagine. I hope I have kept Florence's gentle personality evident in this story. From all accounts, she was simple, genuine, and truly kind. It was never my wish to sully her reputation or turn her story into something she'd be embarrassed to read. I hope she'd smile, in her quiet way, upon reading this story—though, I would guess she wouldn't tell me if I was anywhere near the truth.

I hope you enjoyed reading this story as much as I enjoyed writing it.

Yours affectionately,
Gabrielle Meyer

About the Author

GABRIELLE MEYER LIVES ON THE banks of the upper Mississippi River in central Minnesota with her husband and four children. By day, she's a homeschooling mama, but at night, she escapes to imaginary worlds to pen tales of hope and inspiration. As an employee of the Minnesota Historical Society, Gabrielle fell in love with history and enjoys writing fictional stories inspired by real people, places, and events. You can learn more about her and her books by visiting gabriellemeyer.com, or connect with her on Facebook at facebook.com/AuthorGabrielleMeyer.

The Truth Behind the Fiction

FLORENCE WAS A VERY REAL and wonderful citizen of Savannah. Much of the history I gave to her and her family is completely true, to the best of my knowledge. Her father, John, was an ordnance sergeant at Fort Pulaski, where Florence was born in 1868. She and her brother, George, eventually moved to Elba Island, where they cared for the lighthouse and Florence waved at the ships for forty-four years.

It's true that she and George saved over thirty men from a burning dredge, and it's also true that she destroyed her diary before they retired to the Bona Bella neighborhood in Savannah in 1931, though she never gave a reason why. Florence was honored at Fort Pulaski for her seventieth birthday with over three thousand guests, and she was often sent telegrams and letters from seamen from around the world who wanted to thank her for her kindness. There is a wonderful statue of her at the end of River Street in Savannah, there was a World War II Liberty Ship christened the *SS Florence Martus*, and one of the Savannah Belles Ferry boats is named after her. No matter what gift shop you enter in Savannah, you will find a book, an ornament, or a miniature statue of Florence available for purchase. She's well known and well loved by Savannahians.

But one thing no one knows for certain: Why did she start to wave? Her simple explanation was that she was a lonely girl and it gave her something to fill her days. As an author with a wild imagination, I couldn't let it rest there. I had to come up with a more compelling reason! I created the character of Hai Ching because I needed someone Florence's parents wouldn't approve of. Unfortunately, at the time the story takes place, Chinese Americans were not being treated well. The stories I shared about their persecution are true. Not only did I want to use Hai Ching because of his origins, but I wanted to shed a light on a problem we've faced with countless people groups throughout American history. I'm so happy Florence could see past Hai Ching's nationality, even if her love was fictitious.

Alas, there is no evidence that Florence actually had a love affair, and her explanation for the waving is probably true. She was likely simply a lonely girl, looking for a way to connect with a bigger world.

But isn't it fun to imagine what might have been?

SOMETHING DELICIOUS FROM A
Downhome Southern Kitchen

SOUR CREAM BLUEBERRY PIE

Fresh Blueberry Filling Ingredients:

4 pints fresh blueberries

¼ cup granulated sugar

1½ tablespoons cornstarch

1 teaspoon ground cinnamon

¼ cup water

2 tablespoons cold butter, cut
   into pieces

Blueberry Filling Instructions:

Cook 3 pints of the blueberries, sugar, cornstarch, cinnamon, and water in saucepan over medium-low heat, stirring constantly, until sugar is dissolved, and mixture is slightly thickened (10 to 15 minutes). Remove saucepan from heat. Add butter and remaining pint of blueberries; stir gently so blueberries stay whole. Allow to cool.

Remaining Pie Ingredients:

1 baked 9-inch piecrust,
   regular or graham cracker
   (cooled before filling)

1 cup sugar

3½ tablespoons cornstarch

1 cup whole milk

1 tablespoon lemon zest

½ cup fresh lemon juice
   (2 to 3 lemons)

3 egg yolks, slightly beaten

¼ cup butter

1 cup sour cream

Pie Topping Ingredients:

1 cup heavy whipping cream, whipped

2 tablespoons powdered sugar

Instructions for Sour Cream Pie Filling:

Combine sugar and cornstarch together in heavy saucepan. Whisk in milk, lemon zest, and lemon juice. Add egg yolks in a thin stream, whisking vigorously. Cook over medium heat, stirring until thickened. Remove from heat and stir in butter until melted.

Allow mixture to cool to room temperature. Stir in sour cream and pour filling into prebaked piecrust. Refrigerate for two to three hours until well chilled.

Spoon cooled blueberry pie filling evenly over top.

Instructions for Pie Topping:

Whip the heavy whipping cream using hand or electric-stand mixer for 2 or 3 minutes, until it begins to thicken. Add powdered sugar and whip again until stiff peaks form. Top pie with whipped cream and serve.

*Read on for a sneak peek of another exciting book
in the Savannah Secrets series!*

Beneath a Dragon Moon
BY SHIRLEY RAYE REDMOND

MEREDITH HAD JUST FINISHED ADDING fresh water to the lavish Mother's Day bouquet gracing the corner of her desk when she heard the tinkling of the bell indicating that someone had come in through the front door of Magnolia Investigations. Stepping out of her office into the reception area, she took one look at the two women lingering in a hesitant manner near the door and came to two conclusions at once: One, they were sisters. They might even be fraternal twins, who appeared to be in their midseventies. They had fine, intelligent eyes and chiseled features with traces of past youthful beauty. And two, they seemed flustered, even a little apprehensive. Had they been arguing?

The silver-haired sister appeared flushed, her blue eyes snapping. The other one, who obviously colored her short dark brown hair, had a tight-knuckled grip on the yellow Savannah Bananas canvas tote bag in her left hand.

"Bernadette Florek?" Meredith stepped forward with a smile. She glanced from one woman to the other. Carmen had been careful to write down the name of the woman who had called earlier in the week to make an appointment for four o'clock this Thursday afternoon. Carmen had also made a point of reminding Meredith about the scheduled appointment before leaving early for a Zumba lesson.

The woman with the silver hair, dressed in an attractive salmon-colored linen pantsuit, took a step forward. "I'm Bernadette Florek." She spoke with a soft Georgian drawl. Tipping her head, she added, "This is my sister, Irene Crews." Her tone was brittle, her eyelids swollen and red. Meredith now felt certain the two women had been arguing before coming into the office.

Irene gave a slight nod as she retrieved a dog-eared business card from the pocket of her navy blue blazer. "We have an appointment with Ron Bellefontaine."

Meredith's heart gave a small but pleasant flutter as it always did when someone mentioned her late husband's name. She missed Ron. Every day. Still.

"Actually, you have an appointment with me. I'm Meredith Bellefontaine." The door to Julia's office opened then, and Julia stepped out, smiling. Meredith said, "This is my business partner, Julia Foley."

Julia looked crisply professional—as usual—in a lime-green seersucker sheath. She had a white cardigan flung around her shoulders and a Diet Dr Pepper clutched in one hand. She lifted it and said, "May I offer you all something cold to drink? Soda or sweet tea? I can brew fresh coffee, if you prefer."

The two sisters exchanged troubled glances. Guessing the reason for their uncertainty, Meredith explained, "My husband passed away a couple of years ago. Didn't our receptionist explain when you asked to make an appointment with Ron?"

"No," Bernadette said with a shake of her head. "I didn't ask for him specifically—I simply asked to make an appointment." She flicked an anxious glance at her sister. "I don't think we want…well, there's been a mistake. We should go. Sorry for any inconvenience."

"You see, we were expecting a man—a private investigator," Irene explained.

"We *are* licensed investigators," Meredith hastened to assure them.

The sisters stared at her doubtfully. "We understood the agency was run by a man—Mr. Ron Bellefontaine, a former police officer. We've heard such good things about him." Irene waved the business card. "That's why we called this agency and not some other."

Meredith nodded. "My husband did work for the police department before setting up his own agency. Julia and I took over the business after Ron passed away."

"We should go." Bernadette touched her sister lightly on the arm. "We're sorry about your husband," she added, giving Meredith a sympathetic nod. "We didn't know." She allowed her troubled glance to slide over to Julia.

"No, wait." Julia stepped forward, placing the soda can on Carmen's desk. "Since you're here, why not come into Meredith's office and tell us what you wanted to see Ron about?"

"Do you carry guns?" Irene demanded. She gave Meredith a piercing glance.

Meredith blinked. Was this a trick question? She'd never had to use her weapon while on a case, and she hoped she never would. "We are licensed to do so," she answered cautiously.

"We also know how to use them, if necessary," Julia added. "Please come in and tell us why you need a PI." She extended her arm, indicating the open door to Meredith's private office.

"Yes, please." Now more than a little intrigued, Meredith wanted to hear their story. She suspected it would prove to be something out of the ordinary.

Bernadette cleared her throat. "We came to consult your husband about a murder our late father may have committed."

Meredith stared. Out of the ordinary, indeed. She could feel her eyebrows rise as she turned to regard Julia with quiet astonishment. Julia blinked. "If you suspect a murder has been committed, you must report it to the police," Julia told them.

"We thought about that," Irene replied. "But our father passed away, and there isn't a body—at least not one that we know of. We have no evidence that Dad actually killed anyone at all. There's no body, no confession. It's just that…well…we have concerns."

"How long has your father been deceased?" Meredith asked. For a brief moment she had a quirky feeling that she and Julia were trapped in another bizarre episode of *The Twilight Zone*. How often had they been hired to investigate a crime when both the alleged victim and the alleged suspect were deceased? She'd lost count.

"Dad died ten years ago," Irene said.

"And you think he may have committed a murder?" Julia asked, emphasizing the word *may*.

After heaving a sigh, Bernadette breathed, "Yes, we do."

"Please, come in, won't you?" Again, Meredith indicated her office with a sweep of her arm. "If we can't help you, I'll tell you so."

Julia stepped aside to allow the two women to precede her through the open door.

The sisters exchanged meaningful glances. Obviously, neither of them felt comfortable employing a woman—two women—to carry out whatever task they had in mind. Perhaps they considered it too dangerous. But dangerous how? They'd inquired about guns after all. Meredith certainly didn't want them to leave until she found out what the case might be.

Bernadette gave another ragged sigh before taking the first step into Meredith's office. Irene followed while Julia dashed into her own office and returned with a yellow legal pad to take notes. The sisters took the two chairs Meredith indicated before seating herself behind her desk. She laced her fingers together and rested her elbows on the edge of the desk.

"So, your father is deceased, and you believe he may have committed a murder before he died," Meredith prompted. The sisters nodded. "And it's my understanding that you have not taken your suspicions to the police. Is that correct?"

"No, we haven't gone to the police. We aren't certain, and we don't want to stir up a hornet's nest without sufficient evidence," Irene replied.

"But why do you think your father may have killed someone?" Meredith pressed.

Bernadette met her gaze with eyes watering. Her lip quivered. "Because of something we found. We've been cleaning out the attic in our house—Momma died this past December, and we're putting the house up for sale—clearing things out, getting ready to put it on the market. Then we found…something." She gave Irene a curt nod.

From the bright yellow tote bag, Irene retrieved a rectangular box—an old cookie tin, from the looks of it. She handed it to Meredith, who placed it on her desk and tugged off the lid. Inside, she found a piece of plain thin stationery, yellowed with age and folded over. The words Connie is Dead had been typed in all caps in the center of the page. The letter *o* appeared incomplete as though the typewriter key had been chipped. Underneath the words was a large zero drawn in pencil. Meredith handed the paper to Julia. Next came a page apparently torn from a sketchbook with a pencil drawing of a man's face—a young Asian man. It was quite well done. The artist had gone to the trouble of noting the crinkles around the man's eyes, the slight curling of the lip as though the subject had been trying not to smile.

"Do you know who this is?" Meredith held up the portrait.

Irene shook her head.

Meredith handed the drawing to Julia before removing a rather worn brown envelope addressed to someone named Judson Crews. "Is this your father's name?" Meredith glanced up at Irene. This time both she and Bernadette nodded.

Meredith lifted the unsealed flap, reached inside, and pulled out a pair of somewhat battered military identification tags attached to a ball chain. The name on the tags was Conway Fite. Connie is Dead, the note read. Connie could be a nickname for Conway. It was intriguing, to say the least. Why would Judson Crews have another man's ID tags? Had he taken them to remember a lost war buddy? Was that even allowed? When Julia held out her hand, Meredith dropped the chain and tags into it.

Then she reached into the envelope again. This time she pulled out what appeared to be a gold medallion with a square hole in the middle. Foreign looking—probably Asian, the size of a half dollar. From the weight of it, Meredith guessed it to be solid gold. And it appeared to be old. Really, really old.

"Do you see why we're concerned?" Bernadette asked, leaning forward. "Why did our father have these tags? Why would he keep a note that says a man is dead? Is the drawing a portrait of the dead man? We can't bear not knowing if Dad killed him or not."

Irene cleared her throat. Running a hand over one sleeve of her blazer, she said hesitantly, "Sometimes murderers keep souvenirs—from their victims. Or so we've heard. What if these things…?" She left her question unfinished.

Meredith's heart went out to the two sisters. Their distress was obvious. She wanted to help them. She just wasn't sure how. "Do you know this Conway Fite? Do you think this man in the drawing is him?"

Bernadette sniffed. "We have no idea."

"So your father never mentioned him?" Julia asked, examining the medallion.

"Not that we recall," Irene said.

"And now that Momma has passed, we can't ask her either," Bernadette added.

Meredith pointed to the note. "What is this zero for? Do you have any idea what it means?"

"We don't know anything," Irene insisted. "Our father was a welder after the war ended. He wasn't much for books and that sort of thing. He read the paper—on Sundays. And he never spoke of his war experiences to us. Said it wouldn't be fitting for young ears."

"Girls' ears," Bernadette added. "Give her the other envelope."

Irene reached into the yellow tote bag again and pulled out a medium-sized padded mailer. "We found these too."

Meredith removed a faded obituary of World War II correspondent Ernie Pyle clipped from a newspaper along with one of the reporter's columns about the battle of Okinawa. Both were yellow and brittle with age. The mailer also contained a photograph of four young men in sepia tones—all in World War II army fatigues. The foursome—in a spirit of camaraderie—appeared to be standing casually in front of a row of sagging canvas tents. Meredith turned the picture over. The names of the men had been scribbled there in pencil: *Jud, Sarge, Butters, Zobrest.* Underneath the names the words PASSED BY ARMY CENSORS had been rubber-stamped.

"That's Dad," Irene said indicating the lanky, dark-haired youth on the far left.

"So your father was in the army during World War II," Julia said, taking the photograph from Meredith.

"Momma said he never did leave that war behind." Bernadette swallowed hard. "He had bad dreams, don't you know? Slept poorly. Had a mean streak too." She shrugged.

Irene added, "Dad fought in the Pacific theater—Okinawa, Bougainville, Guadalcanal."

Meredith picked up the brown envelope, the one addressed to Judson Crews. She studied the postmark. "This is rather curious. The war was over in 1945. This envelope was postmarked in 1981." She frowned. "You found these inside?" Meredith indicated the note, the ID tags, and the medallion.

Irene nodded. "Of course, we have no way of knowing if these things were mailed to him or if Dad simply kept these items in the envelope for safekeeping."

Bernadette's face contorted with grief. Her dark eyes sparkled with unshed tears. "We want to know—what happened." Irene reached over to clasp her sister's hand.

"You may be worried for nothing," Julia said kindly. "Let's give your father the benefit of the doubt, shall we? Do you know anything about the other men in the photograph?"

The sisters shook their heads. "That's why we wanted to see Mr. Bellefontaine," Irene replied. "A friend recommended his services. She'd hired him several years ago to look into a personal matter. She still had his business card." With a sigh, she added, "Bernie and I don't even know where to begin or what to do. We thought Mr. Bellefontaine could discover the identity of the men in the photograph and maybe look into…the other matter."

Fascinated by the medallion, Meredith picked it up from the desk where Julia had placed it. "This is intriguing too. Is it a coin? A medal of some sort? It appears to be Asian. I've never seen anything like it before."

A Note from the Editors

WE HOPE YOU ENJOY THE Savannah Secrets series, created by the Books and Inspirational Media Division of Guideposts, a nonprofit organization that touches millions of lives every day through products and services that inspire, encourage, help you grow in your faith, and celebrate God's love in every aspect of your daily life.

Thank you for making a difference with your purchase of this book, which helps fund our many outreach programs to military personnel, prisons, hospitals, nursing homes, and educational institutions. To learn more, visit GuidepostsFoundation.org.

We also maintain many useful and uplifting online resources. Visit Guideposts.org to read true stories of hope and inspiration, access OurPrayer network, sign up for free newsletters, download free e-books, join our Facebook community, and follow our stimulating blogs.

To learn about other Guideposts publications, including the bestselling devotional *Daily Guideposts*, go to ShopGuideposts.org, call (800) 932-2145, or write to Guideposts, PO Box 5815, Harlan, Iowa 51593.

Sign up for the Guideposts Fiction Newsletter

and stay up-to-date on the books you love!

You'll get sneak peeks of new releases, recommendations from other Guideposts readers, and special offers just for you . . .

and it's FREE!

Just go to Guideposts.org/Newsletters today to sign up.

Find more inspiring stories in these best-loved Guideposts fiction series!

Mysteries of Lancaster County

Follow the Classen sisters as they unravel clues and uncover hidden secrets in Mysteries of Lancaster County. As you get to know these women and their friends, you'll see how God brings each of them together for a fresh start in life.

Secrets of Wayfarers Inn

Retired schoolteachers find themselves owners of an old warehouse-turned-inn that is filled with hidden passages, buried secrets, and stunning surprises that will set them on a course to puzzling mysteries from the Underground Railroad.

Tearoom Mysteries Series

Mix one stately Victorian home, a charming lakeside town in Maine, and two adventurous cousins with a passion for tea and hospitality. Add a large scoop of intriguing mystery, and sprinkle generously with faith, family, and friends, and you have the recipe for *Tearoom Mysteries*.

Ordinary Women of the Bible

Richly imagined stories—based on facts from the Bible—have all the plot twists and suspense of a great mystery, while bringing you fascinating insights on what it was like to be a woman living in the ancient world.

To learn more about these books, visit Guideposts.org/Shop